Jacob's heart stood still.

Cathryn O'Malley.

If he'd thought he'd forgotten her, he'd been mistaken. The old feeling of longing rushed through him. Longing tinged with a dozen questions. Questions and, yes, anger and hurt pride. If the townsfolk could see inside him now, they'd have no doubts that he was flesh and blood.

For five years he'd tried to understand why Cathryn had run from him. What had made her stay away. Had made her put up a wall of silence even her close and loving family had been unable to penetrate.

And now, suddenly, she appeared before him, as beautiful and as puzzling as ever. Holding the child he and she should be raising. Together.

Dear Reader,

It wouldn't be summer without romance, or June without a wedding—and Special Edition brings you both this month!

Our very romantic THAT'S MY BABY! title for June is *Happy Father's Day,* by Barbara Faith. In fact, this daddy has *six* adopted children he calls his own! Now he has to convince the woman of his dreams to become part of his family.

What would June be without blushing brides? Well, first we have book two of Christine Flynn's miniseries, THE WHITAKER BRIDES. In *The Rebel's Bride,* it's renegade Caleb Whitaker's turn to walk down the aisle. And *Waiting at the Altar* is where you'll find ever-faithful Jacob Matthews—this time, he's determined to be a groom at last in book two of Amy Frazier's series, SWEET HOPE WEDDINGS. In Gail Link's *Marriage-To-Be?* the nuptials are still in question—it's up to the bride to choose between two brothers.

Rounding out the month are two authors new to Special Edition. Janis Reams Hudson has a sexy tale in store when two sparring lovers issue the challenge, *Resist Me if You Can.* And after Lois Faye Dyer's *Lonesome Cowboy* meets his match in a spirited schoolteacher, his lonely days just might be over.

So don't miss a moment of these wonderful books. It's just the beginning of a summer filled with love and romance from Special Edition!

Sincerely,

Tara Gavin,
Senior Editor

AMY FRAZIER

WAITING AT THE ALTAR

Published by Silhouette Books
America's Publisher of Contemporary Romance

To my mother, Drusilla Landry,
who embodies the spirit
of love, compassion and wisdom.

SILHOUETTE BOOKS

ISBN 0-373-24036-8

WAITING AT THE ALTAR

This edition published by arrangement with Harlequin Books S.A.

Printed in U.S.A.

Books by Amy Frazier

Silhouette Special Edition

The Secret Baby #954
**New Bride in Town* #1030
**Waiting at the Altar* #1036

*Sweet Hope Weddings

AMY FRAZIER

has loved to listen to, read, and tell stories from the time she was a very young child. With the support of a loving family, she grew up believing she could accomplish anything she set her mind to. It was with this attitude that she tackled various careers as teacher, librarian, free-lance artist, professional storyteller, wife and mother. Above all else, the stories always beckoned. It is with a contented sigh that she settles into the romance field where she can weave stories in which love conquers all.

Amy now lives with her husband, son and daughter in northwest Georgia, where the kudzu grows high as an elephant's eye. When not writing, she loves reading, music, painting, gardening, bird-watching and the Atlanta Braves.

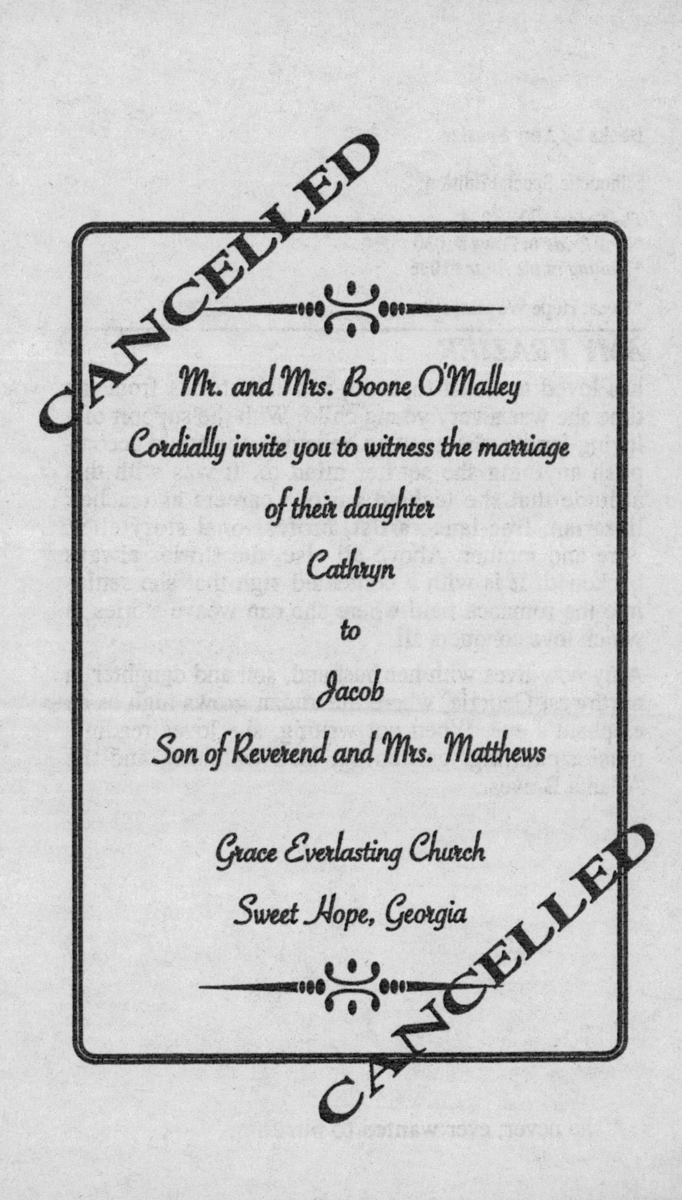
CANCELLED
Mr. and Mrs. Boone O'Malley
Cordially invite you to witness the marriage
of their daughter
Cathryn
to
Jacob
Son of Reverend and Mrs. Matthews
Grace Everlasting Church
Sweet Hope, Georgia
CANCELLED

Prologue

With her hand protectively covering her abdomen and the new life within, Cathryn O'Malley prepared to walk down the aisle to marry a man she didn't love. This was certainly not the romantic hearts-and-flowers wedding she'd always envisioned.

"Oh, Jacob." She sighed aloud, twisting a wayward wisp of hair into the daisy crown that secured her simple bridal veil. "How can you be so sure you want me... and another man's child?"

As the strains of organ music wafted through Grace Everlasting Church, reaching Cathryn, alone, in the tiny bride's room, she leaned her forehead against the cool, sturdy wall and silently debated for the umpteenth time the rightness of her present course. She was eighteen years old, and three months pregnant. Pregnant with the child of a man she'd never again see. And no, she didn't love Jacob Matthews, the man she was about to marry. He knew that. But he was the best friend she'd ever had. And because of that, she never, ever wanted to hurt him.

If she could only get past this moment—this moment that somehow, even with the frankness Jacob and she shared, felt like duplicity—she could foresee herself coming to love Jacob. Certainly a spouse's love. Perhaps even a lover's love. More than just the sometimes protective friendship she now felt. And the gratitude...the gratitude. Dear Lord, she owed Jacob Matthews more than she could ever repay. And that, precisely, was why she must not make the wrong decision today.

A sharp knock sounded at the door. It would be her father, come to walk her down the aisle. Come to usher her into her new life. Inhaling deeply, Cathryn moved slowly toward the door. Her father, stepmother and grandmother hadn't wanted to leave her alone before the ceremony, but she'd desperately needed a few moments to herself. A few moments to sort, once again, her feelings. To ascertain that what she was doing was for the best.

It was. It had to be. Arrgh! Overcerebration could thwart the firmest of decisions.

A rueful smile stealing across her lips, she moved quickly toward the door, eager for action not thought. Eager now to greet her golden bear of a father. Eager to take his arm. To walk down the aisle. To begin a marriage with her best friend. Strong, patient and loving Jacob.

"Now, Daddy, you see I'll not be late for my own wedding...." The words froze on Cathryn's tongue as she opened the door to reveal, not her father, but Ellie Able, a middle-aged parishioner of Grace Everlasting and the mother of a classmate of Cathryn's—a classmate who had, unsuccessfully, set her cap for Jacob.

Jacob's father being the pastor of Grace Everlasting, and Jacob his likely successor, the entire congregation had been invited to today's wedding. Even so, Ellie Able's sudden visit was a puzzling one. Regaining her composure, Cathryn said, "Miss Ellie, do come in."

"No need," Ellie replied, her look and words tart as she stood firmly in the hallway. "What I have to say can be said right here."

Cathryn flinched inwardly at the implied threat in the woman's tone. "Ma'am?"

"Cathryn O'Malley, you are making a grave mistake here today, and you know it."

Cathryn felt her pulse begin to race, but for the life of her she could find no words to answer.

"You, young lady—" the words *young lady* were said in a honeyed sneer "—are about to pull down the finest family in Sweet Hope, Georgia. All because of your tramping ways and that fatherless child you bear."

Cathryn sucked in her breath and felt the bottom fall out of her stomach. No one—*no one* with the exception of Jacob, her immediate family and *that man*—knew about the baby. No one else. Or so she'd believed.

"Miss Ellie," she managed haltingly, "I do believe you're mistaken."

The woman narrowed her eyes. "Oh, am I? Well... you may have attended classes with my Missy, but my Sonny attended classes with Drew Paxton. And my family, for one, knows the whole story."

At the mention of Drew Paxton, a flood of ugly remembrance and unwanted emotion washed over Cathryn. Ellie Able faded into near oblivion, her voice becoming nothing more than that of an annoying insect buzzing in Cathryn's ear. The near past overwhelmed her so, pulling her into a maelstrom of resurgent fear and shame, that she forgot she was not alone until a hand gripped her arm and Ellie Able's face, close to her own, swam into focus.

"Just what do you plan to do now, girl?" the woman snapped, shaking Cathryn's arm. "If you've a shred of decency left in you, you'll leave *now* or risk dragging down Jacob Matthews, his calling and his family."

As abruptly as she'd appeared at the door, Ellie Able released Cathryn's arm and disappeared into the shadows of the hallway, leaving Cathryn alone with her disintegrating world.

All her inner debate, all her plans, all her resolutions were for naught. Now, if she truly cared for Jacob and the unborn child she carried, she had only once choice. She couldn't risk destroying her best friend, the family and the calling he so loved. Couldn't risk having her child learn that he or she had been conceived not in love, but in violence.

Drew Paxton had already damaged Cathryn's life. She wouldn't allow him to harm two more.

Removing her wedding veil and the antique ring Jacob had given her when she'd agreed to marry him, she placed them both on the settee in the corner of the room. On the back of a discarded church envelope she hastily scribbled a note and left it with the other objects.

Then, without hesitation, without a glance backward, Cathryn O'Malley, eighteen and pregnant, left Grace Everlasting Church and Jacob Matthews waiting at the altar.

Chapter One

The message on the overpass read, Cassie O'Malley, I Love You! Lord, was that thing still there after all these years?

Cathryn clenched the wheel of her small car and harrumphed softly as she recalled Jacob, who'd painted it years ago, and the reaction of her conservative family. Having spotted it for the first time, one uncle, a farmer, had snorted, "At least the boy had sense enough to paint it John Deere green."

Glancing over her shoulder at her four-year-old son, Aiden, asleep in his car seat, she smiled. The little tyke was too young to understand that his rock-solid mama had been the scandal of Sweet Hope, Georgia, less than five years ago.

As if she'd discuss it, even if he were old enough. Cassie O'Malley was, for all intents and purposes, dead. In her place lived Cathryn O'Malley whose squeaky-clean present repudiated her past.

Perhaps that's why the butterflies in her stomach had turned to hummingbirds and then to frenzied bats, struggling to burst free. Oh, why had she let Alice Rose talk her into coming home?

Turning off the highway onto a two-lane road, Cathryn squinted against the bright April morning sunshine and adjusted the car's visor. Only her grandmother *and* a natural disaster could have convinced her to return to Sweet Hope. And for a week, no less. How she hoped she wouldn't run into Jacob Matthews. Perhaps the fact that the overpass message hadn't been painted out meant that Jacob was no longer living in Sweet Hope, either. Surely he'd want the evidence of his emotional folly erased. If he'd stayed. If... For a moment Cathryn wished she hadn't made the subject of Jacob Matthews off limits with her family for the past five years. Right now she'd feel much more at ease knowing the situation—Jacob's whereabouts—in advance.

Too, she now wished she hadn't agreed to meet her family at the Grace Everlasting Church complex—some of the few remaining untouched buildings in the county, and the center for tornado relief efforts. If Jacob, with his love of family, was anywhere today, he'd be at his father's church.

Cathryn slowed for a team of men clearing an enormous oak that had fallen by the roadside. Coming out of her introspective reverie, she scanned the fields on either side of the road. The devastation left in the wake of the killer twister appalled her. Tree trunks snapped twenty feet off the ground. Barn roofs missing. Farm equipment tumbled like Tinkertoys. Utility trucks swarming over the landscape. Ah, yes, Tornado Alley, she thought grimly.

"Girl," Cathryn murmured aloud, "stop whining about your own self. These people need you. That's why you came back. As for Jacob Matthews, well..."

"Mama?" Aiden's sleepy voice came to her from the back seat.

"Almost there, sweet baby. Almost there."

"Am *not* a baby, Mama," he protested softly, indignantly.

"Oh, that's right." Cathryn smiled. "I forget what a little man you've become."

"Am not *little,*" he grumbled.

Cathryn tried not to laugh as she glanced in the rearview mirror at her sober son. The love of her life, this child. This far too serious child. No, he was definitely not a little baby. He was far too sturdy and far too old—far older than his four years—to be a little baby. He'd been born old. And sober as a judge. Perhaps, Cathryn thought with a sigh, there must be balance in the universe: for every young impulsive Cassie O'Malley, an Aiden O'Malley.

"All right, my big man...we're almost there. I can see Grammy's church steeple now."

"Grammy?" Cathryn could hear her son rustling in his car seat. "Will Red be there, too?"

"No, sweets. This is Grammy's church, not her farm. And horses are definitely not allowed in church."

The silence told Cathryn he was weighing this new bit of information. Soberly. Intently. As intently as he weighed everything in his small life.

She took the moment of quiet to concentrate on the turn into Grace Everlasting's crowded parking lot. Amid the haphazardly parked cars she immediately recognized her father's pickup truck and breathed a sigh of relief. At least one ally in uncharted territory.

Dozens of people, working in teams and line brigades, unloaded bottled water, foodstuffs and clothing from several rental vans. But despite the confusing blur of activity, Cathryn's gaze was drawn to the front steps of the church where Jacob Matthews, his shirtsleeves rolled up, two small children clinging timidly to his pants legs, conducted an interview with a reporter from an Atlanta television station.

Cathryn inhaled sharply and applied the brake.

That could and couldn't be the Jacob Matthews she'd known.

Yes, the familiar, straight, untrainable lock of dark hair fell boyishly over one eye. Yes, the clear gaze with which he fixed the reporter and the expression of genuine concern were pure Jacob. Yes, the all-American good looks were still there...with a difference. Five years ago, at twenty-two, Jacob Matthews had looked like a boy. The boy next door. Today, standing on the church steps, above the crowd, he looked like a man. But larger than life. Larger, and with an aura of passion and power.

Passion and power? Cathryn wrinkled her nose. Where did that image come from? Surely the strain of her homecoming was making her melodramatic. She blinked and looked again and was startled to see that the compelling aura still surrounded her one-time best friend.

"Mama?" Aiden asked gravely from the back of the car. "Is that man important?"

Glancing over her shoulder, Cathryn could see her son's chubby little finger pointed directly at Jacob and the surrounding television crew.

"Yes, sweetcakes," she replied softly, remembering. "That man is important." But not for the reasons a four-year-old might think.

Opening the car door quickly to quell a sudden, unwanted flush of emotion, she moved to release Aiden from his car seat. Infusing her voice with a deliberate lightness, she said, "Let's see if we can find Grammy."

As he spoke with the reporter about his parish's needs, Jacob Matthews caught sight of the woman removing a young child from a car that had seen better days. Probably another tornado victim seeking shelter or assistance from his church. Would the flood of displaced never end? He needed to cut this interview short. The media could report the news of the storm without his analysis. His congregation needed him. Now.

Having politely but firmly dismissed the television crew, and having pried loose the Edwards twins from his legs and sent them on their way to the kitchen with the promise of Alice Rose's chocolate chip cookies, he strode toward the newcomer still standing next to her car.

Tall and slender, she cradled a sleepy child. She bent her head, capped with short blond hair, to kiss the boy's cheek. Shifting the child to her hip, she raised her head and started toward the church administration building.

Jacob's heart stood still.

Cassie O'Malley.

If he'd thought he'd forgotten her, he'd been mistaken. The old feeling of longing rushed through him. Longing tinged with a dozen questions. Questions and, yes, anger and hurt pride. If his parishioners could see inside him now, they'd have no doubts that he was flesh and blood. Imperfect as his flock. Human. A man like any other. His calling didn't ask him to deny that. It only asked that he struggle to be the best man he could be. Asked him to understand, too, the struggles of others.

Well, for five years he'd tried to understand what in Cassie O'Malley's struggles had made her run from him. Had made her stay away. Had made her put up a wall of silence even her close and loving family had been unable to penetrate. In five years he hadn't understood. That lack of understanding had galled him mightily.

And now, suddenly, she appeared before him, as beautiful and as puzzling as ever. Holding the child he and she should be raising. Together.

"Cassie," he breathed, half in greeting, half in remembrance.

She looked up, an uneasiness flitting across her features. "I prefer to go by Cathryn now, Jacob," she said softly.

She might prefer Cathryn, but she would always be his Cassie.

"You cut your hair," he murmured, then immediately could have kicked himself for the inanity.

She smiled, a brief smile that didn't reach her eyes, then glanced at the sober, watchful boy she carried in her arms. "I thought the time had come to shed the Alice in Wonderland locks. We all have to grow up sometime."

So she wanted a more mature look. She may have thought she'd achieved it by cutting her hair, but to Jacob the new short look made her seem even more vulnerable. A vulnerability tinged with a faraway sadness suggesting a heavy burden still carried. In his profession, he'd seen that look before. But never on a face so beautiful.

The boy squirmed in Cathryn's arms, silently but clearly demanding attention. "Your son?" Jacob asked simply, belying the rat-a-tat of his heart. He knew the child was her son. Knew, too, he should have been, by now, *their* son.

"Yes." Her arm circled in firm protection about the boy. "Aiden."

"How do you do, Aiden?" Jacob said, smiling and extending his hand.

In an almost too old gesture, the boy reached out to put his tiny, rounded hand into Jacob's long, lean one. "How do," Aiden murmured with a gravity that tugged at Jacob's heartstrings.

With reluctance Jacob released the boy's hand and sober gaze. "Have you come to check on your family?" Cathryn's stiffened posture told him she was eager to move on. He wanted to hold her, if only with words. "If you have, they're fine. Unscathed. And, as usual, the first in line to help. Right now Boone's out with a work crew. Belle's heading up the temporary day care, and Alice Rose is in charge of the kitchen and the volunteer roster." He lowered his voice dramatically. "Her word is *law.*"

At the mention of Alice Rose, a genuine smile passed over Cathryn's full lips, and for a moment Jacob caught a glimpse of the old Cassie.

"The matriarch of the O'Malley clan and the undisputed grande dame of Sweet Hope, Grammy never changes," she said in that lilting voice he'd never forgotten.

"Grammy?" The boy's serious face came to life. "You promised Grammy."

Cathryn kissed the boy's forehead. "So I did. If I have only one week to volunteer, I'd better check in with Grammy...and with Pastor Matthews." Her voice faltered as she turned to Jacob. "Is your father's office still in the same place?"

Jacob took a deep breath. "Yes...but he's no longer pastor. He retired, and is now on a mission trip to China with my mother."

Cathryn's face went pale. "Does that mean...?"

"That I'm pastor of Grace Everlasting?" He smiled a smile that Cathryn didn't reciprocate. "Yes. I am. If you've come to volunteer, you'll be working with me."

Was the prospect so unutterably horrible? The bleak look on Cathryn's face said yes. A look that said she was ready to run from him. Once more.

"Grammy!" Aiden squealed and pointed. Across the parking lot Alice Rose stood on the steps of the administration building, scanning the crowd. "I see Grammy. Mama, can I go?"

"Not alone, sweet thing," Cathryn replied evenly, her eyes still riveted to Jacob's. "Not across the parking lot. We'll go together. Now." She nodded at Jacob, and unease flickered in her eyes. "Perhaps we'll see each other again in the coming week. Right now I need to see my family."

"Of course."

She turned and, with her son held firmly on her hip, threaded her way through the press of people in Grace Everlasting's parking lot.

She didn't want to be here. That was clear. And, clearly too, she hadn't expected him to be here. Surely not as the pastor of Grace Everlasting. With that glitch in the program, her expectations for the week had obviously turned uneasy.

And what were his expectations? Could he handle the old feelings he had for her? Could he control the hurt he felt at her rejection? Could he ever again act as her friend to help her with the nameless hurt she so obviously still bore? He stuffed his hands deep into his pants pockets. Hah! And he had thought all he had to contend with was the aftermath of a tornado.

He watched across the parking lot as Alice Rose threw her arms around her granddaughter and her great-grandson.

Cathryn had said *perhaps* they'd see each other again in the coming week. Jacob smiled. If he could count on nothing else, he could count on the fact that Alice Rose would use her weight as matriarch of the O'Malley clan and grande dame of the volunteer roster to thrust Cathryn and him together at every turn.

His smile broadened. Despite his conflicting expectations, that thought was not unwelcome. No, not unwelcome at all.

Jacob started as Homer Martin patted him on the back in passing. "Better watch yourself, Pastor Matthews," the man said, chuckling. "For a man of God, that's one devilish grin you're sportin'."

As Cathryn felt herself and Aiden encircled in the strong, warm arms of her grandmother, she could also feel the gaze of Jacob Matthews, still hot upon her. Where in heaven's name had he developed such intensity?

"Cathryn! Aiden! Bless me, but you're a sight for sore eyes." Alice Rose stood back, held the two at arm's length and regarded them lovingly.

"Grammy," Aiden said earnestly, "I met the important man."

"The important man, dear?"

Cathryn lowered Aiden to the ground to give the flush in her cheeks time to subside. "Jacob Matthews." She shook her head and mentally upbraided herself for her ridiculously flustered state. "When we arrived, your new pastor was giving a television interview from the top of the church steps. Whether it was the crew and equipment or the height of the steps or the children clinging to his legs, I must admit he did look rather imposing."

Alice Rose smiled at Aiden and ruffled his hair, but her words were for Cathryn. "You will find, my dear, that Jacob Matthews has come into his own."

"You could have warned me, Grammy." Cathryn uttered the words softly, without accusation. What was the point of accusation? If she'd been warned, she'd have been no less unnerved.

Aiden tugged at Alice Rose's hand. "Mama says Red's not allowed in church. Why not?"

"Ah, lovey," Alice Rose replied with a chuckle, "if the Important Man had his way, we'd have all of God's creatures at services. Red included." She bent to whisper conspiratorially in the boy's ear. "But a few parishioners are still very stuffy. Won't hear of it."

Aiden nodded his head solemnly, in obvious, total understanding.

"Aiden!" With a jubilant shriek four-year-old Margaret O'Malley emerged from the administration doorway and flung herself at the boy.

A flustered teenage girl followed closely behind. When she saw Alice Rose, she tried to explain. "Miss Belle sent us to see if Margaret's relations had arrived yet. I told Margaret we needed to hold hands and use our Sunday manners through the halls, but you know Margaret. . . ."

Both Alice Rose and Cathryn laughed aloud. Yes, they knew Margaret.

The little girl was Cathryn's sister by marriage. Just a few months younger than Aiden, the daughter of Cathryn's father, Boone, and her stepmother, Belle, Margaret was impetuosity itself. Where Aiden was as fair and as constant as the sun, Margaret was as dark and as changing as dappled shadows. Whereas Aiden had been born old, Margaret would be a girl at ninety-two. Aiden seldom laughed. Margaret seldom didn't. But despite their differences the two children adored each other. Technically aunt and nephew, they were closer than the closest cousins.

Although Cathryn had returned to Sweet Hope for no more than a few brief visits, the O'Malley clan had regularly visited her and Aiden in south Georgia. Family was of the utmost importance. Although Cathryn wished to avoid her hometown, the O'Malleys were determined to keep their circle of love unbroken. The obvious bond between Aiden and Margaret was proof positive of their success.

"Come, Aiden," Margaret cooed in his ear. "We have guinea pigs in our classroom."

Although he didn't smile, Aiden's eyes widened. "Can I go, Mama?"

The teenage escort spoke to Cathryn. "Miss Belle said I was to bring the two of them back to the day care so that you could go with Miss Alice Rose and get your assignment." The girl smiled. "She said you could even sneak a glass of tea as long as you came straight after to see her."

"Thank you, Brie," Alice Rose replied. "Tell Belle I won't keep Cathryn more than a half hour."

"Come on, you two." Brie placed her hands on Aiden's and Margaret's heads. "I suppose it'd be too much to ask you to hold hands and walk."

Margaret shot the teenager the most dazzling of four-year-old smiles, grasped Aiden's hand, then, with a yelp of joy, darted into the building. With a shrug and a roll of her eyes toward Alice Rose, the teenager turned and followed.

"Come on." Alice Rose winked slyly and took Cathryn's hand. "Shall we run through the halls, too?"

"Oh, sure, Grammy. Let's just call attention to my return." Cathryn kept her tone of voice lighthearted, but her heart was not light.

This return, especially after having met Jacob earlier, was proving to be one of the most difficult things she'd ever attempted. A real turning point in her life. A real exercise in growth, it was going to take all her strength to be able to keep her head up, to keep her distance—from Jacob and from his parishioners—for a whole week.

Who could guess what Grace Everlasting's parishioners knew or thought they knew about the circumstances of her life? About Drew Paxton. About Jacob Matthews and his humiliation at the altar five years ago. About Aiden and the ugliness surrounding his conception. Did they know or suspect the truth? Did they even care after all this time?

Whether they did or not, Cathryn did care. As if it were yesterday.

She felt her grandmother tug her hand, and realized she'd been lost in thought.

"Tea, Grammy," she said with a sigh. "I could use some sweet tea."

Alice Rose led the way through the cavernous hallways of the church administration building. Led the way through the cot-filled gymnasium to the enormous kitchen at the rear of the complex. Everywhere along their way people clustered together, the adults working purposefully, the children playing together as if this disaster had merely provided a holiday for their benefit, and the very old sitting quietly with sad, watchful eyes. They'd seen this before, this awesome power of nature. If they watched and waited long enough, they'd see it again, surely.

A few curious glances settled on Alice Rose and Cathryn. A few whispers could be heard as they passed. That would be all for now. No matter what people thought, they would never dare utter a hurtful word in Alice Rose's presence. The woman commanded too much respect, Cathryn thought ruefully. Grammy was her talisman.

In the kitchen Alice Rose spoke cheerfully to the crew of men and women busily preparing box lunches. Pouring two tall glasses of iced tea, she swooped past the activity and out the back door into the late-morning spring sunshine. Crossing the new grass, she sat finally at a picnic table under an ancient flowering dogwood.

"Sit, dear." She patted the bench beside her. "You must be tired after your drive."

Cathryn sat and, wrapping her hands around the tall, cool glass of tea, felt her muscles relax. Until now she hadn't realized how tightly she'd clenched her fists on the seemingly endless walk through the church buildings. How hot her palms had become. What a most ridiculous reaction to a perfectly normal homecoming.

Homecomings should be joyous occasions. No one could love their family more than Cathryn loved hers. And she must remember the joy her homecomings brought them, that this particular one was especially for them.

She turned to her grandmother and insisted, "I'm not tired. How could I be tired when I look around and see how y'all must have worked nonstop for the past couple days?"

Alice Rose sighed deeply. "It has been a forty-eight hours to remember." Patting Cathryn's hand, she added, "Just having you home again, though, gives me renewed strength. You're like a tonic to me, Cathryn girl. Always have been."

Cathryn leaned her head onto her grandmother's shoulder. "And you have been my strength, Grammy."

"Posh and bother!" Alice Rose protested, squeezing Cathryn about the shoulders. "You're strong all on your own."

Nearby, someone cleared his voice very deliberately.

The two women looked up, startled. Jacob Matthews stood at the end of the picnic table.

"Sorry to interrupt." His clear, sincere gray eyes said his apology was no mere formality. "But, Alice Rose, did you ever find me that administrative assistant? I've been in touch with the federal emergency agency...and we're going to need someone who knows the ins and outs of government red tape. More so, certainly, than I do."

Cathryn did not care for the Cheshire-cat grin that stole across her grandmother's face.

"Why, yes," Alice Rose fairly purred. "From the start I had just the person in mind, although I wasn't certain we could get her. But now...well, Pastor Matthews, meet your new administrative assistant."

With a sinking heart Cathryn looked over her shoulder, hoping against hope that some professional-looking woman, a briefcase loaded with government documents under one arm, would be standing off to the side. No such luck. Turning to look again at her grandmother, she was appalled to see the look of unabashed glee on the older woman's face.

Cathryn clenched her back teeth till she could feel the muscles of her jaw pulse. The O'Malley women were notorious, incorrigible matchmakers. Herself included. She thought of Boone and Belle, and how Alice Rose and she had fairly thrown the two of them together. But, until now, Cathryn had avoided being the object of any romantic schemes. Dear Lord, she prayed in silent haste, get me off the hook now, and I'll never plot again. Ever.

Too late.

"Terrific," Jacob said, his tone level and cool, but his gaze too warm and far too intense. "I had visions of being buried in paperwork. One disaster's enough, thank you very much."

"No!" Cathryn managed to squeak. "Grammy promised Belle I'd help with the temporary day care. So that I could be near Aiden." She swung her gaze to an unrepentant Alice Rose. "You promised," she hissed.

Alice Rose fluttered her hands airily. "That was before Brie and her classmates offered to be Belle's helpers." She patted Cathryn on the arm. "Really, love, you can't expect us to hold positions open in a disaster. We grab willing hands and put them to work as they come through the door. Anyway, with your experience, you will be a far greater help to Jacob. And Aiden will love being with his Nonny Belle and little Margaret."

He would. He'd see it as a grand holiday. There was no valid objection there. No valid objection, either, to helping Jacob with the parish's federal disaster aid applications. For the past five years she'd held down a position as clerk in the town offices of Albany, Georgia. Two years ago Albany, because of the worst floods on record, had forged its own intimate relationship with the federal emergency agency. If Cathryn knew anything, she knew the ins and outs of government red tape. No, there were no valid objections there, *but...*

She narrowed her eyes and glared at her smugly smiling grandmother. This had been Alice Rose's outrageous plan from the beginning. Feeling increasingly cornered, she swung her gaze to Jacob, who stood patiently waiting, offering no assistance, his expression unreadable.

"Well?" he asked finally.

"Well, what?" Cathryn felt dread bog her down.

"Will you accept the position?"

"Where is your parish-paid secretary? Doesn't this job fall in his or her domain?" Surely he had qualified help who would get her off the hook.

Jacob shrugged and seemed to suppress a smile. "Martha's on maternity leave. I was fast becoming swamped even before the tornado."

"I can only stay a week." He'd really need someone more permanent. "I had to take vacation time. The wheels of government grind very slowly. I doubt we could accomplish much in only a week."

"Believe me, I'll take what I can get."

His words jolted her. He'd said the very same thing over five years ago. Under very different circumstances and with disastrous results. She almost asked him if he knew what he was getting himself into this time. Almost asked, but didn't. She'd hurt him once, but never again. Not even flippantly to get herself out of an uncomfortable situation.

She took a deep breath and thought of the victims of the tornado. What was a little personal discomfort compared to their distress?

She set her chin. "When do I start?"

It appeared that both Jacob and her grandmother had been holding their breath. They exhaled sharply, simultaneously.

"Have you seen Belle yet?" Jacob asked.

"No."

"She'd kill me if I didn't let you say hello. When you have, meet me in my office. We'll get right to work. And Alice Rose... thanks. I didn't realize you had an expert up your sleeve."

As he turned and strode purposefully across the grass, Cathryn couldn't help but wonder how he felt about being thrust together with her. After all these years. After all the hurt. Once, they'd been best friends, but she'd ruined that. Now she could only hope that even if she couldn't mend that painful rift, she could help him and the people he'd sworn to lead. Surely he'd recognize the gesture as an attempt at repaying all he'd been willing to do for her.

She watched him, tall, straight and powerful, enter the church kitchen. It was hard to believe that this man had been the all-too-trusting boy of her past. This man was in charge. Of his parish. Of himself and his emotions. That was evident. Evident in his authoritative carriage. Evident in his confident smile. Evident in the way he assumed everyone would pitch in willingly for a just cause.

No, this Jacob Matthews had left the naive and adoring boy in him behind. Cathryn must be careful. Whatever happened this week, this man would not be befriended easily or casually. For, laced with his aura of authority and confidence was an intensity that spoke of forever after. Forever after... or nothing at all.

* * *

Standing behind his desk, gazing out the window, Jacob heard the creak of the office door opening. It could only be Cassie. He never felt electricity in the air except when Cassie was near. Without even seeing her, he felt the humming charge so intensely now that he wondered how he would ever get through the coming week and still maintain his professional cool.

Turning slowly, he stared into the widest eyes. The color of cornflowers. Wide, blue and not a little willful.

After all these years, she still had the ability to tie his tongue.

She shook her head. "Well, where do we start?"

He inhaled sharply, then looked at the mounds of paper on his desk. Paperwork, as necessary as it was, could wait a few minutes longer. With the craziness of the tornado's aftermath, he might not see her alone again in the coming week. This chance might never come again. And he needed the answer to a question that had burned a hole in his heart for five years.

"Why did you leave me?" he asked without preamble. "Your note told me very little. Except that you couldn't marry me."

Shock and something else—the desire to flee?—flickered for an instant in her eyes. When she spoke, however, her voice was calm, controlled. "Is this the pastor of Grace Everlasting asking?"

"No, this is the man asking. Jacob Matthews. Do you remember him, Cassie? He used to be your friend."

"Yes, Jacob," she replied quietly, never taking her clear gaze from his. "I remember him. You were the best friend I ever had."

It was his turn to be shocked. He hadn't expected this soft, touchingly frank reaction from her. He'd expected passionate defiance, yes. A story of self-reliance, perhaps. But this softness, never. Cassie O'Malley had been many things. Bright as a shooting star. Alluring. Aggravating. But soft? Never soft.

"Why, then? Why did you run?" He tried to maintain an open mind, but, despite her present softness and look of vulnerability that cried for understanding, the old hurt in him—the old barely suppressed anger—bubbled to the surface, catching his words, giving them an edge he didn't want her to hear.

"Because it wouldn't have worked between us." As she spoke, her eyes clouded, showing him just enough uncertainty to give him leave to pursue the matter.

"Hogwash." He took several steps closer to her until she took a barely noticeable quarter step backward. He stopped, not wanting to force her to flee. "That was the one thing we agreed upon. Right from the beginning. That we'd make it work."

She smiled. A tired smile that curved her sensuous lips, but didn't light the cool blue of her eyes. "Oh, Jacob, we were so young."

She'd been eighteen, he twenty-two when he'd found her, crumpled and crying in her car in the parking lot behind the drugstore. One pregnancy test had come up positive. In disbelief, she'd gone to buy a second. Passing, he'd seen her slumped over in the driver's seat. A mere acquaintance then, he'd seen—had felt—her desolation. He'd slipped into the passenger seat of her car to comfort her, and had soon found his life altered inexorably.

"Yes, young," he replied, his voice husky. "Young, but right, all the same."

Her eyes lost their softness, took on the willfulness he remembered. Flashed a challenge as she spoke. "I didn't love you."

The words still hurt, but, even today, they were only half the story. Half the truth. He knew it. And knew beneath her show of strength and self-reliance that she knew it, too. "You cared for me," he insisted.

She lowered her lashes, as if it somehow hurt to admit it. "I did. But I didn't love you."

"I loved you enough for the two of us."

"My baby wasn't yours," she declared, raising her gaze to his. Masking, he thought, her real feelings with a false frankness.

"He was as mine as you would have allowed."

She threw up her hands, then turned her back on him. "You never knew the whole story. If you had..."

"If I had, what?" Jacob moved close behind her. Putting his hands firmly on her shoulders he felt her flinch, but wouldn't let her move away.

"If you had," she whispered raggedly, "you never would have offered to marry me."

Oh, he'd have offered to marry her under any circumstances. The young Jacob Matthews had been that crazy in love with her. But the memory hurt. And now his pride wouldn't allow him to admit his juvenile devotion—even to prove an important point.

"You never gave me a chance to prove myself, Cassie. As passionate and as energetic as you were, as open and frank, you always kept a part of yourself...apart. Never shared all of yourself. Not with me. Not even with your family."

Her silence, the stiff set of her shoulders told him he'd rubbed the truth. And the truth was raw.

"You were strong, Cassie O'Malley. Too strong, perhaps. I always suspected that you felt you could *will* hurt away. Alone."

She turned slowly to face him. "I would have made a terrible pastor's wife. My past would have sapped the strength you needed to lead your congregation. Would have hurt your calling and your family. You may have loved me, but you loved them, as well. I couldn't shame you. Or them. At the last moment I was convinced of that awful truth. That's why I left."

The word *shame* reverberated in the air between them.

There was no false frankness in her regard now. Jacob felt as if he could see to the depths of her very soul. And what he saw was selfless. The hurt she'd inflicted had not been capricious. It amazed him to realize that a gnawing suspicion of her capriciousness had been the cornerstone of his pain these past five years.

He took a deep, clean breath as his blood ran hot in his veins. "That said, you'll let me show you how none of it's true?" For the first time in five years he saw the possibility of mending the rift between them. Between him and the woman he still loved.

Ashen shock registered on her face, as if she'd recognized immediately the full import of his suggestion. "Nothing's changed, Jacob," she countered breathlessly. "I'd have been the ruin of you five years ago. I'd be the ruin of you today." The color began to return to her cheeks. "I agreed to help you with your paperwork because of my family. I agreed to this conversation because you deserved to hear the truth. But tongues are probably already wagging outside this very door. Anything more between us will court disaster."

Her fingers fluttered to her cheeks, now flushed bright pink. "I'm afraid I need to freshen up before we begin."

Before we begin. Yes, thought Jacob with an inner peace he hadn't known in years, with this small bit of candor, we've only just begun.

Chapter Two

Cathryn blotted her face with a cold, damp paper towel, then leaned against the sink in the church lavatory. Her reflection in the mirror stared back with a physical disarray that duplicated her inner turmoil. How long had she been back in Sweet Hope? An hour, maybe? Just long enough to hug Alice Rose and Belle . . . and have her emotions shaken topsy-turvy by one Jacob Matthews.

She pressed the damp paper towel to the flush in her cheeks. Why he had her so flustered was beyond her comprehension. He shouldn't matter. She didn't love him.

Five years ago she'd cared enough for him that she'd set him free. Free from the taint of possible scandal. Better to be left at the altar than saddled with a wife whose past would come to haunt him. Why couldn't he understand that she'd done it for his own good? He, of all people. Wasn't he in the business of sacrifice? A little discomfort now for the common good down the road?

She raised her eyes heavenward. Dear Lord, she wasn't being sacrilegious. It's just that Jacob, as a man of God, should understand the difference between what could be and what ought to be. If five years ago there had been any chance that those two concepts could possibly have coincided, Cathryn O'Malley would have married Jacob Matthews, the soon-to-be pastor. Would have worked at being a loving wife.

Cathryn flushed anew at the thought of his strong hands on her shoulders earlier. Strong. He'd been a strong boy. Had grown into an even stronger man. And there was a definite allure to strength. She'd felt it just now in his office. A woman could be content to spend her life under the protection of a strong, compassionate man.

Some other woman. Not Cathryn. At the thought of the intimacy such a relationship would naturally bring, an involuntary shiver ran through her.

Despite the one dark area in her existence, she'd done well on her own for the past five years, thank you very much. Away from Sweet Hope. Away from Jacob's all too intent gaze. Away from his inevitable questions. Like those just now in his office.

All things considered, his questioning could have been harsh after all the years of silence between them. But it hadn't been. He hadn't been. Angry, yes, at first. But controlled in his anger. Obviously, he'd truly wanted to hear her side of the story before he passed judgment. She'd had the distinct impression that he'd actually suspended judgment for five long years until he could hear her explanations. Remarkable.

Remarkable, too, but a little frightening, was the very non-pastor-like way in which he'd looked at her. As if, somehow, the past five years had been swept away. As if he were still the young man who'd obviously loved her. As if the arguments had been argued and the decisions made. As if she and he were meant to be together.

Despite all reason.

Cathryn started as the lavatory door to the hall swung open, and her stepmother, Belle, entered the room.

Cathryn smiled. Then smiled even more widely as she thought how no one could *not* smile in the presence of her stepmother, Arabella Sherman O'Malley, a woman of such unorthodox grace, charm and warmth she'd captured the cold and rebellious heart of Boone O'Malley.

"I thought I just saw you. Checking up on me, hmm?" Cathryn asked, feeling a swell of not totally unpleasant exasperation at the lengths her family would go to protect one of their own.

"Even volunteers are allowed breaks." Belle pretended to primp in the mirror. "This is a break, dear heart. It has nothing to do with you."

Cathryn cocked an eyebrow. "No lavatories in the school wing?"

Belle flashed her stepdaughter a brilliant smile. "So I'm concerned about you. You and Jacob. So sue me."

"There is no *Jacob and me.*"

Belle ignored Cathryn's protest. "How did it go just now?"

How did it go? How *did* it go? "Have you noticed that Jacob Matthews has become a very intense man?" Cathryn asked by way of temporary evasion.

Belle hesitated before she spoke. "Let's just say he's not a man to be trifled with."

Bristling, Cathryn retorted, "I have no intention of trifling with him!"

"I think, if you're going to work with him this week, you owe him some kind of explanation. . . ."

"We took care of that just now." Cathryn didn't want to discuss it.

"You explained *everything?*"

"Yes."

A look of sad reproach crept into Belle's eyes. "Well, then, perhaps after all these years, you could explain it to me."

Oh, how Cathryn hated to see that look in her stepmother's eyes. And not just in Belle's eyes. She'd seen the look before in her father's eyes. And in her grandmother's. But as much as the looks hurt Cathryn, she could not hurt her family by telling the whole sordid story. They only thought they wanted to know the truth, but they wouldn't. And so she'd never told it—not to a soul. Not even, fully, to Jacob.

"Only if you explain to me," Cathryn offered, making her words deliberately light, "why, after years of being one of my best friends, you're now playing the part of the wicked, interrogating stepmother."

Belle's eyes widened. "Oh, dear. You know how I hate the *S* word."

Cathryn did know. And she'd used the word knowing it would make Belle back off. Jacob had been right. There always had been a part of Cathryn that needed to remain apart.

"I'm sorry. I didn't mean to hurt you." Truly she hadn't. Tossing the paper towel in the trash, Cathryn kissed Belle's cheek. "I have to go. Jacob doesn't even suspect the government red tape he's in for. Come by with Aiden when you're ready to head home. I presume I'll be staying out at Grammy's, as usual?"

Belle laid a restraining hand on Cathryn's arm. "Sweetheart . . . didn't Alice Rose tell you?"

"Tell me what?" Cathryn didn't like the serious look on Belle's face. Had the tornado destroyed the farm? Panic began to rise like bitter bile.

"Although the farm—the house itself—sustained very little damage," Belle replied quickly, reassuringly, "the power's out, as is the power at our house in town."

Cathryn looked above at the well-lit lavatory ceiling. "But . . . ?"

"Several years ago Jacob had the foresight to have generators installed at the church. He's always seen Grace Everlasting as a necessary center of the community. Lucky, now, for us."

"Yes, lucky," Cathryn replied distractedly. "But I want to get home. Aiden will need the stability of familiar surroundings. . . ." She felt too old to mention that she needed that same stability. "We can use candles."

"Sorry, love. The county commissioner's asked for a temporary ban on all but emergency travel. Too many power lines down. To many weakened gas lines in damaged houses.

Too great a risk for the mere pleasure of sleeping in your own bed."

"But what are we supposed to do?" Cathryn took a deep, cleansing breath. This had not been in the cards. She'd counted on the idea of being able to get through this week by retreating occasionally to the safety of her grandmother's house. She was not prepared for life in a community goldfish bowl.

Belle smiled and wrapped her arm around Cathryn's shoulders. "I'll tell you what you're going to do—you're going to work till you're tired. Then you're going to join the pajama party in the gymnasium. I've saved two cots for you and Aiden." Her eyes flashed mischievously. "And cheer up. I feel sure Jacob isn't as hard a taskmaster as rumored. Remember, it's only gossip that he worked his secretary so hard she decided to have a baby to escape."

Great.

It wasn't the thought of hard work that made Cathryn's stomach flip-flop. She was used to hard work. Relished it, in fact. But here she'd thought she'd only have to make it through one long day at a time under the scrutiny of the good folk at Grace Everlasting. Now, with her grandmother's assignment and her stepmother's too-cheerful announcement, she was faced with an unremitting week of elbow-to-elbow life with Jacob Matthews.

As Jacob talked on the phone to his congressman, Cathryn slowly pushed open the door to the office. When she saw him engaged, she appeared ready to retreat. Unwilling to let her slip away, he silently beckoned her into the room. She'd seen her family. It was obvious she'd freshened up. She had no more excuses. Now she was his. He wasn't about to let her go again.

He quickly wrapped up his conversation, hung up, then rose to his feet. "Cas . . . Cathryn. Ready to start? I wasn't kidding when I said I was going to need your help. That was Representative Hoyt on the phone. It seems there are preliminaries to the preliminaries of applying for federal aid."

"Too true." Cathryn rolled her eyes. "The government makes you jump through hoops just to get to the obstacle course. As if the victims of a disaster hadn't gone through enough."

"That's why I want us to do as much as we can. The people in this county are struggling right now to piece their present together. When they've done that, we need to be ready to help forge a future. We can do that by easing the paperwork."

A faintly puzzled look spread across her face. "I would think that was the duty of the local elected officials. You don't even need to involve yourself. Not with paperwork."

He snorted softly. "Bureaucracy seldom wears a human face. The victims of this tornado are people. People who deserve to be treated with dignity and kindness. That's where I come in, as an advocate for these people—my people."

The corners of her sensuous mouth turned up in a small smile. "You always were the great protector."

They were no longer talking about the tornado, about the people of his parish. They were talking about a five-year-old storm of an entirely different nature. About an eighteen-year-old girl...and his own need to have her. She might correct him and say he'd only demonstrated a need to protect her. She hadn't known that his motives hadn't been wholly altruistic.

He looked at her now. Looked deep into the blue of her challenging gaze, and realized with shock that his desire for her had not diminished.

With great restraint he answered. "I've learned to protect now only when my protection is wanted."

"Is this the man speaking or the pastor?"

A jolt of disappointment arced through him. "That's the second time you've distinguished between the two. Why should one preclude the other?"

She tilted her chin in obvious provocation. "Should? Is that the case?"

He could see through her ruse—push him to distraction so that he'd think the walking away was his idea. Well, he wouldn't be baited. Or pushed, for that matter.

"Ah, Cathryn O'Malley," he replied softly, "that I can't tell you. If you stick around Sweet Hope long enough for the dust to settle around your heels, you can decide for yourself."

It satisfied him to see the quick quirk of one slender eyebrow. He'd made his point. For now. He turned to the pile of papers on his desk. "This morning," he continued, all business, "we need to make a list of contact people. Find out from them exactly what we do and the order in which we do it. I don't want anyone in this parish rejected for aid because of sloppy paperwork. Do you understand?"

"Yes, I think I do," she answered breathily. He had the distinct impression she wasn't referring to paperwork.

For an hour they worked side by side, searching for every available name that could be of help in relief efforts. Phoning—thank goodness the phone lines were up and running—setting up a network. Silence reigned between the two of them except for the sparse conversation necessary to conduct strict business.

It was the kind of business, however, that Jacob could conduct on autopilot. Business that allowed too much time to observe his new assistant. Observation that was, at the same time, pleasurable and painful.

What had she been doing all these years? He hadn't a clue. She'd left word in her scrawled note and through her family that he was not to follow her. He hadn't. For too many unsatisfactory reasons. One of which had been his male ego. To be left at the altar was one thing. To possibly be used as a doormat was quite another. Forgiveness might be divine, but self-abnegating foolishness, well . . . he didn't think even the Lord suffered fools gladly.

Yes, the pleasure of having Cassie O'Malley by his side again was tempered with the still-sharp pain of rejection. And her words and body language of this morning told him not to expect the future to be any different from the past.

He pinched the bridge of his nose and tried to focus on the business at hand. But the room had become too small, Cathryn's palpable aura taking up too much of it. It seemed that too often their hands touched in a reach for a stack of papers or the phone receiver. Electricity hummed in the air. He felt a stifling need to break free.

Relief came from an unexpected source.

Just as Jacob felt he could stand the confinement not one second longer, Homer Martin poked his head around the office door to exclaim, "Jacob! Come quick! The kitchen! We got an emergency!" The man disappeared as quickly as he'd appeared.

Thoughts racing through his head of fire or an explosion or ptomaine poisoning, at the very least, Jacob sprang to his feet. "Cassie, come on! Who knows how many extra hands we'll need."

Cathryn struggled to keep up with Jacob's sprinting form. The physical exertion was exhilarating after the tension in the office. If Homer Martin hadn't burst into the room, surely she herself would have burst. The unspoken words between Jacob and her had been that explosive.

She'd said some strong words in there. Words that had been designed to push him away. But he'd held his own. Even, if she'd read him right, had initiated a gentle offense. She thought of his challenge to stay in town long enough for the dust to settle about her heels. As she established what she hoped was a dignified jog in pursuit of the pastor on the run, the corner of her mouth quirked in a wry smile. Why, he'd as much as accused her of running from confrontation.

And hadn't that been the very case?

Well, she might have run in the past, but now, for whatever reason, she'd returned. And not for just a stealthy overnight visit. She was here for a week. In plain sight.

She glanced to the side as she wound her way through the cots in the gymnasium. Jacob held a lead the entire length of the enormous room. People stared. First at their pastor. Then at Cathryn in full pursuit. Cathryn blew out her cheeks. If any bystander had a sense of poetic irony, how odd this chase must look. Especially after her flight from Jacob five years ago.

Oh, let them look, she thought with irritation. What did or did not go on between Jacob and her was nobody's business but their own. She was not the pastor's wife. She was simply a volunteer in her hometown. The O'Malley name gave her as much right to be here as the next person.

As she pushed through the doors to the kitchen, it hit her: This was the first time in five years she'd declared, even to herself, her right to take up breathing room in Sweet Hope.

She had no time for her delicious little epiphany to sink in. Once inside the crowded kitchen, she was deluged in a babble of voices. Jacob, at the center of the mob, standing head and shoulders above the gesticulating volunteers, seemed totally unflustered, seemed satisfied and able, even, to listen to everyone at once.

Homer Martin stood, hands on bony hips, an expectant look on his face, by the open back door.

Cathryn, despite the din, could see no indication of an emergency. She smelled no smoke, saw no evidence of an explosion, nor any prone body on the floor. What could have caused all this excitement?

Whatever it was, Jacob held it and the entire body of kitchen volunteers at bay. Alone.

Instinctively, Cathryn pushed through the crowd to his side.

Laying a hand on his arm and stretching on tiptoe to gain his attention, she fairly shouted in his ear, "What's going on here?"

As he turned to her, she saw on his face not worry but the most heavenly of boyish grins. The warm gray of his eyes caught her and held her. Before she could guard against it, her heart pounded pleasurably in response.

Turning slowly, as if unwilling to release her, he held up a hand to silence the crowd. Once he had everyone's attention, he again turned to Cathryn.

"It seems," he said, his grin undiminished, "that the generators at Chumley's Supermarket are malfunctioning.

Mr. Chumley is donating as much frozen food as we can store here at Grace Everlasting."

"That's wonderful," Cathryn replied. "What's the problem?" She remembered the church suppers of her youth. Suppers that seemed to feed a multitude. Remembered how impressed as a child she'd been with the mammoth size of the industrial-strength appliances used to prepare and store the food. Certainly, Grace Everlasting couldn't take in a supermarket's entire frozen food section, but it could take in enough to feed the tornado's homeless for days to come.

"The problem," replied Jacob, mischief creeping into his grin, "is the ice cream. We need room in the freezers for the 'real' food. But Chumley has dozens and dozens of gallons of ice cream he needs to dispose of before it spoils."

"Why can't you serve it after the box lunch?" Cathryn asked, glancing at her watch. It was almost eleven.

"That's what I say," came a woman's voice from the group of volunteers.

"Because," Jacob explained patiently, "by the time we assemble several hundred people for lunch, pass out the box lunches and allow for everyone to eat, the ice cream will have melted."

"Y'all seem to forget," Homer Martin, still by the door, piped up. "Chumley's men didn't ask permission before they unloaded the ice cream with the other frozen food. It's stacked up on pallets in the shade by the back door here, just waitin' for seventy-five degrees' worth of April sunshine to turn it into fly soup."

A groan went up from the parishioners. All eyes turned to Jacob for an answer.

"It seems to me," suggested Jacob, a definite twinkle sparking his gray gaze, "the only solution is to ring the bell to assemble everyone who's on the grounds. We'll break out the toppings we keep for the sundae socials and have a party."

Cathryn had to suppress a smile as she saw the reaction of Jacob's flock to his suggestion. Except for the look of pure glee on Homer Martin's face, the others appeared as if Jacob had suggested they dance naked in the streets.

"What about the box lunches?"

"There's nothing in the box lunches that won't keep till midafternoon," Jacob replied. "We can send them with everyone after ice cream, and people can eat wherever and whenever they feel hungry."

"Why, Pastor Matthews!" one woman squeaked. "The children, too?"

Jacob cocked one dark eyebrow. "I was thinking of the children *especially.*"

"But it's *before* lunch," someone else sputtered. "We'll ruin their little appetites!"

"They—we—have been through a lot in the past forty-eight hours," Jacob responded patiently. "Instead of ruining anything, I think an impromptu sundae social will brighten our day considerably."

"Amen!" Homer Martin shouted.

One woman, a scowl on her face, elbowed her way to the front of the group. "Pastor Matthews," she admonished tartly, "this smacks of a celebration. Do you really think, in the midst of this serious disaster—of all this loss—it's seemly to be throwing a party?"

Ah, Pastor Matthews, thought Cathryn, how do you extricate yourself from this with dignity?

Jacob smiled, this time gently, making the glowering parishioner the sole beneficiary. "Mrs. Singleton, I'm reminded of the old saying, 'Man thinks. God laughs.' Now, I think, we've been given a wonderful opportunity to laugh with him."

The woman, still scowling but silent, looked around for support from the crowd.

Before she could get it, Jacob added, "It's either that or form work crews to bury the melting ice cream. It will, if left uneaten, eventually form one enormous pest-attracting mess."

"I, for one," chimed in Homer Martin, "would rather eat it than bury it. Preferably, eat it with chocolate sauce and marshmallows!"

Cathryn watched the group slowly come to grudging agreement. Watched the roguish twinkle in Jacob's eyes as his parishioners began to turn their attention from objections and complaint to the task of organizing a quick sundae social.

Jacob's solution had been an unexpected and unorthodox one, but, thinking of Aiden and Margaret, she had to conclude it would be welcome. A fun departure from the ordinary. Jacob had always been a warm and fun-loving young man. Why had Cathryn assumed he'd have to leave these qualities at the threshold of his career as a man of God?

Man thinks, God laughs, he'd said. What a refreshing thought. In her own recent experience she'd never once thought of God laughing. If she'd pictured him at all, it had been with a disapproving scowl on his face, like the one on the parishioner who didn't think parties seemly in the face of disaster.

Cathryn much preferred Jacob's interpretation.

Jacob squeezed the sides of the carton to get the last of the Rocky Road ice cream for little Cindy Makum. "That's it, Miss Cindy," he said with a wink. "If you come back for thirds, you'll have to switch flavors."

The five-year-old giggled as she headed for the end of the table and the sundae toppings.

Glancing at the table piled with empty cartons, Jacob then gazed out across the athletic field with satisfaction. At the dozens of children, faces smeared with ice cream, chasing each other in the warm April sun. At the mostly women and elderly adults who, although marooned, chatted amiably. As if their lives had not been turned upside down. His decision that they all spoil their appetites with ice cream had been right. For a few brief moments they'd forgotten the enormity of the task that lay ahead of them. For a few brief moments they'd kept dark thoughts at bay and had embraced simple joy and spontaneity. And life.

"Under normal circumstances, does your congregation have this much fun?" Cathryn's voice broke into his thoughts.

He turned to look at her, ice cream scoop in her hand, a bemused expression on her beautiful face.

"You know," he replied seriously, "in the two years that I've been pastor here, my hardest task has been to convince my congregation that joy isn't a sin."

A shadow passed over her blue eyes, leaving them dark and faintly troubled. "Aren't you afraid of being considered a lightweight?"

He smiled gently, remembering that hot July day when he'd assumed the pulpit for the first time. Had asked those assembled to join him in his favorite anthem, "Joy to the World." Had seen the disapproving glances. Had known the parishioners saw him as a definite lightweight. He'd had to prove to them over the past two years how an exuberant love of life and a spiritual calling were not mutually exclusive.

"You know me well enough," he declared softly, "to know I don't much worry about gossip."

As she looked away, he saw the set of her shoulders grow stiff. He might not care about rumor and innuendo, but it was clear that Cathryn O'Malley still did. Despite her strong demeanor, some secret part of her still lay vulnerable.

"What a luxury," she breathed almost inaudibly.

"Why?" Jacob felt troubled that thoughtless words had the ability to wound this woman. "Why would you consider ignoring gossip a luxury?"

He followed her intense gaze out over the athletic field to a small, sturdy four-year-old boy. Her son. Tethered to Cassie by an invisible but absolute filament of love and devotion.

"I want nothing to touch him. To hurt him," she answered, her voice strong, protective. "Nothing."

Jacob understood. Partly. Aiden had been a love child. The living embodiment of a youthful, impetuous act. But an unwed pregnancy and single parenthood didn't carry quite the disapproving punch it had years ago. Especially not if the mother had clearly made good. Had clearly accepted her responsibilities. Had raised the child with guidance and love. As Cathryn had.

"You've no need to give a thought to wagging tongues," he declared, that old protective feeling rising in him. "You've done a fine job, raising a fine son, Cassie O'Malley." He said her name—her old nickname—lovingly.

She turned to him. And turned on him a smile of such incredible beauty, he inhaled sharply. Selfishly he filed away this bit of information: If ever he wanted to receive one of these rare magical smiles, he had the key. Her pride in her son made her radiant.

She was so beautiful he wanted to touch her. Wanted to reach out and stroke the softness of her cheek, and by his touch command that golden smile to stay.

Perhaps she saw the longing in his eyes, because, too quickly, her smile faded. Looking down at the remains of the sundae social, she said, "We'd better start cleaning up."

He didn't want the moment to end. Didn't want the inevitable distance to come between them. Mischief pure and simple overtook him.

"You have ice cream on your cheek," he said. She didn't.

"I do?" Her eyes crossed adorably in an attempt to see it.

"Here, let me." Slowly trailing a finger through a puddle of strawberry on the table in front of him, he moved closer. Reached up, touched her cheek, smeared the melted pink where he touched.

She started at the intimate contact. Stared in disbelief at the telltale mess on his finger. "Why, Jacob Matthews!" Her eyes widened in exasperation, but he could see the hint of a smile touch her lips. "You'll get your mama's fool in trouble!"

It was worth it. Worth it for the reward of her smile. Worth it for the feel of her. Her warmth. Her strength. Her courage.

He was about to throw caution to the wind and say so when a small, nasty *harrumph* led his attention to Ellie Able, who passed by the table to throw her trash in the receptacle. She glowered at Cathryn and muttered something inaudible. He'd bet it wasn't civil.

Cathryn stiffened, and with a paper napkin swiped at the smear of pink on her cheek. The ice cream had been replaced with the hot pink flush of discomfort. To the bottom of his heart, Jacob felt her unease.

Ellie Able was the loose cannon in his congregation. A gossip and a plotter, she made for a very dangerous opponent. Jacob's method of dealing with her had always been openness. An openness geared to head off any malice or subversion on the woman's part.

"Miss Ellie," he said, keeping his voice even, "you know Cathryn O'Malley, of course. My new assistant."

Ellie Able's eyebrows shot up to her hairline. "Whatever would qualify Cathryn O'Malley to be your assistant?" she asked rudely as if Cassie weren't present.

"Now's as good a time as any to let y'all know." Jacob picked up a school bell that rested at the end of the table.

Cathryn shot him a warning look, but he ignored it. He wouldn't hurt her. He did, however, need to let his congregation know, in no uncertain terms, her position here.

He rang the school bell mightily, attracting the attention of everyone on the athletic field. People drew closer. Expectant.

Cathryn couldn't believe what Jacob was doing. Attracting attention. To them. As evidenced by Ellie Able's nastiness, it was a foregone conclusion as to what the majority reaction would be. Glancing out over the field, she spotted Belle with a group of children, Aiden included, at the swing sets. At least her son's attention would be elsewhere. She took a deep breath and steeled herself.

"Could I have your attention, please?" Jacob called out in his deep, rich baritone. "I hope you enjoyed this pleasant break, because we have a lot of work to tackle this afternoon." Heads nodded in resigned agreement. Cathryn noticed how naturally people listened to Jacob. Extended to him an undivided attention that befitted a born leader.

"I've arranged for insurance representatives to set up stations this afternoon in the boardroom. Now, this is separate from any federal aid we might get. And separate, too, from the church emergency fund. We'll let you know about the federal help as soon as we hear. The church emergency fund can be implemented as soon as my assistant and I get a list of your most pressing, immediate needs. We'll be around this afternoon, also."

He stopped and glanced at Cathryn. A tiny shiver ran over her shoulders, whether at the compelling resonance of his voice or the knowledge that he was about to draw her into the public eye, she didn't know. Unexpectedly, he reached for her hand, clasped it in his own and raised it above their heads in a gesture that was disconcertingly triumphant.

"Ladies and gentlemen, my new assistant, Cathryn O'Malley. Fresh to us from Albany's battle with the floods and the federal emergency agency. She knows her stuff, folks, and we're lucky to have her."

He lowered their clasped hands but didn't release her. She stood beside him, amazed at the import of his words. He'd welcomed her to Grace Everlasting at the same time he'd issued an unmistakable warning to his parishioners. She was here as a valued volunteer, yes, he'd made that clear with his words. But, more important, by what he'd left unspoken, by his body language, he'd made it crystal clear that she was here under his protection. If anyone wished her, or by extension Aiden, ill will, they were going to have to come through the Reverend Matthews first.

That thought overwhelmed her.

"If you'll give us a chance to clean up the party," Jacob continued, gesturing to the sundae debris, "we'll get down to business shortly."

People turned toward the church buildings, seemingly eager to get in yet another line, this line, perhaps, a step toward alleviating some of their displacement. Jacob's words had been strong enough that no one groused openly about Cathryn's unlikely placement as assistant to the pastor. But several women cast slanted glances her way. Glances that held the transparent sting of judgment.

Holding her chin up high, she turned to begin the task of cleaning up, and discovered her hand still clasped in Jacob's. Found herself pulled face-to-face with him, his gray eyes intense, studying her.

She returned his gaze unflinchingly. Oh, he thought he knew her. But he didn't. If he knew the truth about her and her past, he wouldn't be so quick to stand up beside her in public. Wouldn't be so quick to offer his protection against all comers. To clasp her hand and stand at her side. If he only knew....

"You didn't need to do that," she said softly, slowly extricating her hand from his warm, powerful grip.

"Hold hands?" A mischievous crinkle appeared at the corners of his eyes.

"No, defend me." Although the hand-holding...her palm still tingled hotly from his touch.

He scowled dramatically. "Did what I just said sound like a defense to you?"

"Yes. Unmistakably." She swallowed her pride. "But I thank you...for Aiden."

"For Aiden," he repeated. Slowly. Too sensuously. "But as far as you're concerned?"

"I'm tough." She forced a smile. "I'm only going to be around here for a week. I think I can fight my own battles for a week."

"A week, huh?" His smile had grown dangerously lazy. Definitely un-pastor-like.

"Yes. Please, remember I leave in a week."

He reached out and grasped her wrist gently but firmly. The pressure of his touch sent warm sensations coursing up her arm. "If you want to leave at the end of the week, Cassie O'Malley, be my guest. If you want to...."

The words *if you want to* hung in the air between them. A challenge and a temptation.

Chapter Three

Cathryn searched Jacob's office for legal pads, pens and his laptop computer. After the impromptu sundae social, the two of them had been halfway to the boardroom to set up a station for emergency church aid when Jacob remembered the materials necessary to keep records. He'd been about to turn around to get them, but Cathryn had volunteered instead, arguing that his parishioners needed the comfort his presence could bring.

In reality, she needed a break from that very same, very powerful presence.

That presence. Intense. Probing. Protective—too protective. Cathryn couldn't allow herself the luxury of Jacob Matthews's protection a second time. He was no longer a young man studying for the ministry. He was now the pastor of the biggest congregation in northwest Georgia. His reputation, as far as she knew, was spotless. His parishioners—obviously—were loyal to the nth degree. A more-than-temporary presence of Cathryn O'Malley and her fatherless son would only complicate, possibly harm Pastor Matthews's life—his calling.

Cathryn had no intention of doing any such thing.

Why had she thought this was a good idea? Coming home, if only to share her skills with her storm-battered community, was craziness itself. Although, even in her most fervent denial, she couldn't shake the ingrained language: *home, her* community. A part of her. As much a part of her as her beautiful son and the pain he'd come from.

Having found all the needed supplies, she turned toward the door, only to discover a man leaning against the doorframe, watching her with an unnervingly insolent smile.

An unruly head of dark auburn waves and a day-old beard gave him a rakish look. Dangerous in a blatantly sexual way. Despite the fact that this man's bulk effectively cut off all exit, it was the languorous, come-hither smile that brought back the old uneasiness. Cathryn felt her pulse pick up in dread, her palms turn clammy.

Quickly pulling herself together, she asked, "May I help you?"

Before he spoke, he gave her a slow once-over. Cathryn felt an unpleasant prickle run along her hairline.

"Are you looking for Pastor Matthews?" She tried again in what she hoped was an unfaltering, efficient voice.

"No, ma'am," he drawled. "I'm looking for Arabella Sherman."

Good Lord, Belle had enough to deal with without this bedroom-eyed, auburn-haired devil. "I'm afraid she's very busy," Cathryn declared protectively. "May I tell her who's here to see her?"

"Honey," he replied, his slow, soft speech reaching out in a blatant, seductive attempt to entangle her, "you may tell her that her baby brother Rhune has come callin'."

Cathryn started, unwilling to believe this man was linked in any way to her beloved stepmother.

He grinned at her silence. "Go on. Lead me to her. You'll see how she welcomes the prodigal brother home."

Oh, she could just bet. No way was she leading this...this macho caricature to Belle before checking out his story. She moved to the large intercom console on the wall. Without turning her back on the man, she checked for the lever marked Nursery, then threw the switch and spoke into the mike. "Belle O'Malley?"

Instead of Belle's alto voice, a perky soprano answered. "This is Brie. Miss Belle's taken the children to the gym for their afternoon naps."

"Thank you." Cathryn's heart fell. She might disturb the entire napping population before she caught Belle's attention in that big room.

Crossing his arms over his chest, the man slouched farther against the doorsill. "The gym's right down the hall. Passed it on my way here. You think it's safe for you to walk me there?"

Cathryn froze. Was this just part of his usual pick-up patter, or could he sense the real unease she felt in his presence? This man was too much like Drew Paxton. A predator.

It was obvious she would be safer with him in a room full of people.

"Come on," she muttered, none too politely. Let's just see if Belle will claim you, she added mentally.

She crossed the room and brushed abruptly by him, his piercing gaze and the inadvertent touch of her body against his making her cringe inwardly. When would those old feelings of revulsion end? she wondered sadly in passing.

Clasping the laptop to her chest, she hurried down the hallway, not waiting to see if the man followed.

He did. Unfortunately. Too quickly. Coming abreast of her, he said, his voice low, the tone suggestive even though the words themselves were innocent enough, "As I said before, I'm Rhune Sherman. And you are?"

Cathryn turned the corner, entered the gymnasium hushed with napping children and elderly parishioners, then stopped. Automatically she scanned the sleeping forms, searching for her son, then breathed more easily when she spotted him curled up next to Margaret. Margaret. As much Aiden's talisman as Alice Rose was Cathryn's.

In one far corner stood Belle talking in whispers with Cathryn's father, Boone. In the opposite corner stood Jacob, engaged in quiet conversation with a parishioner. Apparently he, too, had been sidetracked on his route to the boardroom. Jacob looked her way and smiled, and a comforting sense of safety descended upon her.

Turning to the man beside her, she said coolly, "Mr. Sherman, I'm the pastor's assistant. Cathryn O'Malley."

Interest sparked in his eyes. "O'Malley? Belle's stepdaughter?"

Cathryn tilted her chin proudly. "Yes, I'm her stepdaughter. Although the 'step' part of it seems too cold for our relationship."

"You're close?"

"Very close." She didn't know why she'd told him this, except perhaps in the hope that, if he had any respect for his sister, he'd cut out the oppressive leer.

He didn't. "My, my." He reached a hand out to brush a wayward strand of her hair away from her face. "Now, that would make *us*..."

The unwanted touch of his fingers on her skin sent a jolt of distaste through her entire body. Involuntarily, she jerked away as if pulled by an invisible cord. Jerked away and slammed into the tumbling mats that hung on the gym wall. Managing to hang on to Jacob's laptop, she lost control of the legal pads and pens with a whoosh and a clatter.

Heads turned. Including Jacob's across the room. His eyes met hers, and seemed to instantly recognize her distress. He coiled as if to spring, but another parishioner, this time a woman surrounded by three young children, grasped Jacob's shirtsleeve, pulled at him and seemed to implore him to hear her tale.

In those few seconds Boone O'Malley came to Cathryn's rescue instead.

"Anything I can help you with, Cathryn?" Her father's strong, deep voice, laced with a definite hint of warning, rumbled around and over them, causing the rakish Mr. Sherman to wipe the self-satisfied grin off his face, to stand up a little straighter.

Inhaling deeply, Cathryn allowed her pulse to return to normal before she spoke. Allowed Mr. Rhune Sherman to remain uncomfortably skewered under her father's piercing gaze.

"Daddy," she replied finally, once she could speak without tremor, "have you met Belle's brother, Rhune Sherman?"

Boone silently shook his head.

"Mr. Sherman, my father—Belle's husband—Boone O'Malley."

Boone scowled.

"Pleased to meet you." Rhune extended his hand.

Her father was saved the formality of shaking the younger man's hand when Belle threw herself into their midst, threw her arms around Rhune's middle and whispered huskily, "Rhune! You devil! I thought never to see you again!"

Too soon for me, thought Cathryn with a grimace.

She felt a hand on her elbow. Her father's. "Let's get out of here," he said quietly, "and leave these two to catch up. We've got our own catching up to do." Stooping to pick up the scattered legal pads and pens, he then ushered her into the hallway.

Casting a final glance over her shoulder in Aiden's direction, Cathryn could also see Jacob still engaged in conversation with the same parishioner surrounded by her children. But he wasn't giving the woman his full attention. Instead, although he obviously carried on a conversation, Jacob's troubled gaze remained riveted upon Cathryn alone.

She turned the corner into the hallway, only to have her father envelop her in a bear hug. "Bless me!" he exclaimed, "I've missed you, Cassie girl!"

"And I've missed you, Daddy." She hugged him back, wondering if he'd picked up on the real meaning of her distress back in the gym. Wondered if it showed how uncomfortable men, with their unwelcome advances, with their inappropriate touching, made her feel. Wondered if anyone could tell how, after Drew Paxton, she felt cold and dead inside. And sexually stalled.

"What gave you the dropsies back there?" he asked simply, holding her at arm's length. "Nervous about coming home?"

"Yes, I guess that's it." She welcomed the half-truth. Felt relieved that her father hadn't picked up on the real reason for her loss of control in the gym.

But Jacob...Jacob had been different in his reaction. There had been something—*something*—in his troubled gaze that hinted he suspected, even across an entire gymnasium, the truth. That was ridiculous. How could he? He knew nothing of her relationships or lack thereof in the past five years. And as for Drew Paxton, well, Jacob had always assumed it had been a love affair gone sour. Heartbreaking for the moment, sad because of her pregnancy, but nothing more insidious than failed judgment.

She shivered.

"Cathryn, are you all right?" Her father's warm, concerned voice brought her back to the here and now. "Do you need to sit down? You're pale as all get-out. Has anyone given you a hard time since you've been back?"

"No, I'm fine. Really. Just fine now." It seemed too small a matter in face of the public destructive aftermath of the tornado to mention Ellie Able and Rhune Sherman and her own private uneasiness.

"'Cause if they have..."

"Daddy, I can fight my own battles."

Boone shook his shaggy blond head. "You've always tried, I'll give you that." He pinched her cheek affectionately. "But, darlin', you do have a great backup team. Me, Belle, Alice Rose...and Jacob."

Cathryn's eyes widened involuntarily. "What does Jacob have to do with this?"

"Seems to me, he could have as much to do with your life as you allow."

Yes, she felt it, too. Trouble was, Jacob didn't know all that he'd be getting into. If he did...

"Cathryn!" Jacob's voice broke in to her thoughts. "I need you to help me. Sorry to interrupt your reunion, Boone, but this can't wait."

"Oh, I understand," Boone replied with a grin. Too ready a grin, thought Cathryn.

Jacob scooped the laptop out of Cathryn's arms and dumped it in Boone's. "Boone, can you head to the boardroom? Start making a list of all the parishioners' immediate needs. Food, medicine, clothing, small amounts of cash. Stuff like that. Cathryn and I need to drive out to Mrs. Wegman's."

"I could drive out," Boone offered. "Seems to me, you and Cathryn are more suited to taking care of parish records."

"Normally, I'd agree." Jacob glanced at Cathryn. "But Mrs. Wegman's daughter Sadie's in the gym with her three kids. Even though Mrs. Wegman's home is in a shambles, she won't leave it. Sadie can't stay with her because of the children, but she's worried sick. Seems to think I can talk her into the shelter here."

"Sounds like a plan," Cathryn agreed. "But why do you need me?"

"Backup. A woman's voice. A voice not related by blood. You know how we sometimes tune out those closest to us?"

Oh, how she knew. "Do you really need me?"

"Believe me," Jacob assured her, "you could only help." His words were controlled, ultraprofessional, but his look...his intense look spoke of yet another need. A need too personal. It was all she could do not to avert her eyes from his.

"Hey," she answered carefully, "I did sign on to be your assistant for the week."

"Then let's go."

Jacob led Cathryn to his mud-spattered Blazer in the parking lot. As the caked mud attested, this wasn't his first mission of mercy outside the confines of the church complex. In the immediate aftermath of the storm, he'd spent twenty-four sleepless hours on teams pulling survivors out of the tornado wreckage. Pulling them out and transporting them to the hospital or to the church shelter, depending upon their circumstances.

As Cathryn and he made their way around the cars in the crowded parking lot, a weariness crept into his muscles. Come to think of it, the second twenty-four hours as well had brought blessed little sleep.

He opened the passenger door of his vehicle and held it for Cathryn. Despite his fatigue, he welcomed this time alone with her. Something unpleasant had gone on between her and the redheaded stranger in the gym. So that it didn't occur again, he needed to know what. If he'd had more time, he would have approached the man himself. But Mrs. Wegman needed him. And Belle seemed to have a tight grip on the stranger...and Jacob had Cathryn safe beside him.

Hopping into his side of the vehicle, he started it and looked over at Cathryn. Her body language had placed an unmistakable chasm between them. He needed to bridge that chasm—for her sake and for his own. Despite her cursory explanation of her actions five years ago, he had a vague, uneasy feeling that she hadn't told him the crux of the issue. He needed to hear that—from her—before he could ever bring closure to the part of his life that was Cassie O'Malley.

As much as he hated to admit it, he suspected closure was the only satisfaction she'd afford him.

"Ready?" he asked, just to hear her voice.

She looked not at him but out the window. "Ready."

He pulled slowly out of the church parking lot and onto the two-lane road strewn with debris.

He'd gone no more than a mile when a highway patrol officer pulled them over to question their intent in the face of the driving ban. But recognizing the pastor of Grace Everlasting, the officer soon waved them on with no further delay.

A tiny spark of mischief ignited in Cathryn's eyes. "I guess I know the person to help bail me out if I'm ever in trouble with the law in Sweet Hope. Your position brings unexpected perks, Pastor Matthews."

"Ah, this position brings perks far greater than an 'in' with law enforcement."

From the corner of his eye he could see her looking intently at him. "You really mean that, don't you?"

"Are you surprised I'm content in my calling?"

"No. Just happy—for you. As for me..."

"As for you?"

"As for me, I'd find your calling particularly difficult. The goldfish-bowl aspect of it, that is."

Jacob chuckled. "Cassie, you're beginning to sound like your father. We all know how private a man he is. But you...you used to thrive in the limelight."

Her voice was soft and not a little wistful when she answered. "That was a long time ago. A very long time ago. Now, like my father, I value my privacy."

"There's a difference." He didn't want to hurt her with what he had to say. He only wanted her to open up to him. "A big difference between the desire for privacy and the compulsion to run."

An icy silence descended upon the interior of the vehicle. If they hadn't been in motion, Jacob felt certain Cathryn would have bolted.

"Cassie, something happened earlier in the gym. With that man, that newcomer. Something that made me believe you're struggling with something very painful."

"Whatever are you talking about?"

"I'm talking about the way you jumped when he touched you."

"Of course I jumped. No one is comfortable with that kind of familiarity. The man was a stranger, for goodness sakes."

"You didn't just jump, Cassie," Jacob contradicted softly. "You recoiled. And the look on your face was one of revulsion."

"I think many women are outraged when men treat them as objects, make uninvited advances. I gave Mr. Sherman no invitation to touch me."

"I'm sure you didn't." Jacob thought of their conversation in his office earlier that morning. He'd reached out and held her by her shoulders to make her talk to him. Thought of their clasped hands at the ice cream social. "But you didn't recoil this morning when I touched you. Why not?"

She paused before answering. "I trust you, Jacob. You've been a friend to me."

Ah, so this was a sexual thing. He was a friend, therefore she felt safe. But with men who might possibly have more than friendship in mind... What had happened to her to make her so skittish of events that some women might consider harmless flirting? No, he didn't actually know that the encounter between Cassie and this Mr. Sherman had been harmless. Cassie, by her reaction, certainly hadn't thought it was. But her reaction, in the safety of the gym with dozens of people around, had seemed an overreaction. Why?

He wouldn't press her right now. He knew her well enough to have experienced her stubborn silent streak. But he certainly wasn't going to let her struggle alone.

They drove the rest of the way to Mrs. Wegman's place without conversation.

The sight of the ruined property in front of her splashed the cold water of reality in Cathryn's face. A reality in which her inner turmoil necessarily paled in light of nature's chaos. She needed to push aside the distress she felt at Jacob's uncanny ability to probe too close to the truth. Considering what little remained of the Wegman place, the task at hand was not her own emotional self-preservation. Instead, Jacob and she needed to convince the elderly woman to return with them to the church shelter.

Without thinking, as Jacob stopped the Blazer on the side of the road and pulled the keys from the ignition, Cathryn laid her hand on his arm and declared, "We *can't* leave here without Mrs. Wegman."

He turned to look at her with a smile so beatific Cathryn's heart skipped a beat. "We always did think alike, Cassie O'Malley. Glad to see we still do." Winking, he opened his door, then slid to the ground in one smooth, sensuous movement.

Trying to ignore the smile, the wink and the poetry of his body movements, Cathryn harrumphed softly. Now, *when* had they ever thought alike? Not in this lifetime, certainly. It was nice, however, she thought as she hopped to the ground from the high passenger seat, to feel a part of something again. If only an agreement on the fate of Mrs. Wegman.

With great care Cathryn followed Jacob over what used to be a front yard. Now, uprooted trees, Realtors' signs from the subdivision down the road, bits of wire and broken glass formed an obstacle course that required attention to every footstep. Miraculously, the house still stood, but a large part of the roof had been blown away.

"Mrs. Wegman!" Jacob called as he climbed the porch steps, his voice deep and booming. A voice to reassure. "Mrs. Wegman, it's Jacob Matthews!"

Cathryn caught a wraithlike movement behind one of the windows. Seconds afterward, a tiny, frail woman clutching a length of lead pipe opened the front door.

Fear clouded the woman's eyes until she did indeed seem to recognize Jacob. "Thank the Lord. Pastor Matthews, it is you."

Jacob stepped to her side immediately, put a comforting arm about her shoulders, then a hand on the lead pipe. "Why, Mrs. Wegman, whom did you expect?"

"Oh, no one, really," she answered, slumping against him, her eyes brimming with tears. "It's just the TV you watch these days is enough to put the fear of God in you. Punks and violence and what all."

"Your television is working?" Jacob asked, a surprised look on his face.

"No, no. No television. No power. No nothing except an old woman's fears magnified."

"Oh, Mrs. Wegman," Cathryn broke in, "you've been through a terrible ordeal. You need to let us take you back to the church. You need to be around people—your family—until we can help you get this mess straightened up."

"She's right, you know," Jacob agreed.

Mrs. Wegman's eyes brightened. She looked at Jacob. "Who's *she?* Your wife? Very pretty, young man. Very pretty."

Jacob smiled. "Mrs. Wegman, you know I'm not married."

"Well, you should be!" the elderly woman declared emphatically. "You should be. And this young lady seems as good a candidate as any." She pierced Cathryn with a flinty gaze. "What's your name, child?"

"Cathryn O'Malley, ma'am."

"Cathryn's a volunteer from Albany," Jacob added. "She's agreed to be my assistant—temporarily—in the wake of the tornado."

"Cathryn O'Malley from Albany, hmm?" Mrs. Wegman seemed to mull this bit of information over. "You wouldn't be Boone O'Malley's girl? Boone O'Malley from Sweet Hope?"

"Yes'm."

"Ah, Boone. A lonely man who finally saw the light. You married, Cathryn?"

"No, ma'am, I'm not."

"Well, you ought to be. The Lord never intended for us to be lonely."

Cathryn felt a blush creep into her cheeks unbidden. "I don't think of myself as lonely." It seemed her entire hometown was possessed by the matchmaking demon.

"That's not what your eyes tell me," Mrs. Wegman insisted. "Yours...or *his*." She turned to Jacob, who looked as startled as Cathryn felt. "Maybe the Lord's seen fit to bring you back to Sweet Hope for a reason."

"Maybe," Cathryn agreed quickly, trying to recover her equanimity. "But the reason Jacob and I are here right now is to bring you back to the safety of Grace Everlasting."

"Sorry. Won't go," the elderly woman insisted with finality.

"Mrs. Wegman," Jacob implored, "your daughter Sadie is worried sick about you."

"I know she is, bless her. She'd be out here with me if it weren't for those young'uns. We both agreed they needed to be at the shelter."

"But you, Mrs. Wegman," Cathryn urged, "*you* need to be at the shelter where you can get a good meal and a decent night's sleep."

"Girl, that's mighty tempting, but there are two obstacles. Number one, this is my home. No, more than my home, this is who I am. I can't abandon it in this shape. It wouldn't be right. Number two, Molly's missing. Even if I could bring myself to leave the property, I couldn't ever leave Molly. Not with her pregnant and all."

Jacob and Cathryn looked at each other, stunned.

"Molly?" Jacob asked. "I wasn't aware anyone else lived with you."

"Molly's my cat, Pastor Matthews. The day before the storm she disappeared. Haven't laid eyes on her since."

"She probably went off somewhere to have her kittens," Cathryn ventured, realization dawning.

"Well, she's nowhere in the house, that's for sure," Mrs. Wegman declared. "I've looked. But I can't get around outside. I just can't clamber up and over that mess." The elderly woman flung one arm out toward the disaster that was her yard. "She'll be back, Molly will. I know it. And when she comes back, I aim to be here for her."

"Of course." Jacob nodded. "I understand now." He rubbed his chin and thought. And while he thought, Cathryn observed.

He did understand. That was obvious. He understood the attachment this woman had to her home, to the land, to one missing pregnant cat. And understanding, he hadn't run roughshod over Mrs. Wegman's wishes. He hadn't insisted he knew best where her safety and priorities were concerned. He hadn't patronized the elderly woman. He had listened, and he had understood.

"If Cathryn and I climb around on the mess out here," Jacob said finally, "if we can locate your cat, will you and the cat come to the shelter?"

Mrs. Wegman shook her head. "That wouldn't work. Molly doesn't much like people. Only me. My grandchildren call her Molly-the-Snit. She'd throw a hissy fit with all those people around."

"Oh, Mrs. Wegman," Cathryn offered, certain that the bargain was close to being sealed, "I'm sure we could find her some quiet spot . . . like . . . like Jacob's office."

Jacob's dark eyebrows shot upward.

"You'd do that, Pastor Matthews? You'd let my Molly stay in your office till we could get back in our home?"

"If it would mean getting you to come to the shelter," Jacob replied evenly, one eyebrow settling slowly back into its normal position. The other remained cocked as he skewered Cathryn with a penetrating look.

"Then, yes," Mrs. Wegman exclaimed, clapping her hands together, "if you children can find Molly, we'll come back with you to the shelter. Bless you. Bless you both."

"Bless you!" Cathryn exclaimed as Jacob sneezed for the fifth time.

"Thank you. We must be getting close," he replied as they made their way carefully through a dusty, musty toolshed that sat precariously on the edge of Mrs. Wegman's property.

"Why do you say that?"

"I'm allergic to cats."

Cathryn stopped short and Jacob bumped into her. "Oh, great," she said with a snort. "And I just offered Molly room and board in your office. Why didn't you speak up?"

"Because I thought it was more important that we find a way to get Mrs. Wegman to the shelter." And because, he added mentally, it felt so good to be working together, if only to convince one elderly woman to come with us. It felt so good that I would have promised the devil himself equal time in the church bulletin . . . if it meant you and I, Cathryn and Jacob, working as a team. It felt that good.

Cathryn looked up at him and shrugged apologetically. "It's just that Alice Rose said earlier that if you had your way, you'd have all God's creatures—Red the horse included—at services. I just thought . . ."

As she stared at him her voice trailed off and her eyes took on a softness that nearly made him forget their mission. Her mouth parted slightly, and the corners turned up in a quizzical smile.

The urge to kiss her overwhelmed him.

He coughed to clear his throat and shook his head to clear her sensuous aura from his thoughts. "What Alice Rose told you is partly right," he began gruffly, "only I'd make all the cats sit out in the narthex."

Cathryn laughed. A lovely, clear, appealing laugh that almost turned his thoughts to kisses again. Almost. Instead, a violent sneeze nearly turned his body inside out.

This sneeze was answered by a pitiful cry from the far corner of the dilapidated shed. Bending, Jacob could see a dusky feline shape and two large glowing eyes. Beneath the cat wriggled several tiny mewling shapes. "I think we've found Molly," he murmured. "Let's hope her instinct to preserve her kittens outweighs her distrust of humans."

When he stood, Jacob discovered Cathryn observing him with the most unsettling intensity. Without as much as a blink, he returned her gaze. "Well, Miss O'Malley, any suggestions?"

Glancing away at the cat, Cathryn cleared her throat. When she did speak, her voice cracked. "I . . . saw a plastic laundry basket amid the rubble outside. I'll get it. Perhaps you could see if Mrs. Wegman has a large towel. If we can get Molly and her kittens into something protected and portable, I think we can get her back to the church."

The unevenness of her voice suggested more than just a reaction to the dust in the shed. Jacob was about to ask if she was all right when she brushed abruptly past him on her way outside.

He followed, expecting to find her halfway to the house. She wasn't. Instead, she was leaning against the weathered siding of the shed, covering her eyes with one hand. Her shoulders slumped, her body slack, she appeared ineffably weary.

"Cassie!" He moved to her side and slipped an arm around her shoulders. She didn't flinch or withdraw. "What's wrong?"

She said nothing but sighed deeply and leaned against him, filling him with a delicious warmth.

Smiling, he tilted her chin so that he could look into her eyes. "Remind me to give you a raise when this is all over."

Although tears pooled under her lashes, she smiled back at him. "I guess I'm just having one of those greeting card moments."

"I'm afraid I don't understand."

She dabbed at her eyes and sighed softly. "Oh, you know...emotions. Nothing but emotions."

"Brought on by a shed on its last legs and an ornery mother cat?"

This conversation was crazy. Crazier still was the fact that Cathryn hadn't moved from the protection of his arms. It reminded him of five years ago when all he'd had to offer her had been the protection of his arms. And his good name. Funny how none of that had changed.

Unexpectedly, she thumped him on his chest. "Jacob Matthews, did you engineer this whole afternoon just to wear me down?"

He drew back to look at her smiling sadly through tears.

Her shoulders heaved in an enormous sigh. "First Mrs. Wegman tells us she can't leave her home because it's who she is. Home, home, home. I can't get away from the concept. Then there's the whole chain of protectiveness. Mrs. Wegman for her cat. The cat for her kittens. You for Mrs. Wegman, the cat and her kittens...and me."

"Me," Jacob repeated. "You, as in standing in line to be protected, or you helping to protect."

"Both. All this home and hearth and protectiveness is driving me nuts." She threw her arms in the air in obvious exasperation. "And just look at *us* working together as if nothing had ever happened between us."

He shrugged his shoulders in exaggerated resignation. "Gosh, golly," he said, scratching his head in imitation of a country hayseed, "this sure sounds like a list of things to start one crying." He teased her affectionately, not maliciously.

"Don't make fun, Jacob Matthews." She moved away from him, and Jacob felt a moment of remorse. He hadn't meant to make fun of her, only to make her smile.

She wrapped her arms around herself in a protective hug. "There's sad crying. And there's happy crying...and there's confused crying."

"And yours was?"

"Confused, Jacob. Confused."

"Why?" Dear Lord, he wanted to understand.

"Because with all that's happened to me in Sweet Hope, you'd think I'd never want to come back. But here's where I feel like *me*. Here's where I feel most comfortable...and most uncomfortable."

"And this whole chain of unwanted protection just exacerbates the whole dilemma?"

"As an independent woman, it drives me crazy. As a mother, it feels like the most natural thing in the world."

"And us? What about us?" He felt compelled to ask, although he feared her answer.

"That's the most confusing part. Why would it feel good and natural working alongside you after what happened five years ago?"

"Let's get this straight, Cassie." Jacob took a step closer to her, reached out and cupped her soft, soft cheek in his hand. "*Nothing* happened five years ago. That's the real problem. You left before anything could happen between us. Maybe your confusion stems from the fact that you and I have unfinished business."

Her eyes widened, and he saw confirmation and reluctance and fear waging war within her. Surprisingly, he saw neither revulsion nor denial.

Emboldened, he stroked her cheek and added, "Your instincts are telling you to go in one direction, but you're trying to run in the other. Give in to your instincts, Cassie. They're good and true."

Suddenly all emotion left her eyes. They became shuttered and unreadable. She pulled away from his touch, shivered and said brusquely, "Let's get Mrs. Wegman and her cat back to Grace Everlasting."

At the total and unexpected change in her, coldness seeped into his bones. The serrated feeling that he'd lost her—again—sawed through his heart.

Chapter Four

All around them the displaced of Sweet Hope settled in for the night.

As Aiden nestled against her on the cot in the crowded church gymnasium, Cathryn quietly read the last page of *Mike Mulligan and his Steam Shovel.* Even at twenty-three, she loved the story as much as Aiden did. The idea of Mike and Mary Anne finally finding a home was heartwarming at any age.

Home. What a loaded concept.

She kissed the top of her son's head and inhaled the pungent little-boy scent of him. He squiggled in her arms so that he could kiss her cheek. A wet and warm four-year-old nuzzle.

"I love you, Mama," he murmured.

"I love you, too." Cathryn's voice caught on the whispered endearment. She had to fight the sting of tears, so overwhelmed with love did she feel.

"Hey, sprout." Boone O'Malley quietly wended his way

through the mass of cots to where Cathryn and Aiden sat. "Got one of those smooches for your Gramps?"

Without a word Aiden flung himself at his grandfather. The man lifted the boy to receive a loud smacking kiss. Boone grinned from ear to ear, while, the corners of his mouth barely curling upward, Aiden's eyes twinkled in what Cathryn had come to recognize as his smile. Sober on the outside, he might not wear his emotions on his sleeve, but her small son had a grand capacity for love.

And how he loved being with the O'Malleys.

In what had become a ritual between them, Boone lowered Aiden to the floor and attempted to tickle him.

Aiden eyed him seriously. "It won't work, Gramps. I'm not ticklish."

"Oh, come on." Boone winked. "You can admit it. Everyone's ticklish *somewhere.*"

Aiden pulled himself up to his full three feet three inches. "*I'm* not. I'm strong," he declared, so solemnly Cathryn bit her lip so as not to laugh.

"He sure is!" Margaret O'Malley danced up behind the trio with her mother, Belle, in tow. She grasped Aiden's biceps and squeezed playfully. "This afternoon he was the only one in our group who could shinny the ropes all the way to the top."

Without a trace of smile Aiden nodded his head in agreement.

"He's strong," cooed Margaret, flashing a grin that had enough wattage to serve both children.

Cathryn reached out and ruffled Aiden's hair. "So, you had fun this afternoon at old Grace Everlasting?" She hoped he had; she wasn't at all certain that she had.

Aiden's eyes widened in response. "It was a 'venture."

"You can say that again," Cathryn agreed, thinking of her work with Jacob and her brush with Rhune. She wasn't quite sure, however, that she wanted to wake up tomorrow and repeat the adventure.

"How 'bout I take these two rug rats," Boone suggested, "and get them washed up for bed. That will leave you women a few minutes to catch up."

"You're an angel," Belle murmured as Boone leaned over to brush her lips with his own.

Cathryn's father smiled roguishly. "Not bad for a creaky old gramps."

Belle returned his mischievous look. "You may be a grandfather, Boone O'Malley, but you're far from creaky."

Cathryn cleared her throat. "Maybe I'd better take the kids and give you two some time alone."

"Hah!" Boone spread his hands to indicate the entire gym. "Alone with five hundred other lost souls. No, thank you. I'll take the kids... and pray for a quick return to the privacy of my own home."

Before he left with the children, Cathryn caught the look of longing Boone cast her stepmother. She sighed. Belle and Boone's story had been one for the romance books. The kind of story she'd wished for herself. But that was not to be. The events of five years ago had shattered any illusion she might have of moonlight and magnolias. Of romantic love.

She shivered and looked at the cot next to hers where Belle now sat, examining Cathryn thoughtfully.

"It will happen for you, too, Cassie... someday."

The old nickname tugged at her heartstrings as much as the promise did. Cathryn attempted a worldly smile. "Now, who says I need *it* to happen to me? I have Aiden, family, friends. That's a lot of love in my life."

"You know what I mean."

Quirking an eyebrow, Cathryn replied, "Yes, I do. And I'd prefer not to discuss it."

"All right." Belle smiled in loving exasperation. "What would you like to discuss in our few responsibility-free minutes?"

Stalling, Cathryn stretched. Funny, but she had an unusual, compelling urge to discuss the day. Everything. Jacob. Rhune. The opposite feelings these two men had invoked in her. She scowled. This wasn't like her. She'd always managed her emotions on her own.

"Well?" Clearly, Belle awaited a real answer.

"For starters, where's your brother?"

Belle rolled her eyes. "At The Red Bait—the one bar in the area that has its own generator."

"He did call himself the prodigal brother." Cathryn could think of a few other things to call that disturbing man, but she wasn't about to voice them to his sister.

"He's a prodigal, for sure!" Belle shook her head and laughed, and the bell earrings she wore tinkled merrily. "Don't get me wrong. I love him dearly... but..."

"But?"

"But what can you say about a man who describes himself as an emergency-room doctor *slash* recovering surfer?"

Despite her uncomfortable feelings for Rhune in the flesh, Cathryn had to chuckle at the description of the absent Mr. Sherman.

"Now I get to ask a question," Belle said before Cathryn's smile could die on her lips. "How did things go with Jacob today?"

Cathryn inhaled sharply. At the sound of that man's name, a whole new set of feelings washed over her.

"I think today went well," she offered evasively. "As Aiden says, 'It was a 'venture.' "

"Then why do I get the feeling that Aiden enjoyed his adventure far more than you enjoyed yours?"

"Oh, Aiden loves being surrounded by family," Cathryn responded in what was obviously a dodge.

"And you, dear? What about you?"

Cathryn reached quickly for Belle's hand. "You know I love seeing you and Daddy and Grammy. There's never been any question of that."

"I've never doubted it for a minute." Belle squeezed Cathryn's hand. "I just wish you were more comfortable in your hometown. With Jacob."

Cathryn looked sharply at Belle. Oh, these relentless matchmaking O'Malleys.

"Cathryn..." Her stepmother pressed on. "Can't you see how happy *Aiden* is here?"

"Yes." Yes, he was. "But... we just don't fit in."

"Because Aiden doesn't have a father?" Belle continued before Cathryn could answer. "There are lots of single parents in Sweet Hope, dear heart. There's no shame in that."

Cathryn shuddered. No, no shame in single parenthood. Her shame went farther back than that.

"And if you really wanted a father for Aiden..." Winking, Belle reached out and gently stroked Cathryn's cheek. "Well, I think Jacob Matthews's offer is still open."

She should object to Belle's assumption. Before today, before Jacob's probing questions and his intense looks and the touching—the touching that, amazingly, hadn't made her want to recoil—she would have objected immediately. But now... after spending the day with Jacob Matthews, Cathryn was unsure of his intentions. And, even more important, unsure of her own reaction to those intentions.

Cathryn sighed in exaggeration. "Arabella Sherman O'Malley." She tried to make her tone admonishing. "Were you by any chance around for the Spanish Inquisition?"

With great affectation, Belle primped her short curly hair and drawled, "Why, sugah, I was *Miss* Spanish Inquisition!"

The two women chuckled companionably, and Cathryn's troubling thoughts were waved aside. Temporarily, she was sure, but aside none the less.

The return of Boone with Aiden and Margaret assured her that Belle's intense questioning, too, had been temporarily put aside.

"Into bed, you two," Boone ordered, his voice a gentle rumble.

"I'm not sleepy," Aiden insisted.

Margaret hopped under the covers of her own cot, then cast a warning look at Aiden. "Well, mister, you'd better pretend to be sleepy or Pastor Matthews will pass you by."

"The Important Man?"

"No. The sandman. He's got a giant bag of cherry suckers, and last night he put one under the pillow of every boy and girl who went right to sleep without a fuss." Margaret rolled onto her side and shut her eyes tight. "Maybe if I go to sleep *early*, he'll leave me two."

Aiden needed no more encouragement. He slipped under the covers of his own cot and quickly closed his eyes. "Kiss me good-night, Mama," he instructed, squinty eyed and very sober.

Smiling, Cathryn bent to do as she was told, then joined Belle and Boone, who'd gone to stand with other adults near the outer walls of the gymnasium.

The men and women, most of whom had been separated during the day, spoke in low tones, catching up on news as they watched their children settling down for the night.

Cathryn whispered to Belle, "What was Margaret talking about? About Jacob and the sandman?"

Belle simply smiled and nodded in the direction of the gym doors. There Jacob, a large sack in his hand, stood watching, waiting.

Cathryn felt shock at the little frisson of pleasure that accompanied his appearance. What was he up to now?

As she watched, he reached out a hand to a bank of switches on the gym wall. A row at a time, he turned off the lights until only a single row over the farthest bleachers remained lit. The enormous room was bathed in a strangely comforting half-light. Sighs went up all around. Adults and children, tired from the unusual circumstances and activities, seemed glad someone had declared the day officially over. Only a dozen or so adults, Cathryn, Belle and Boone included, remained standing at the edges of the room.

After a few moments Jacob began to thread his way around the cots, gently slipping something under the pillow of every sleeping child.

"Cherry suckers?" Cathryn looked to Belle.

"Cherry suckers. His favorite."

How well Cathryn remembered. Back when they'd been best of friends, Jacob had tried not to push her into loving him. But how obviously he'd wanted to win her over. For her birthday, he hadn't presumed to send her flowers; instead he'd sent her a dozen "long-stemmed" cherry suckers. Even unwed and pregnant, she'd smiled the entire rest of the day.

He'd always known how to sow joy. And here he was, years later, playing sandman to dozens of displaced kids. Sowing a little happiness. A little magic. Knowing the magic came from a very real Pastor Matthews didn't seem to diminish it one whit with the children.

Cathryn cast her gaze heavenward. I know, she admitted inwardly. There's a lesson in all this if only I'd care to examine it.

When she lowered her eyes, she saw Jacob coming down the row of adults, stopping briefly to say a few quiet words. People nodded, then began to head for the exits.

Suddenly he was in front of her. With a mischievous grin he half whispered, "Full-moon softball. Ten minutes. Diamond number two," and then moved on.

Ready to beg off, Cathryn looked at Belle and Boone.

"Come on," murmured Boone. "Our team lacks a decent shortstop. We need you, Cassie girl. I'm not losing to Jacob again tonight." He and Belle grasped her by each wrist and pulled her gently toward the exit.

"But the children," she protested softly.

"No problem. Alice Rose has volunteered to play dorm mother."

"But—"

"No buts," prodded Belle. "Boone keeps that state championship trophy of yours buffed and polished. Tonight I get to see your stuff."

Cathryn groaned good-naturedly. That old trophy was seven years old. She hadn't held a softball in her hand since then. Heck, she might not have an ounce of stuff left in her. She harrumphed. Serve them right if she didn't. Perhaps they'd put her out on waivers, and she could return to help Alice Rose supervise the sleeping children.

With her father and her stepmother on either side of her, Cathryn stepped reluctantly through the gym doorway and into the moonlight.

* * *

As the spring peepers sang in loud chorus, Jacob loped through the moonlight toward diamond number two. He sure hoped Boone and Belle had convinced Cathryn to join the game. Last night with a dozen adults who couldn't sleep, he'd organized a pickup game of softball. It had been so relaxing after the stress of the storm cleanup, the players had vowed to do it every night as long as they were stranded at the shelter. Had dubbed it the tornado tourney.

Now, for more than just relaxation, Jacob needed the ball game. He needed to see Cathryn again. Needed to see her in a group of people after their attempt at working alone together this afternoon had ended with her withdrawal. As soon as they'd returned to Grace Everlasting with Mrs. Wegman, Molly the cat and her kittens, Cathryn had disappeared. Jacob had briefly seen her helping Alice Rose in the kitchen during supper.

He hoped this evening to ease tensions between them so that tomorrow she'd still be his temporary assistant. He felt strongly that, if he could remain close to her, he could discover the hurt she so obviously harbored within. Could help her heal. And that done, could convince her that he and she still had a future—together.

As he approached diamond number two, good-natured ball chatter competed with the spring peepers' song. And there, in the midst of the motley crew of moonlit players, was Cassie. Not Cathryn, but Cassie. Tossing the ball around as if it were yesterday and she was still on the Sweet Hope girls' state championship softball team.

Jacob inhaled sharply. It had been at the finals that he'd first seen her. He'd arrived home from college for the weekend, and, like all small towns everywhere, Sweet Hope had been *into* high school sports, especially those that had a shot at a state title. His family had pressed him into accompanying them to the girls' softball game. And that's where he'd seen her.

Cassie O'Malley. Ace shortstop. All moxie. And laughter. And fluid poetry in motion. Cassie O'Malley, the obvious leader of the team. Full of spirit and energy. And passion.

Although he was four years older than her and a college senior at the time, he'd been a goner since that moment seven years ago.

"Jacob!" Boone O'Malley's voice rang out in the clear evening air. "You going to stare or play ball?" The older man chuckled heartily. "Hope you're planning to play ball, because our team's fixin' to plow you under tonight."

"Oh, I'm planning to play ball for sure...despite the fact you've brought in a ringer."

Even in the moonlight, Jacob thought he could see color creep into Cassie's cheeks. Good. It meant she felt something when he noticed her. Even if it was irritation. Some feeling was better than no feeling at all. If he'd seen indifference, he'd know his cause was lost.

But she'd blushed, and his heart leapt.

He grabbed a worn glove from the church's recreation supply box and headed onto the field. "Five innings. Agreed?" he shouted. "It's already nine o'clock."

Boone wasn't about to let him off the hook. "Aw, pastor, aren't you afraid of what your flock might think if you leave the game unfinished?"

Jacob laughed and easily caught the ball Homer Martin lobbed at him. "I'm more afraid, Boone O'Malley, of what the Lord might think if I left his sermon for tomorrow unfinished."

"Can't argue with that." Boone chuckled. As the opposing team's unofficial captain, he approached for the toss of the bat. "Let's play five innings of ball, then."

Out of the corner of his eye Jacob could see Cassie intently observing the banter between himself and her father. Just having her back in town was hope, sweet hope indeed. But to play ball with her in the moonlight was provocative magic.

He hoped the Lord understood that his heart was more in softball than in finishing that sermon.

* * *

Cathryn leapt in the air. Heard and felt the snap of the ball in her glove. Settled back to earth with a feeling of pure, unadulterated, childlike joy.

"Dang!" Homer Martin kicked the dirt. He hadn't even had a chance to drop his bat to the ground before Cathryn had caught his line drive. "Boone O'Malley, you should be shot for bringin' in a ringer."

Boone on the pitcher's mound grinned as he caught the ball Cathryn threw him. "Y'all have had nothing but gripes since my baby took the field. You don't watch out, you're going to give her a complex."

Cathryn grinned, too. Really grinned for the first time since she'd returned to Sweet Hope. Despite the opposing team's good-natured griping at her still-intact softball skills, she didn't feel any animosity coming from the assembled adults. Only grudging admiration. And from inside herself a happiness and a sense of freedom that she hadn't felt in a long, long time. Her muscles thrilled to the forgotten rhythms of the game. Her heart rose with the banter, and the strategy, ragtag as it was tonight, and the sense of belonging to a team.

For the first time in what seemed like forever, Cathryn felt good.

Blame it on softball. Blame it on the moonlight. Or, more close to the truth, she thought as she watched Jacob come to the plate, blame it on the pastor of Grace Everlasting for thinking to put the two together. For softball and moonlight were proving to be a potent combination.

"Easy out!" Boone pointed his glove at Jacob, stretched lazily on the mound, then turned to look at his team in the field. "But don't fall asleep out there, me hearties. Ole Pastor Matthews may surprise us yet."

"Oh, yeah." Jacob grinned right back at Boone. "I may've had my problems batting tonight, but the inning's not over yet, Boone O'Malley. The inning's not over yet."

"Planning on a miracle, Jacob?" a voice behind Cathryn called out.

Jacob hunched over the plate. "Aha! Blasphemy in the outfield. Just the incentive I needed." He shook his head, trying to remove an errant lock of midnight dark hair that had fallen over one eye. "Put it right here, O'Malley."

Expectantly, Cathryn hunkered down in her position at shortstop. It was the bottom of the fifth—the last inning they'd agreed to play. One out. Jacob represented the tying run.

True, he'd had his problems batting this evening. Unusual problems for the natural athlete Cathryn knew him to be. But tonight he'd seemed distracted at the plate. At first she'd thought his distraction the inevitable result of his responsibilities as supervisor of the temporary storm shelter. But later she'd noticed his distraction seemed to be of an unusually cheerful nature. He seemed as wound up as a kid at his own birthday party. Maybe that's why he hadn't had a hit all evening.

Lost in thought, Cathryn never heard the crack of the bat. She only heard the whiz of the ball as it flew past her. Right through the hole between her and third base. By the time she'd recovered, Jacob stood on first base, panting and smiling to beat the band. His teammates whooped and hollered on the sidelines.

"Tell me how that looked, Boone, my man!" Jacob's voice rang out with obvious satisfaction. His stance emphasized the power in his lean body. He looked boyish and cocky and very little like a man of the cloth. "Guess the *ole pastor* has some life in him yet."

I should say so! thought Cathryn as she dusted herself off and tried to get her mind back on the game. Back on the game and off the game's central energy. As much as she tried, it was getting harder and harder to dismiss thoughts of Jacob.

She looked his way, only to discover his gaze riveted disconcertingly upon her. She felt color rise to her cheeks and blessed the appearance-altering moonlight. There was *nothing* between the two of them...so why did she feel so drawn to him?

"Look alive out there!" Boone's voice jarred the cobwebs out of Cathryn's thoughts. "It's home-run Harriet."

Harriet Madison, the only teenager on the two teams, stepped to the plate. She'd already knocked two home runs over the fence this evening for Jacob's team. By the look on her face, she intended to go for a third. Boone's team began a spirited patter.

Cathryn's muscles tensed. Out of the corner of her eye she could see Jacob take a lead off the first base bag as Boone wound up.

On the very first pitch Harriet swung and connected, smacking the ball in a line drive toward the gap between second base and first. The second baseman made a diving stop as Cathryn moved to cover second. Swiftly scooping up the ball, the second baseman threw it to Cathryn, who stepped on second base and prepared to throw to first as Jacob, in a swirling cloud of red Georgia dust, came sliding into second. She leapt to avoid a collision, and, off balance, threw the ball to first.

She knew the ball had reached first base before the runner only because she heard the cheers of her teammates. All her other senses were involved in tumbling. Tumbling from her leap to avoid the sliding Jacob. Into a heap. A heap directly on top of the now laughing Jacob sprawled on second base.

He caught her as she fell. Caught her and held her and laughed a deep, rich laugh into her hair.

She coughed as the thick red Georgia dust entered her mouth and nostrils and lungs. Still chuckling, Jacob sat, pulled Cathryn onto his lap and gently patted her on the back.

"You okay?" he asked, not letting her free. "Could someone get some water?" he called to anyone in general.

Cathryn struggled ineffectually to get up. "No, please. I'm fine." As soon as she said the words, the dust tickled her throat and she began a new series of helpless coughs and sneezes.

"Oh, I'd say you're fine, all right." Jacob's voice rumbled with admiration in her ear. "And that double play was fantastic."

Cathryn caught her breath and looked into Jacob's eyes. She saw amusement and joy and something else. Genuine affection? No, what she saw in his eyes made affection pale. Made her tremble.

The smile left his face. "Cassie, are you certain you're okay?"

She would be once she could move away from his touch. Could hide from his too-intense regard. Could cool the heat she felt spreading throughout her entire body. She struggled to her feet, and this time Jacob let her go.

Her teammates surrounded her in a congratulatory rain of voices. She couldn't see Jacob. But she still felt enveloped in his joy and his laughter. Felt his warmth. His strength. Still felt the piercing heat of his longing, and the disconcerting pull of attraction for him that she seemed to always feel now in his presence.

What was this attraction after all these years? Years of separation and years of mere friendship before that.

Perhaps, she thought as she threw her glove into the equipment box, it had to do with Jacob's obvious love of life. As with the impromptu sundae social this morning, as with the sandman cherry suckers earlier, Jacob seemed to be constantly proving that adversity need not kill joy.

Cathryn harrumphed softly to herself. Softball and moonlight. Who would have thought they could make her forget for an all too short while? Forget the past. Forget that she didn't really fit into life in Sweet Hope. Forget that she was totally unsuitable for a man like Jacob.

No matter how attractive he was.

She looked up to see the two teams heading toward the church gymnasium. Silence and the solitude settled blessedly over her.

Jacob cleared his throat, not wanting to startle Cathryn. But she jumped anyway. He'd actually not wanted to disturb her at all. Had wanted to stand and watch her lost in thought. Lovely in the moonlight. Smudged with the dust of red Georgia clay. Flushed from her triumphant double play. And now, very pensive.

He reached into his pocket for the large ring of church keys. "I just need to lock up the equipment box for the night."

"Oh." She stood aside self-consciously, as if he'd pried into her very thoughts.

"Great game," he offered, merely wanting to extend the moment without frightening her away.

She smiled. A truly happy smile. "Yes. I'd forgotten just how much I enjoy playing ball."

Oh, yes. Her enjoyment, her relaxation, her return to the Cassie of seven years ago had been obvious. Obvious and enchanting. He'd do anything to make her feel all the time the way she'd seemed to feel tonight, for the rest of her life.

She gave him a quizzical look, and he realized his thoughts had been wandering. He recovered quickly. "Do you play with Aiden?"

"Catch. But I can't really play all-out softball with a four-year-old, now, can I?" Her smile turned wistful.

"You should move back home to Sweet Hope. This year for the first time Grace Everlasting's fielding a co-ed team. Slow-pitch."

A cloud seemed to pass over her pale features. "Aiden and I have a home. In Albany." Her words were a rebuke to him.

Blame it on the moonlight; he couldn't dance this dance of implied steps. "Cassie..." He reached out and touched her arm. "This is Jacob Matthews, remember? How many times have we walked and talked down by the brook at Alice Rose's farm? *Talk* to me, now. Please."

She didn't look at him, but she didn't pull away from his touch, either. "There's nothing to talk about. For a couple hours tonight you worked the old Matthews magic and kept reality at bay." She looked at him, and her blue eyes seemed enormous in the moonlight. "But now it's back to business as usual."

"Which is?"

"I'm here for a week. To help with relief efforts. A week from today, Aiden and I get in my car and return to Albany and our life there."

"What kind of life can it be away from the family you love and your hometown?"

She slipped her arm out from under his hand. Her skin felt silky and cool as she withdrew. She sighed, and he knew she definitely did not want to have this conversation.

Because he had only one week to break through her resistance, he couldn't withstand the urge to press. "Is there someone special in Albany? Is that why you feel the need to stay there?" He steeled himself to hear the answer.

She ran a hand through her tousled blond hair and sighed. "No. There's no one."

Her silence left him no opportunity to broach his next question easily. "Do you ever see Aiden's father?" He paused. "Is that why you left me at the altar...because you thought you had a chance at reconciliation with him?"

She looked as if he'd physically slapped her. Her eyes widened and darkened in distress. Her mouth and cheeks looked unnaturally red against the pallor of her skin. He didn't want to hurt her. He wanted instead to pull her to him and comfort her. Stroke her hair and tell her, as he had five years ago, that everything was going to work out. That his strength and his love would make it work out.

"I haven't ever seen...Aiden's father. Not since... never." Her voice was barely a whisper. Her shuttered eyes guarded a hurt that she obviously was unwilling to share. "I never *ever* wanted . . . want . . . to see him."

"Then *what,* Cassie? What hurt keeps you from us?"

She turned away from him. Her head high, her shoulders ramrod stiff, she hugged herself and remained silent.

He'd have none of this. He'd never let another person hurt her. Neither would he allow her to shoulder this burden—whatever it turned out to be—alone. For, by doing so, she hurt herself.

"Cassie . . ." He said her name in quiet supplication.

Slowly she turned to face him. Her blue eyes were full of life's unshared pain. "Jacob..." The sound of his name on her lips warmed him. "I've shared more with you than with any other living being. But I'll not share this. This is mine alone."

"It doesn't have to be."

She reached out and gently laid a hand on his arm, causing the warmth he already felt to increase dramatically. "If I shared this with you... if I let you into my life..."

"What?" He couldn't wait for her to finish. "What could be the harm in it?"

Smiling sadly, she let her hand drop. "Jacob Matthews, you always did see the best in people. Always approached every situation as if it could be mastered."

He reached out and wiped away a smudge of dust on her cheek with the pad of his thumb. "And what's wrong with that?"

"Sometimes you overwhelm me with your goodness." She bent her head and studied her hands. "Sometimes... I find your perfection a little daunting."

"My perfection!" Now he'd heard everything. In frustration, he thrust his hands into his own hair and pulled until it hurt. When he looked again at Cathryn, she was watching him solemnly. "I'm thinking you have it in your head I'm not a real man. Do you know how that makes me feel?"

Cathryn lowered her eyes and had the decency to blush. "That's not it at all... quite the contrary...." Her voice faded to a hushed stillness.

Quite the contrary! What was she saying?

He reached out to touch her arm and felt her supple muscles tense. Smothering a soft little moan, she stepped back, beyond his grasp.

She swallowed hard and squared her shoulders. "Jacob, please. Can't you see how unsuitable I am for you?"

No, he couldn't. He could only see Cassie. See the one woman who'd ever held his love. The one woman he knew with certainty was meant to stand by his side. The only woman who'd ever felt *right.*

And he wasn't about to give her up—again—without a fight.

He moved closer to her until he left her no personal space at all, then gently grasped her upper arms. Held her firmly so that she wouldn't attempt to retreat. "When you look at me with those sad eyes and talk about me in terms of goodness and perfection, I hear you putting yourself down."

"I'm not." With an admirable candor, she looked him square in the eyes. The tensing of her jaw, however, betrayed her inner turmoil. "It's just that other people could still use our...unsuitability...to harm your career. To harm you."

He slid his hands down the length of her arms and laced her fingers through his own, and thought about her professed reasons for leaving him at the altar those many years ago. "Ah, Cassie O'Malley, when will you ever stop protecting me?"

A hint of a smile curled the corners of her full mouth. "When you stop trying to protect me."

"Touché." They shared a smile, and Jacob's very being warmed. He'd pushed enough tonight. "Truce?"

"Truce." She squeezed his fingers gently. "Now, Jacob Matthews, you may walk me home."

Still holding hands, they fell into step and headed toward the gymnasium. He inhaled deeply in satisfaction. "All right. But answer me this. Who's protecting whom on this walk?"

"Nobody," she replied, a trace of genuine laughter infusing her words. "Just old friends out for a moonlit stroll."

Just friends? Not likely, he thought as a determined glow settled over his heart.

Chapter Five

As the last verse of "Amazing Grace" swelled to the rafters of the Sunday-filled sanctuary, Cathryn tried desperately to hold back the sting of unbidden tears. What was it about group singing that brought tears? Not tears of sorrow, but tears of immense joy and belonging. She dabbed at her eyes and thought what a basket case she must seem. Was she the only person in the world whose vocal cords were directly connected to her tear ducts?

Jacob, walking up the aisle to the back of the church where he'd give the final benediction, smiled at her and jump-started the feeling all over again. Goodness, to get through the service, she'd have to mouth the last chorus of the closing hymn.

Oh, that feeling.

The feeling especially of belonging. Of being pulled by roots sunk deeply into the northwest Georgia soil. Of needing these assembled people as much as they temporarily needed her services. Of wanting her son to grow up surrounded by loving O'Malleys.

The nascent feeling that, had circumstances been different, a marriage to Jacob Matthews would have felt right. So right.

That last thought lingered uncomfortably as Cathryn remembered the just-finished service. Remembered how, from behind the pulpit, Jacob had commanded his audience. How he'd obviously grown from a fine young man to a compelling adult.

He'd spoken of God's gifts in the face of adversity. Of family and of community and of a place to call home. He'd spoken of the resilience of the human spirit, of faith and of the gift to start over that each new minute brings. Surprisingly, in the face of events, the service had been one of thanksgiving and hope. And as he'd spoken, Cathryn had felt Jacob aim his words directly at her.

Now, while the strains of the organ faded to nothing, Jacob's strong voice rang out over the congregation in benediction. Cathryn inhaled sharply. She would never *ever* say the words aloud, but in her heart of hearts she began to suspect that, if circumstances were different, she could love this man. This man of strength. Physical strength and, more important, strength of character. This man who embraced life with unbridled joy and laughter and optimism.

As things now stood, however, she could *not* allow herself the luxury of loving Jacob.

"Shall we shake the pastor's hand, then see how Aiden liked Sunday school?" Belle's voice at her side made Cathryn start. Her stepmother gave her a quizzical look. "Not nodding off in church, now, were we, Ms. O'Malley?"

Cathryn pulled her thoughts back into the present and smiled. "No, ma'am."

"Don't 'ma'am' your stepmama, Cathryn," Boone warned playfully over Belle's shoulder. "It makes her feel old as sin." To his wife he said, "You forget we have noon-meal duty. No shaking the pastor's hand for us. Let's see if we can slide out the side door."

As Belle and Boone turned against the tide of exiting parishioners, Cathryn was swept into the aisle. Into the swell of people heading toward the church doorway where Jacob stood greeting the morning congregation. People all around Cathryn spoke of the incredible events of the previous week, of their misfortune or of their luck, of the sermon and of the sense of hope Pastor Matthews always inspired. Cathryn barely heard a word. Her thoughts were on the churchyard where she'd be reunited with her son. But her gaze couldn't get past the imposing figure silhouetted in the doorway. The figure of a man who was goodness and temptation all rolled into one.

Cathryn harrumphed softly to herself as she thought of her past and what that past would mean to a man like Jacob and his calling. No, Cathryn O'Malley, she thought, put Jacob Matthews out of your mind. He is definitely forbidden fruit.

Suddenly she found herself face-to-face with him. Not Jacob the pastor, but Jacob the man. And a far too appealing man, at that. A lock of his dark hair had begun to slip over his forehead. His gray eyes pierced hers with a mischievous twinkle. The corners of his mouth turned up in a beckoning smile. A smile that could be as boyishly affectionate as Aiden's...or as sensuous as a lover's. He reached out to take her hand in his, and, for a moment, Cathryn stood not in the doorway of Grace Everlasting but in that long-ago meadow, alone with Jacob. And he had just asked her to marry him.

"Thank you for your help." His voice enveloped her, pulled her back to the present, shaking her out of her reverie. "Perhaps, you'll choose to stay in Sweet Hope." His words had depth and a final note of certainty.

An electrifying shiver reverberated through her. She would not give in to the unspoken promise in his words. A relationship between Jacob and her would not work. It simply would not.

She withdrew her hand from his. "You're welcome for the help. It's not much . . . because Aiden and I *will* be leaving at the end of the week."

Just then an enraged squeal echoed through the churchyard.

From her height at the top of the front steps, Cathryn looked down and could see the source. Two little boys engaged in a dusty scuffle. And, dear Lord, one of them was Aiden.

"Aiden!" Between her son and her was an immense sea of people frustrating her attempts to get to him. To stop the fight. How she instinctively hated violence of any kind. Even the four-year-old-boy kind. In heaven's name, what could four-year-olds find to fight over with such intensity? Her heart began to pound as she fought her way with difficulty through the crowd.

"Make way!" Jacob's voice rumbled with authority directly behind her, and the crowd quickly parted.

Jacob arrived at the still-scuffling boys a split second before Cathryn. Before she could reach her arms out, he'd pulled the two young combatants apart. "Do you want to tell me what's going on?" he asked, his voice stern, his face a scowl that brooked no false excuses.

As the other boy began to cry, Aiden stood, then shoved his hands deep into his pants pockets, his expression truculent. Cathryn reached for him, but he stiffened. The other child, still in Jacob's grasp, increased the intensity of his wails.

"What on earth happened?" Cathryn's heart began to sink. Aiden remained fiercely silent. It was obvious they would get no answers from the other, now loudly howling boy.

"Answer your mother, Aiden." Not harsh, Jacob's command was still just that—a command. Obvious over the shrieks of the boy he held.

Aiden squinched the features of his face in a movement Cathryn knew was designed to hold back tears. He pointed a stubby finger at the boy in Jacob's grasp. "He lied."

"What lie could he tell that would make you fight? You know how I feel about fighting." Kneeling, Cathryn reached out for Aiden's hand as the other boy wriggled free from Jacob and dashed into the gathering crowd.

Aiden didn't pull away from Cathryn this time. This time he threw himself upon her. Wrapped his sturdy arms around her neck, buried his face and hung on for dear life.

"Sweet baby, what did he say?" She heard the snuffle that meant tears.

"He said...he said I didn't have a daddy because my mama was bad. Real bad."

Dynamite could not have caused more destruction than her son's words.

She tightened her protective embrace and felt Aiden's little body shudder with sobs. The old anger welled up inside her. She'd been a fool to bring him here. Here where he was vulnerable to the ugly thoughts of others. This child who had never harmed a soul. This child who was love itself. He should never have to suffer for the fact that he had been conceived under force and a rain of hateful words. She should never have brought him here, where her past might come to haunt her. And to scar him.

She felt Jacob's strong hands on her shoulders, lifting her. His voice was quiet but strong and reassuring. "Take Aiden to walk by the stream behind the ball diamonds. I'll meet you as soon as I've followed Howie to his parents."

Comforted by his voice, she started when she looked into gray eyes full of barely controlled fury. "Jacob. Please, let me handle this with Howie's parents. You may tell them I'll search them out as soon as I've talked to Aiden." She reached out and touched his arm. "It's *my* place, however, to handle this."

Jacob, in turn, reached out and brushed tears from Aiden's cheek. "Go talk to your son, Cassie. I'll meet you in a few minutes." He then turned abruptly and left.

Jacob was not a man quick to anger, but neither was he a man who avoided confrontation. And when cruelty necessitated confrontation...well, his wrath could be fearsome. He could prove a powerful ally. But as easy as it would be to slip under the mantle of his protection, Cathryn needed to remind herself that she was the head of her family of two. *She* made the decisions and smoothed troubled waters. To let Jacob handle this scuffle would set a dangerous precedent.

As she turned, the crowd parted as if she and her son were not quite clean.

Damn! No one had the right to pass old venom on to the next generation.

Jacob had just finished dealing with the Mapes family—cousins to Ellie Able. Of course, he thought bitterly. They would be.

He'd made clear his displeasure at this particular family's cruelty toward Cathryn O'Malley and her son, who were essentially guests in his house. Perhaps, after his outburst, Grace Everlasting would be several families short in the congregation by evening, but, still, he didn't regret his words.

He couldn't save the world. He wasn't that naive. But within his domain he could make certain that his parishioners made an attempt at brotherly love. Even if he had to play the enforcer, he thought with chagrin.

He crossed the now-empty ball diamonds. Everyone should be settling down for midday Sunday dinner at tables set up in the dining hall. Everyone except Cathryn and Aiden. He hoped to find them down by the stream. Hoped to be able to salve the hurt. There was nothing in the world he wouldn't do to keep hurt away from that woman and that boy, her son. Who should have been his son.

Descending the grassy bank that led to the stream, Jacob felt the air change from sun warmed to a blessed shade cooled, just cool enough to compose his overheated sense of protectiveness. He knew enough to rein his true feelings in. Cathryn O'Malley would have none of them.

Just ahead of him on the stream's edge, their bare feet dangling in the water, sat Cathryn and her son.

"Hey," he said softly, sitting down beside Aiden. "May I join you?"

Aiden looked up, his round face blotchy and tearstained. "I guess."

"Want to talk?"

"I don't think that's a good idea," Cathryn replied quickly but not before Aiden murmured softly, "Yes."

Cathryn shot a warning glance at Jacob over the top of her son's head. Jacob looked from the woman to the boy.

Aiden screwed up his face. "Why did Howie Mapes call my mama *bad?*"

"I tried to tell him not to pay attention to everything others say." Cathryn put her arm protectively around Aiden's small shoulders. "That it doesn't matter."

"It mattered to me," Aiden insisted, then looked directly at Jacob. "Did it matter to you?"

Jacob's heart somersaulted. "Yes, Aiden, it mattered to me."

"But it's a lie."

"It most definitely is a lie."

Aiden jumped to his feet. Standing, he was barely taller than Jacob seated, but he towered with four-year-old fury. "Then *do* something. You're important. Howie Mapes would listen to you."

Jacob smiled. "Believe me, Howie Mapes and the entire Mapes family listened to me just now."

"Jacob!" Cathryn, too, jumped to her feet, as outraged as Aiden but, Jacob felt certain, for very different reasons. "You shouldn't have," she protested.

"Why not, Mama?" Aiden dug his fists into his hips and looked up at his mother. "They needed to be told."

Cathryn looked the picture of exasperation. She answered her son, but she stared irately at Jacob. "If any telling needs to be done, I'll do it. That's why not."

"But you couldn't tell 'em. You were taking care of me. Who was gonna take care of you?"

Jacob, smiling at Aiden's pint-size wisdom, shielded his eyes from the dappled sunlight and stared up at Cathryn. "He's got you there."

Before kneeling beside her son, Cathryn flashed Jacob a final look of blue-eyed indignation. "We've gone over this before, Aiden. I take care of you *and* me. That's how it works. That's enough. It always has been and always will be."

Despite the strength of her words, Jacob didn't believe her. Neither, it seemed, did Aiden.

"But don't you ever get tired?" the boy persisted. "Wouldn't you like a helper like Gramps helps Nonny Belle?"

Jacob wondered that, too. Wondered if Cathryn ever got tired or lonely in the life she'd chosen away from Sweet Hope. Wondered what it would be like to be her helpmate. Her best friend and confidant. Her husband. Watching her now, uncomfortable under her son's questioning, he felt his heart fill with longing.

Cathryn said nothing, but Aiden, tugging on her hand, would have none of her silence. "Mama, I didn't hear you thank Pastor Jacob. Today he was your helper."

The look she shot Jacob was definitely not filled with gratitude. "Thank you," she said, her words tight.

Aiden scampered away from the adults, and Jacob couldn't help wishing all problems could be resolved as easily as this one had been in the boy's mind. Believing in his heart that Howie Mapes had told a lie, Aiden had stood up for his mother as best he could. He'd then reached out and found another soul who believed Howie's accusation a lie. And he'd been relieved that that kindred spirit had set the Mapes family to rights. A piece of cake. The icing was his mother's thank-you. Now Aiden was content that justice had been done, and his world could proceed. If only life were that simple.

As Aiden splashed barefoot in the shallow stream, chasing water striders, Cathryn slipped into her shoes, her face an unreadable mask.

Jacob rose from his seat on the ground. "You think I stuck my nose where it didn't belong, don't you?"

Her eyes flashing, Cathryn looked up at him. "If it were only me, I wouldn't care what you did. But now... how do you expect Aiden to fit in with the other children for the rest of the week, if the pastor appears to play favorites?"

"I don't consider what I did *playing favorites.* I consider it pastoral counseling. As for Aiden... if he has any difficulty moving right back into the stream of things, I'll show him where there's a huge mass of tadpole eggs. He can show his classmates, and I bet within minutes bygones will be bygones."

Cathryn threw up her hands in exasperation. "Jacob Matthews, you cannot go around solving life's problems with sundae socials, cherry suckers and *tadpoles.*"

Jacob smiled. "You're not the first to tell me that."

"Then don't you think there might be a grain of truth in it?"

He shook his head. "Cassie O'Malley, where's your sense of wonder?"

"My sense of wonder has taken a back seat to my sense of responsibility." Her blue gaze clouded. "My sense of survival."

Jacob's heart constricted. He knew so little of her past five years. Had they been survival years? Surely the O'Malleys would have helped out. Surely they wouldn't have allowed two of their own to suffer. At least, not where the essentials were concerned. Food, shelter, health care. Love. But, Jacob suspected, Cathryn, as always, would keep her innermost thoughts and struggles to herself. If she talked of surviving, Jacob would bet his last dollar that her struggle with survival was internal. And hers alone.

He vowed again to discover the root of her obvious distress. To discover it and to do his best to help her master it. For her sake and for Aiden's sake. And, a cloistered voice reminded him, for his very own sake, too.

"Well, then, if you've misplaced your sense of wonder," he said carefully, "I think I need to show *you* my hidden cache of tadpole eggs."

"But dinner... I really should get back to feed Aiden."

Jacob nodded at the child who stood calf-deep in water, bent over, examining a submerged rock with boyish intensity. "Aiden looks as if he'll hold up for a few minutes longer." He checked his watch. "It's quarter to. Dinner's being served till one."

"But we'll be late."

"There'll be *something* to eat, I assure you. You forget..." He quickly raised his gaze heavenward, then lowered it and winked at her. "I know someone in authority."

Cathryn's face relaxed as she actually smiled. "Jacob Matthews, does the Lord ever find you an exasperation?"

"Daily, most probably."

She gazed deep into his eyes, setting his heart to thumping, before she called, "Aiden! Do you want to see Pastor Jacob's secret tadpole eggs?"

The boy's serious face seemed to glow, and, although he didn't smile, Aiden radiated interest. Jacob kicked off his shoes and socks, then held his hand out to the child, who took it readily.

"Can Mama come?"

"Oh, yes." Jacob turned to look at Cathryn, whose gaze was momentarily riveted on the clasped hands of the man and the boy. "These eggs are especially for your mama."

"Why's that?"

"Because they're just about to hatch. You and your mama, being here for the week, will get to see it. We'll check back every day. They'll go from little dots in jelly to wriggly little creatures. A minor miracle." He smiled down at Aiden. "Your mama, especially, needs to see that miracles do happen."

In the almost empty church dining hall, Aiden played under the long table with Margaret while Cathryn sat and thought about this roller-coaster day so far. About how Jacob had been a part of each twist and turn. About how she'd not asked for or wanted his protection... but how good it had felt. Ah, Jacob, her persistent protector. It was as if fate—or someone with a keen sense of irony—kept plopping him in her path. Ever since the first time she'd met him, he'd seemed as if he belonged in her life. He'd certainly made it easy and natural for her to lean on him. A part of her rebelled at giving up one single ounce of her independence, while another part of her never seemed to mind with Jacob. With him, she never thought of it as giving up anything. Rather thought of it as sharing.

As this morning.

Once she'd thought it through, she hadn't minded Jacob talking to the Mapes family. Not really, despite the fuss she'd automatically made. He had, in fact, given her an opportunity to spirit Aiden away, to talk to him, to calm him. Her child, of course, was her first and foremost concern. Then, when Jacob had shown up at the stream, Cathryn initially hadn't wanted him to say any more to her son. She'd taken care of everything. Or so she'd thought. But Jacob's few words to Aiden on top of her own had seemed to satisfy him as her words alone had not been able to do.

And those tadpole eggs. She had to admit that Jacob had been right there. Aiden had been enthralled. And she...well, she'd felt that old, almost forgotten sense of wonder begin to surface at the sight of the simple but miraculous continuation of nature's cycle. A cycle she'd experienced since her own childhood, as had her parents and their parents before. A cycle that never failed to nurture hope within her.

She listened to the happy sounds coming from under the table, and thought, Yes, Jacob Matthews, once again you've smoothed the rough edges of my life. Although it was a bit much that he'd insisted on having her sit here upon their return to the dining hall while he foraged for a late midday meal. She smiled. Oh, he'd said he knew someone in authority, but she doubted even the Lord would get a late dinner out of Alice Rose and her kitchen crew without a lecture.

"A penny for your thoughts."

Cathryn looked up into the come-hither gaze of Rhune Sherman, who stood, loose hipped and sure of himself, directly across the table from her.

"Mr. Sherman—"

"Rhune."

"Rhune, then. You startled me."

"You seemed deep in pleasant thoughts." His voice was low and husky and honey rich. Seductive. And very practiced.

Cathryn shivered. She was no longer a schoolgirl for whom a sexy voice and a smooth delivery made the day a little brighter. If anything, such moves made her withdraw into herself. Away from the ugly memories such meaningless flirtation invoked.

"I was...resting. Pastor Matthews and I have a lot of paperwork to deal with this afternoon." Rhune's blatant male regard made her uncomfortable. Made her feel somehow exposed. "If you don't mind..."

"If you don't mind," Jacob's reassuring baritone broke in, "Cathryn and Aiden and I were just catching a quick bite before we get back to work." He slid two heavily loaded trays onto the table, then stood behind Cathryn, eye-to-eye with Rhune. "Cassie, I brought you extras on the squash casserole. I know you love it. Aiden, soup's on, son."

A lazy-smiled, quizzical expression on his face, Rhune eyed first Cathryn, then Jacob. "I don't mean to interrupt."

Jacob slid his hand onto Cathryn's shoulder. His use of her nickname, his proprietary stance, the deliberate way in which he spoke to Rhune, letting the other man know he had somehow broken in on an almost-family unit surprised Cathryn. The territoriality on Jacob's part was sudden and unexpected. And not unpleasant, she thought as heat crept into her cheeks.

"You're not interrupting," Jacob said at last. Evenly. "You're welcome to join us. I just wanted you to know we won't be lingering."

Abruptly, Aiden climbed out from under the table. "Mama, can Margaret eat again with us? She's hungry."

"Again!" Margaret's cherubic face popped up next to Aiden's.

Glad for the distraction, Cathryn smiled at the two children and patted the bench beside her. "Yes, munchkins. Climb up here. I think Pastor Jacob's brought enough to feed an army."

"Yes, indeed," Rhune agreed. "Looks like the pastor's good at taking care of his own."

Cathryn's heart skipped a beat at Rhune's tonal implication of more than pastorly interest on Jacob's part. Was that how it appeared? That Cathryn, the children and Jacob belonged together? Or was Rhune just scoping out the situation? Determining whether he could make a move or should move on. Jacob, surprisingly, neither denied nor confirmed that he was *taking care of his own.*

He sat next to Aiden, comfortably sandwiching the two children between the adults, and motioned to the bench across the table. "As I said, you're welcome to join us."

Rhune smiled. A sexy, cat-who-ate-the-canary smile. "Thanks. But I think I'll locate my sister. It seems I scheduled an inappropriate time for a vacation. If she puts me to work, she'll feel better about my insensitivity." He nodded at Jacob, but winked at Cathryn. "I'll be seeing you."

Cathryn watched Rhune's lanky retreat and thought, Sweet mamas, lock up your daughters. She turned back to the dinner at hand, only to discover Jacob staring at her with a piercing gray intensity above the heads of the two children intent on their meals.

She flushed. "Yes?"

"Do you suppose he has an effect on *every* woman?"

Cathryn's flush deepened, but not for the reasons Jacob would assume. Rhune affected her, yes, but the effect was not attraction. No, the effect was unease and a wariness born of experience. Yet, she had no reason to reassure Jacob. She might not wish to encourage Rhune, but she could not encourage Jacob.

She swallowed hard, then managed to say, "Margaret seems immune."

Turning to eat, Jacob inhaled deeply as a cautious, shuttered look passed over his face.

The children's occasional giggles broke the awkward silence that followed as the four ate.

"Eeuwww!" Aiden squirmed in his seat and tugged at Cathryn's sleeve. "Can I go with Margaret to the kitchen? She says Gramps and Nonny Belle are making tapioca pudding for supper, and if we ask, they'll let us help pour in the fish eyes."

Margaret shrieked with delight. "I was just foolin' 'bout the fish eyes, Aiden. Tapioca just looks like it's made with fish eyes."

"Eeuwww!" Aiden repeated with enthusiasm. "This I gotta see. Can I go, Mama? Can I?"

"*May* I," Cathryn corrected. And although she wanted the children to stay—to act as a buffer between her and Jacob—she made a show of checking their hastily cleaned plates, then finally said, "Yes."

The children raced, hand in hand, toward the kitchen as a deafening silence again enveloped Cathryn and Jacob.

They were alone in the dining hall except for three women chatting quietly over coffee at the next table. The atmosphere at her own table was so hushed with tension that Cathryn could hear every word of the women's conversation without trying to do so.

She looked at Jacob. Something had changed between them. Somewhere along the line, the very air between them had become strained. Somewhere...about the time Rhune had left her in blushes. Could Jacob really have misinterpreted her reaction as attraction to Belle's brother? And had it mattered? Could Jacob still care for her enough to be jealous of another man's attentions? The thought gave her pause.

"Jacob..."

As if he'd read her thoughts, he swung his gaze to hers and said, "If you want the afternoon off...to socialize...I can handle the paperwork alone. There's no need for you to be tied to me."

A flicker of pride and of hurt in his eyes made her catch her breath. She wanted desperately to reach across the short space between them and touch him. Smooth the furrow between his brows. Reassure him she had no interest in Rhune Sherman. But that would mean admitting she still cared about him—Jacob. That her caring was beginning to take on troubling new aspects. She couldn't do that.

"Jacob...it's not what you think...."

"Pastor Matthews?" A woman's voice broke into Cathryn's attempt at explanation.

"Yes?"

The young woman, dressed in cutoff jeans and a tight T-shirt, stood respectfully before Jacob. "I want to thank you. For me and my family." She tugged at the too-short jeans, perhaps the only clothing she had left from the storm's wrath. "We're not from your parish, but if it weren't for you and your church, I don't know where we'd be."

Jacob rose and extended his hand. "Glad we could be of help. You do know we're helping residents fill out insurance claims. We'll be helping with federal assistance claims, too. Until any compensation starts, you can apply for some small immediate church relief from me or Cathryn." He motioned to Cathryn, and the two women exchanged polite nods.

"Even if we're not members of your congregation?" the woman asked.

Jacob smiled that smile Cathryn knew could calm the devil himself. "Looks like we're all one congregation in this mess."

The woman nervously smoothed her clothing. "You don't know what that means to us. We're going out with a crew tomorrow to see what we can salvage from our home. If we could but stay here till we see what we'll be needing..."

"Now, that's one thing you don't have to worry about. You and your family are welcome to stay as long as necessary."

The woman's face broke into a relieved smile. "Thank you." She turned to Cathryn. "Thank you. My family sure will be comforted, knowing we're welcomed by the pastor himself...and his wife. Thank you." She turned quickly and fairly ran from the dining hall.

Before Cathryn could digest the idea that yet another person had thrown Jacob and her together, she heard one of the women at the next table hiss, "Can you imagine standing before the pastor in that trampy outfit?"

"No," one of the other women answered in a stage whisper. "Now, there's a woman who's *asking for it.*"

"Deserves anything she gets," the third added none too quietly.

The edges of Cathryn's vision went dark.

She tried to assure herself the women's words were just cattiness born of nothing to do. She tried to find words—a rebuttal—to speak, to show these women the cruelty of their casual remarks. She needed to come to the stranger's defense, but she felt paralysis creep through her body. She'd been unable to defend herself against similar charges five years ago and had run instead.

The old sickness welled up inside her. The old doubt. Had the sharp tongues, in her own case, been right? Had she, indeed, received exactly what she'd asked for?

"Cassie..." Jacob's worried voice broke softly into her darkness.

Pushing away his extended hand, she stood abruptly, bumping the table, rattling empty dinner dishes. She needed air. She needed to remind herself that, no matter if those past voices had been right or wrong, their sharpness could slice into the present. Could harm Aiden if she remained in Sweet Hope. Could harm Jacob and his calling. Could make him lose whatever feeling he still held for her. Selfishly, she didn't want to lose what little they had.

"Cassie!"

She fled.

She needed to find her son and her family. She needed to surround herself with their strength. Needed to distance herself from Jacob and what he might come to know of her.

What in heaven's name had gotten into Cathryn? He'd been so caught up in her reaction to the stranger's assumption that they were a married couple that Jacob hadn't discerned the words the three women at the next table had spoken. But clearly, from the anguished look Cathryn had shot them, they had been the ones to upset her.

He fired a look of his own at the women, only to see three guilty pairs of downcast eyes.

For Pete's sake! It seemed that since Cathryn's return, in her defense, he'd been fairly showering his parishioners with hellfire-and-brimstone looks and admonitions. First Ellie Able, then the Mapes family, now these three. He needed to get his act together—in more ways than with just his parishioners.

He needed to control the growing battle within himself. The growing desire for a woman who seemed intent on having nothing to do with him after this week.

Oh, but he still wanted Cathryn O'Malley. Wanted her as his wife. Wanted her son as his son. Wanted the three of them to build a life together. Here in Sweet Hope. As a family.

He raked his fingers through his hair and quelled the urge to go after her. He had a parish to run. A parish in the aftermath of disaster. He had people who depended on him. Who *welcomed* his help. Who came to him and asked that he help ease their pain.

So why was he still hung up on the one woman who refused his help? Who had shown by her desertion of him five years ago that she wanted neither his help nor his love.

In frustration, Jacob stormed out of the dining hall and headed toward his office. It had been so blasted easy being pastorly these past five years when Cathryn wasn't right in front of him. Roiling up the old yearnings. The old hurt. The old pride. Now he felt torn between the needs of his parishioners, Cathryn's needs and his own not-to-be-quieted needs.

His own needs were the most disturbing. He hadn't cared a fig for them in five years. He'd thrown himself into his studies, into service to this church and this community. In his incredibly busy schedule he'd thought he was whole. Had thought he was over the pain Cathryn's leaving had brought him.

He'd been wrong.

Where else could he be wrong?

He turned the corner to his office and saw Ellie Able and several members of the Mapes family standing with Deacon Rush before the closed office door. They didn't look as if they'd come to tea.

Chapter Six

With every footstep away from her family in the kitchen and toward Jacob in his office, Cathryn upbraided herself for her earlier flight reaction to the remarks of the three cruelly catty women in the dining hall.

The women had, in a few sharp words, made it clear that they thought the stranger's dress provocative. Had made it clear they thought that she was asking for trouble. Sexual trouble. They'd been talking about the stranger, but Cathryn had heard their words as if they'd been aimed directly at her.

The three women were ignorant fools. No matter what others might think, Cathryn had not *asked* for the brutal treatment she'd received from Drew Paxton five years ago. Neither her manner of dress nor her realistic and vocal support of sexual preparedness had warranted such an attack. She'd said, "No." Clearly. Firmly. Insistently. She'd known in her heart of hearts that Drew Paxton, although exciting as a date, had not been the one with whom she'd wished to share her virginity.

He'd called her a prude, then a tease. Then worse.

She'd fought, but he'd been too strong.

And now, five years later, despite all reason, she still felt shame. Still felt an instinctive reaction to flee whenever her past, or the reminder of it, threatened to surface. Revulsion pooled in the bottom of her heart. It wasn't that she was a wimp. No, she was strong. O'Malley strong. She'd been taught, and felt to her core, that she could withstand anything life threw her way.

But Aiden...

She'd fled that first time—from Grace Everlasting's altar—because of an unborn Aiden... and because of Jacob. Because Ellie Able, whether she'd really known the whole story or not, had threatened to lay Cathryn's past open for inspection. And if that had happened, her child and her best friend stood to suffer much more than Cathryn.

She shivered as she marched down the corridor to Jacob's office. She must stop running. She had nothing to fear. Aiden was safe in their life in Albany. Jacob would never be a part of that life. And, if she could get through the next five days, Sweet Hope would be nothing but a memory.

The noise from within Jacob's office drew her up short outside the closed door. Voices—loud, angry voices—rose and swelled through door and walls to descend upon her. The anger surprised her. She'd never thought a pastor's life all milk and honey, but she'd never thought of it in terms of acrimony, either. The voices coming from within the office were definitely acrimonious. Bitter. Demanding. The aftermath of the tornado had certainly caused enough escalating worry and tension to overheat the coolest heads, but knowing that didn't make the din any more pleasant.

In the center of the uproar was Jacob's deep baritone. Powerful. Passionate. Persuasive. The voice of reason. Reason with a backbone.

But the wave of loud, angry voices overwhelmed reason. Voices tumbling pell-mell one over the other so that Cathryn could hear only snatches of the argument. Bitter words flung into the fray. *A divided congregation. Misplaced loy-*

alties. Inappropriate behavior. And the final few that brought a deadly silence: *Not the kind of man we want to lead us.*

Unexpectedly, the door to the office swung open with a whoosh and a bang. Cathryn stepped back so as not to be trampled by a red-faced Deacon Rush, followed by Ellie Able, and Edwina and Harry Mapes, all of whom looked as if they'd tangled with the devil himself.

Harry glowered at Cathryn, then turned to snarl over his shoulder, "This isn't finished yet, Matthews. No, sir, this isn't finished yet."

The four adults stormed down the corridor, then disappeared. Cathryn heard an outside door slam, the sound echoing through the too-still air of the hallway. Air that smelled of confrontation and scalded emotions.

It looked as if Jacob might need a friend.

Inhaling deeply, Cathryn stepped through the open doorway into his office.

He stood, his back three-quarters to her, his arms folded tightly across his chest, staring out the window, the quarter of his face that she could see a frozen mask. The taut fabric of his shirt over his broad back indicated a tension within the underlying muscles. A tension within the man. To Cathryn he seemed a tightly wound mechanism restrained only by a hair trigger. This was not the joy-filled, patient Jacob she knew. What had happened in this room to cause such a transformation?

"Jacob?"

At the sound of her voice, he whirled around. His gray gaze pierced her with a look of controlled anger...and pain.

Despite his formidable regard, she took a step closer. "Do you want to talk?"

He unfolded his arms and shook his head, causing a dark lock of hair to fall over one eyebrow. This time he looked anything but boyish. "No." His voice was brusque. "I want to work." He picked up a pile of papers on his desk and scowled at them.

Cathryn responded to the tormented look in his eyes, not to his words. Stepping to his side, she took the papers from his grasp. As she did so, her fingers brushed his, and she could sense his pain with that brief moment of physical contact. Her breath caught in her throat. The years had never dimmed the feeling of connection she retained for this man. They'd always shared an unspoken rhythm, for want of a better word. An understanding, a bond that could neither be defined nor denied.

She forced a smile. "Jacob Matthews, you'd never let *me* off the hook this easily."

"I'm sorry. I can't discuss it." His expression said he wouldn't. "Sometimes, what goes on in this office is confidential. Goes no further than the parties involved."

"Can you tell me truthfully that I'm not one of the parties involved?" As she spoke, she saw the flicker in his eyes that confirmed her suspicions.

He started to turn from her, but she laid a restraining hand on his arm. "Jacob..."

"The tornado and its destruction has us all on edge. Living like sardines hasn't helped tempers." His voice softened, lost its angry edge as he looked deep into her eyes. "This, too, will pass, Cassie. This, too, will pass."

Suddenly Cathryn became overly conscious of her hand on Jacob's arm. She withdrew it. "Not if I remain here as your assistant," she replied softly. "It seems either I go, or the Mapes family and their supporters go."

"It's not an either-or situation."

"I don't believe you." Cathryn could hear the anger rise in her own voice. "I'm driving a wedge between you and members of your congregation. My presence here is making it difficult for you to do your job."

For the first time since she'd entered the room, Jacob smiled. "No. I prefer to think that your presence here is making my job more... challenging."

"Oh, Jacob, don't joke. The four people who just left your office looked as if they were ready to have your job."

He shook his head ruefully. "It'll take a lot more than one argument to unseat me."

"But those people looked mad enough to leave Grace Everlasting for good if they didn't get satisfaction."

"They won't. It's their home."

Cathryn inhaled deeply. "Then Aiden and I should leave."

"It's your home, too. You grew up in it. You have as much right to be here as Ellie Able or any other parishioner, for that matter." He began to pace. "This is a church, not an exclusive club. It's open to all comers."

"Even if everyone can't get along?"

"Within these walls, we become a family. A family doesn't run from discord. It faces it and works toward harmony."

Cathryn felt that old combination of frustration and respect well up within her in the face of Jacob's optimism. "Ellie Able and me in harmony? You fail to change, don't you? You, Jacob Matthews, remain ever the idealist."

The muscles in his jaw pulsed. "You don't think it will work." It wasn't a question.

"No. Call me a realist."

The lighter mood that had begun to creep into the room vanished. Jacob's body again tensed. His gaze became shuttered as if her simple statement had brought him pain, had made him withdraw.

He turned to the window and said, his words flat, "No, it won't work if you don't let it."

The silence that followed felt like an accusation.

When at last Cathryn spoke, her voice felt rusty. "Oh, Jacob, we're so different. You and I. Different in our approaches to life . . . perhaps too different."

"Yes." His simple admission brought her no joy, but somehow released her.

She now turned to the papers on his desk as an excuse, any excuse to move, to break the tension in the room. But her thoughts wouldn't turn to forms and figures and projections. Her thoughts were on his admission that they were too different. By agreeing, he'd made her want to contradict him. Unexpectedly. Made her want to reverse the dead end his admission had brought them to.

How different were they? Jacob merely wanted to take care of his own—the family that was Grace Everlasting—as she wanted to take care of her own. Aiden. How different was that? Both she and Jacob were fiercely loyal. Protective. Wanting only the best for those they cared for.

She looked up at him. He'd turned to his desk also, and was riffling through a notebook. His brow furrowed, he suddenly looked very tired. Good Lord, what he'd been through in the past few days, trying to hold a community—a fractious church family—together in the storm's aftermath.

Suddenly, her insistence that they were different seemed like hairsplitting. Of no consequence. Suddenly, she felt her loyalty encompass him. Felt her protective instincts extend to him. Felt a need to ease his obvious burden. If only a little.

Without thinking, she put both her hands over his. "Jacob, I'm sorry. I didn't mean to sound quarrelsome. Not with you. Not now, in the face of all this trouble."

The look of surprised relief in his eyes melted her contrary mood. Reflexively, she wrapped her arms around his waist in a gesture of comfort and reconciliation.

"Friends, still?" she asked hopefully.

As Jacob felt Cathryn's arms slip unexpectedly about his waist, he inhaled sharply. Five years ago he'd become blissfully accustomed to her natural and easygoing affection. Now the shock of it threw him emotionally off balance.

Her arms resting lightly on his hips, she leaned her head on his chest. "I came to help out for a week, not to cause more trouble." She didn't withdraw, but settled against him in a gesture that brought back far too many memories. "We were such good friends, Jacob..."

Friends.

She'd seen him as only a friend. He'd known that. But the trust she'd shown him, and the ease she'd exhibited in his company...and the genuine affection...had led the younger Jacob to believe that real love could blossom between them. Given time.

He'd believed this so thoroughly that he'd gathered the courage to ask her to marry him that afternoon in the meadow. Then, as today, she'd wrapped herself around him in a feather-light embrace, and had said, "Yes."

Had said, Yes as if she'd truly meant it.

Had made him a man full of happiness and infinite hope for the future.

Then, too soon, she'd disappeared before they could let their love grow. And he'd been too long without her in his arms. Much too long.

Before she could disappear again, he slipped his arms around her shoulders and encompassed the heat and vitality of her slender body. Cassie. Dear Cassie, he thought. Can't you feel that this is where you belong?

Cathryn sighed softly. "We always did balance each other well—me, with my realism and you with your idealism."

Jacob found it difficult to speak. "I used to think of myself as idealistic," he said, his voice husky, "but I realized that, in truth, I'm selfish."

Cathryn harrumphed softly. "You haven't a selfish bone in your body."

"No?" He dared to let his lips brush the top of her head. "What do you call a man who doesn't want to choose between one side or the other? A man who wants it all."

"All?"

"Yeah." The words caught in his throat. "I want to face up to the difficulties of the Ellie Ables of the world . . . with Cathryn O'Malley at my side."

"Oh." Her response came quietly on a little puff of breath. He felt her body stiffen imperceptibly.

"Excuse me." A third voice, tinged with unmistakable pleasure, shook the air in the room.

As Cathryn withdrew quickly from his embrace, Jacob turned to see Alice Rose O'Malley standing in the doorway, an expression of sheer satisfaction bathing her features.

"Grammy!" Cathryn exclaimed, running her fingers through her tousled blond hair.

"Clearly, I've interrupted something." Alice Rose beamed. "My business can wait."

"It's not what you think." Cathryn moved quickly to pull her grandmother into the room. "Jacob's been doling out the comfort non-stop. He needed some himself. A hug. A *friendly* hug. That's all."

Alice Rose looked from Cathryn to Jacob, who felt as if the older woman could see clear down to the bottom of his heart. "It sure looked like more than just a friendly hug to me."

"Grammy, you're the world's most shameless matchmaker." Cathryn's scolding was brittle. Edgy. "There is absolutely *nothing* between Jacob and me. We're just friends. Aren't we, Jacob?" She turned to him, and the blue of her eyes was a chilly, distant blue. Defensive. Not at all like the unguarded moment they'd just shared.

At least, he'd thought they'd shared an unguarded moment. Perhaps he'd deluded himself. Once again.

"Yes, Alice Rose," he replied evenly, trying to suppress the feeling of irony that weighed him down. "Cathryn and I remain just friends."

The look Cathryn shot him was one of infinite relief.

For a few pointed moments Alice Rose stared at the two of them in disbelieving silence. Finally she said, "Jacob, about tonight's service—"

"I was thinking of conducting a community meeting rather than a service," Jacob interrupted, glad for an excuse to talk about anything but his exasperating nonrelationship with Cathryn. "To discuss the next step in storm recovery."

"Good." Alice Rose frowned as she glanced at a Cathryn lost in thought. "Boone wants to discuss a barn raising for Marshall Sims."

Jacob rubbed his hands together. "Precisely the kind of thing I had in mind." Action. Work with a purpose. A clear task to engage him. Unlike the ambiguous and frustrating job of trying to make heads or tails of his obviously unrequited feelings for Cathryn. "In fact, Alice Rose, spread the word that people should come to tonight's meeting prepared to suggest ways to best utilize Grace Everlasting resources in the upcoming days. Cathryn's made it clear to me that government assistance will be slow in coming."

At the sound of her name, Cathryn became attentive once more. "Which reminds me...I'd better get the forms we've completed ready for mailing tomorrow." She stepped to Jacob's desk and made a determined show of activity.

Alice Rose smiled slyly. "I guess I'd better leave you two to your unfinished business."

Cathryn shot her grandmother a look filled with unmistakable warning as the older woman backed out of the room.

"I'll spread the word about the meeting tonight," Alice Rose called in goodbye. "See you there."

"Yes, see you there," Jacob replied mechanically. He turned to look at Cathryn, who eyed him warily.

Alice Rose's interruption and her transparent assumption that something simmered between Jacob and Cathryn had created a thick atmosphere of tension in the room. The afternoon's paperwork that stretched before them held no promise of any real distraction.

Jacob knew it, and so, it seemed, did Cathryn.

"I suppose I should apologize for my grandmother," she offered. "She's a champion at jumping to conclusions."

"No apology necessary." Making his words cool, he reached for his laptop computer. "It was, after all, just a friendly hug."

Just a hug that had made him think once again, *What if...* But the quickness and vehemence with which Cathryn had risen to disabuse her grandmother of any romantic notions had shattered his notions, as well. Had set him straight. Clearly. And had hurt. Again. Deeply.

He was no more to Cathryn than a good friend. The Rhune Shermans of the world might make her blush, but he, Jacob Matthews, would only ever elicit a comforting, *friendly* hug. He should let go the irritation that that fact caused. He should accept Cathryn's presence here for what it was: a week's worth of community service. Nothing more, nothing less. He should forget the feel of her against him.

No, he could never forget the feel of her against him.

And for that reason, he needed to create some emotional distance. The very fact of the matter was that he was no saint. Never claimed to be one. He'd been offered friendship, but had wanted more. Much more. However, if he was no saint, neither was he a man of easy morals. He'd seen people thrown together in adversity seek each other out for temporary physical solace. Although he'd not judged them, he was not one of them. He had a gut feeling that Cathryn, despite her troubled past, was not one of them, either. A hug meant to comfort would never escalate to caresses meant to obliterate reality. Neither he nor, he guessed, Cathryn would be satisfied with solace born of a temporary passion.

He'd speculated that Cathryn's distance and pain now was somehow tied up with a momentary act of passion years ago. He'd bet his bottom dollar she'd guarded against such letting-go ever since.

No, neither one of them would be satisfied with momentary release. Jacob could only speak for himself, but he wanted commitment and love. A real, abiding love. And passion born of that love. But if that was not to be forthcoming from Cathryn O'Malley, he was proud enough not to push. No, the best thing for him right now would be to keep a courteous, businesslike distance.

He looked to Cathryn and said, "Let's get busy. We have a lot to do before tonight's meeting." His words sounded brusque even to his own ears.

She turned a blue gaze on him that was full of question. And for the first time since she'd returned to Sweet Hope, her presence caused him a deep, searing pain, without promise of reprieve.

Belle's words rang in Cathryn's ears. *Jacob Matthews is not a man to be trifled with.* A quaint, country expression. Had she, by her hug meant to comfort, trifled with him? She hadn't intended to. But judging by the emotional distance Jacob had put between them all afternoon, he was not comfortable with...something. But what? The hug? Or her insistence that he and she were just friends? Surely he'd known that. Surely, she'd made that clear from the start.

But his words of this afternoon kept pushing under the edges of her consciousness. *I want it all. I want to face up to the difficulties of the Ellie Ables of the world...with Cathryn O'Malley at my side.* Oh, my. That didn't sound like a man satisfied with friendship.

Cathryn sighed and leaned against the gymnasium's open back door. In what had become a ritual, Boone had taken Margaret and Aiden to wash up before lights out. Belle and Alice Rose were helping with refreshments after tonight's Sunday-service-turned-strategy meeting. The meeting formally adjourned, Jacob would still be in the middle of listening and planning. He'd made it clear that he didn't need Cathryn's assistance. Had insisted she see to Aiden.

It was fortunate she didn't have more time alone to herself on this trip back home. Her thoughts were too troubling.

As people began to file back into the gymnasium in preparation for bedtime, Cathryn heard the first distant, rumbling thunder. Heard, too, the scattered whimpering of children. She turned to see adults exchange worried glances. She understood the unease and the worry, for spring thunderstorms could easily foreshadow tornadoes. And the horror these people had endured only days ago would still be fresh in their minds. She said a quick prayer to the Lord asking comfort for the restless children, and giving thanks that Aiden hadn't been subjected to such an ordeal.

She spotted Boone picking a trail around the cots. Aiden walked easily at his side, but Margaret clung to his neck, her small face squinched into an uncharacteristic expression of apprehension. Cathryn hurried to meet them.

"It's gonna be okay, Margaret, you'll see," Cathryn heard Aiden say as she approached.

"You don't know," Margaret whimpered into her father's neck. "You weren't here, Aiden. You were safe in Albany."

"There, there, lovey." Boone stroked the girl's back. "Aiden's right. It's just a little thunder." But the look Boone cast Cathryn said it could be otherwise.

The air in the gymnasium had become very warm, very still and oppressive. No rain fell as yet, but the thunder continued to rumble ominously, ever closer. Lightning flashed through the narrow windows near the gym roof. With each new thunderclap, children huddled closer to their parents. Parents eyed each other with growing unease.

Cathryn held out her hand to Aiden. "Anything I can do here?" she asked Boone, forcing a cheerful note into her words.

"Perhaps a bedtime story," Boone replied.

"Just what I was thinking," a deep voice behind Cathryn agreed. Jacob's voice.

Cathryn turned to see Jacob and Belle, who immediately reached for Margaret.

While Belle's face clearly showed her worry, Jacob's showed only reassuring calm and control. Cathryn inhaled deeply. Why was it that the mere presence of this man made her believe that everything would turn out just fine? He'd *always* had that capability.

He ruffled Aiden's hair. "I think all the children could use a story. And I could use a cool-headed helper. How about it, Aiden?" He winked. "You look cool as a cucumber."

Without hesitation Aiden transferred his hand from Cathryn's to Jacob's. "Sure."

"Boone," Jacob said quietly, "there's a television and a scanner in the hall storage room. Glue yourself to both and let me know if anything stronger than diversion is necessary." He nodded at Cathryn and Belle. "Would you please gather the children and their parents into a circle in the middle of the floor. Aiden and I have a bedtime story to perform."

Aiden looked the slightest bit worried. "Perform?"

"Don't you worry, son. You just do as I say in the story, and you and I are going to make these kids forget this old thunderstorm."

Aiden nodded solemnly, then trotted off with Jacob.

As Cathryn and Belle, with a very clingy Margaret, hastened to gather children and parents into a makeshift storytelling circle, Cathryn barely had time to reflect with surprise on the ease with which Aiden had given his hand and his trust to Jacob.

Through the years she'd guarded her son carefully. Had kept his circle of intimacy small—confined really to the O'Malley family. He was a cautious and sober child to begin with, not given to openness with strangers. But, from the start, the boy hadn't treated Jacob as a stranger.

Strange.

And neither had Jacob treated Aiden with anything but a natural and easygoing affection. Oh, yes, she'd seen Jacob interact with the children of Grace Everlasting. Had seen his loving nature come through. But with Aiden...with Aiden, there was more. The look he'd given her son just now contained an unmistakable fatherly glow.

And Aiden had responded. Quickly. Easily.

Very strange.

Having gathered the children and parents into a circle in the center of the gymnasium, Cathryn settled herself to watch this unusual performance—of joyous man and cautious child—unfold.

Thunder, lightning and now rain on the roof competed with Jacob for the children's attention. All those elements and fear, too. But Jacob, by sheer force of personality, prevailed.

He spread his arms dramatically. "Tonight I'm going to tell you one of my favorite stories about a cap peddler and a very mischievous monkey." He touched his hand to his chest in a courtly gesture and bowed. "I will be the peddler, and my able assistant, Aiden O'Malley, will be the mischievous monkey." Aiden looked the tiniest bit startled as Jacob continued, happy promise rising in his voice. "And all of you will be monkeys, too. You simply follow Aiden's lead. Do exactly what I say the monkeys do in the story."

The whimpering in the audience subsided as the children stared at a now pink-faced Aiden.

Before beginning the story, Jacob bent to whisper a few words to Aiden.

Cathryn smiled. Aiden *loved* this story. So had she as a child attending Miss Perkins's Saturday morning storytelling sessions in the Sweet Hope library. Surely that's where Jacob, childless, would have heard it. Would have remembered it. And saved it for just the right occasion. So like Jacob.

But lovely, white-haired Miss Perkins had never told the story quite this way.

Instead of just reading the story or telling the story, Jacob acted out the part of the peddler carrying his imaginary wares—caps—on his head. Hamming it up, he went from child to child, offering make-believe caps, commenting on the suitability, the attractiveness of each choice as the children tentatively pretended to try them on, eliciting giggles and blushes as he progressed.

By the time he pretended to take a nap under a tree with the caps on his head, all storm-related whimpering had stopped. All eyes—parents' included—were riveted on the sleeping peddler and on Aiden, the little monkey, who approached on cue in the story Jacob continued to tell softly. The thunder and rat-a-tat rain merely provided a dramatic backdrop as Aiden—very seriously—pretended to steal the hats from the sleeping peddler, passed them out, with a conspirator's stealth, to children in the audience, then encouraged the newly recruited monkeys to climb make-believe trees.

As Jacob, one eye slightly open, told the tale of the monkeys' escape into the camouflaging branches of the trees, the children, suppressing giggles, sure that they were indeed putting something over on the gullible peddler, acted out his words. When at last Aiden and almost every child in the audience were settled in hiding, Jacob awoke, startled to discover his make-believe caps had been stolen.

Oh, the angry antics he went through before discovering the cap-stealing monkeys in the trees. The frustration he displayed in trying to get the cheeky, mimicking varmints to give back his caps. Such hammy fun. Such pure, unadulterated Jacob Matthews joy. By the time the monkeys finally released their booty to an exasperated peddler, every face in the audience—child and adult—wore a smile to obliterate the storm's tension.

Everyone beamed. But Cathryn had eyes for only one child. One small boy with an uncharacteristic grin on his face. Aiden, in charge of monkey business, beat his chest, hopped up and down and grinned to beat the band. A genuine mischievous-boy grin.

Cathryn swallowed hard, trying to quell her rising tears as she now watched her son orchestrate a pig-pile—or monkey-pile—assault on Jacob. Her tears quickly turned to laughter at the impossible task the children had in trying to fell their towering pastor. As Jacob held himself firmly upright, the children managed a joyously writhing heap all their own around his knees. His deep rumbling laughter washed over them like a benediction, and Cathryn sighed as tendrils of that laughter slipped around her own heart. Soothed her. Made her feel once again that unbidden home-again feeling.

In the midst of the finale's mayhem, Jacob looked her way. Caught her gaze. Before she could lose herself in those intense gray eyes and that mesmerizing smile, she glanced quickly to the ceiling and the long row of narrow windows. Glanced away as a diversion, but soon discovered that the typically quick spring storm had passed, and that stars were beginning to peek from behind the night clouds. She smiled.

And when she returned her gaze to Jacob and the children, she found he still stared at her. This time with a peaceful expression on his face that seemed to say, *See. I knew everything would work out.*

She half expected him—wanted him—to approach her. She even heard herself thanking him for her son's unlikely mischievous expression. That would be a good natural conversation starter. Would ease the tension of the afternoon. Would allow her to spend a little time basking in the strength and the confidence and the joy that was Jacob. Yes, she wanted that.

But he didn't approach her. Instead, as smiling parents untangled their children at Jacob's feet, he turned to speak with a young father holding an infant.

Suddenly Cathryn felt chilled. Felt her spirits sag just the tiniest, most unexplainable bit until she saw Aiden emerge, beaming, from the pile of children, saw him give Jacob a joyous knee-high hug, then scamper toward her.

"Mama! Did you see us?" Breathless, he threw himself upon her. "Did you see what a good monkey I was? Did you see the trick we pulled on Pastor Jacob? Did you?"

"Yes!" Cathryn knelt and swept her son into her arms. "You were wonderful monkeys!"

"Was I the *most* wonderful?" He giggled, and Cathryn's heart skipped a beat at the unfamiliar sound.

She buried her face in his warm, moist neck. "Yes. You were the most wonderful monkey who ever stole a cap."

He pulled away from her and skewered her with a stern look. "I was afraid you were going to tell Pastor Matthews where the monkeys were hiding. When he was looking for his caps."

Cathryn feigned hurt. "And spoil such a good trick? Oh, I'd never do that."

Aiden looked over his shoulder. "Margaret was a good monkey, too. I hope she's happy now. The storm scared her."

Cathryn spied Margaret playing an exuberant game of tag around the cots with two other girls. "I think, even as afraid as she was, Margaret has forgotten that old storm."

Aiden sighed. "Pastor Jacob says miracles happen," he declared in a tone of voice so old and solemn Cathryn started.

She regarded her son intently and could find no trace of his former monkeyshines. He'd returned to character. Aiden her thoughtful child. But she'd never forget how he'd blossomed earlier. How Jacob, with a silly story of primate larceny, had made her son smile. Truly smile. If Aiden had abandoned himself to joy this one time, he could do it again.

Yes, she thought, a little in awe, miracles do happen.

Chapter Seven

Cathryn felt as if she and her family were part of a pioneer wagon train.

A police escort led the caravan of Grace Everlasting cars and trucks as the drivers snaked their way on the debris-strewn road from the church to Marshall Sims's dairy farm. Every vehicle had been packed with supplies for the long day of barn raising. Aiden, with Margaret and Belle, rode ahead of her in Alice Rose's station wagon. Boone and Rhune Sherman followed in her father's truck.

Rhune, actually, had asked to ride with Cathryn, but, fortunately, in a rush of frustration charged energy, she'd already packed the passenger seat and the entire back seat with supplies by the time he'd asked.

Her frustration came compliments of Pastor Matthews.

Ever since yesterday afternoon in his office—after she'd hugged him—he'd been coolly distant. Not unkind. Not angry. Not petulant. Simply professional. Businesslike. Certainly not like the warm and tender Jacob Matthews who'd confessed he still wanted her by his side.

Cathryn thrummed her fingers on the steering wheel as the church convoy slowed to yet another temporary stop. Lord, the roads were still a mess. She harrumphed softly. It seemed, contrary to her most recent beliefs, her life was still a mess.

Oh, she'd been able to start anew in Albany. Control her emotions and her daily existence. She'd been able to protect her son and rear him in an atmosphere of love. She'd even been able to stop thinking *every day* about Drew Paxton and that horrible night five years ago.

The mess came with Jacob.

Cathryn bit her lower lip. That man was supposed to remain neatly in the little mental cubicle she'd reserved for friends. Period. Instead, he kept sneaking out and into an undefined gray area of her life. An area inhabited neither by friends nor by family nor by former admirers. That was the problem with Jacob. He commanded a space in her life that was his alone.

And that troubled the hell out of her.

The convoy of vehicles began to move again. "What's a woman supposed to do?" Cathryn muttered aloud. Well, she knew for sure that today she wouldn't have to worry about any tension-packed tête-à-têtes with Jacob. A barn raising required crowds of people and nonstop activity. She might not even see the unsettling pastor.

That hopeful thought was quickly dashed as she pulled into the yard at Marshall Sims's. There, a standout amid the other men, Jacob unloaded lumber and issued instructions. His dark hair glistened in the early-morning sun. His muscles rippled under his already damp chambray shirt, bespeaking the fact that he must have been here working onsite well before many of his parishioners had risen. He spoke with a commanding baritone and moved with a powerful, easy athletic grace. Everyone—men, women and children—automatically looked to him for leadership. It was a picture reminiscent of Saturday morning when Cathryn had pulled into Grace Everlasting for the first time in years and had seen Jacob towering over the Edwards twins on the church steps.

Cathryn inhaled sharply, struck by the fact that this time she was less drawn by Jacob's obvious leadership qualities than by the sheer physical beauty of the man. Lordy. Where had that thought come from?

She'd spent the past five years fairly repulsed by men. How could she now have come to this pretty pass where she sat ogling her former best friend in the midst of a church-sponsored relief effort? As long as she was doing a little mental truth-telling, she might as well ask herself why it was she could insist she and Jacob were just friends at the same time she felt hurt and left out by his most recent cool and professional attitude.

She pinched the bridge of her nose. Cathryn, girl, she mentally chided herself, you're coming unglued.

As the eldest Sims boy directed her to a parking spot, she ticked off the days left in her service to her hometown. Five full days left. She and Aiden would head back to Albany first thing Saturday morning. Who knew? Maybe before then she and her family would be able to move out of the church shelter and back into their homes. She could hope.

Hope. She wouldn't go so far as to pray for that to happen. She wasn't quite sure the Lord would take seriously a prayer that asked for deliverance from one of his most trusted servants.

"Cathryn." Jacob's unexpected voice in her ear made her start. He'd hunkered down beside her car, his face level with hers through the open window.

Hadn't he just been unloading lumber? How the heck had he managed to get from point A to point B so quickly? Or had she been uncharacteristically lost in thought?

"Cathryn?" His voice, so close, was cool and business-like. Unlike the pounding of her heart. "Today you have KP. Check in with Alice Rose and Rita Sims. You'll be setting up a mess tent over there by the front of the house."

Before Cathryn could bring herself to object, Jacob had moved on down the line of parked cars, efficiently directing newcomers to their assigned tasks.

She felt unease at her assignment. Knowing the gossipers among his congregation, how could he relegate her to the "womenfolk"? She could wield a hammer with the best. Hadn't Boone O'Malley, master contractor, raised her? She'd expected to be put on a building crew. A crew that worked in mostly manly silence. Unlike the Grace Everlasting kitchen crew—a group of notoriously voluble women. Women who would expect her to join in conversation. In a camaraderie she didn't feel.

That didn't seem like Jacob to assign tasks according to gender.

Slowly she opened the door and unwound her stiff body from her tiny car. Before heading to the front of the farmhouse, she stretched and surveyed the hubbub of activity. To her surprise, she saw women and men in aprons carrying supplies to the mess tent area, as men and women alike strapped on tool belts. So Jacob hadn't assigned tasks according to gender.

Why wouldn't he put her with a building crew? He knew she had the skills. Knew, too, her dislike of chatty crowds like the kitchen crew. She wanted to spend the day where she could more likely work at her own pace, in silence if she wished. Was Jacob pushing her into the midst of a talkative group as some kind of pastoral counseling?

She glared into the midst of the builders where Jacob now laid out plans. It hit her—he would be working on the barn. She suddenly suspected that he'd merely assigned her as far away from him as he could.

And that thought was supposed to relieve her?

For a moment, Cathryn had to remind herself that she was here to work on a barn raising, *not* on her jumbled feelings for a man who had taken up far too much of her thoughts lately. Why, anyone might think she felt an attraction for him.

In defiance of her own traitorous thoughts, she straightened her spine and marched to the mess tent area.

Jacob looked up from the plans spread in front of him and watched Cathryn sashay across the Sims's yard. Was she ever steamed over her assignment to KP. He could tell. He almost chuckled aloud. He'd bet she'd be thinking her walk to the mess tent was a ramrod-stiff march. But no matter how angry Cassie O'Malley became, no matter how rigidly she tried to walk away, that woman had never been able to suppress the unquestionably womanly way her behind sashayed. *Sashayed.* There was simply no other word for it. And it was a sight to behold.

"Jacob?" Boone's voice recalled his attention. "The barn?"

Jacob sighed deeply, pulled his gaze away from the far too tantalizing Cassie and looked square into the twinkling eyes of the man he hoped against hope to make his father-in-law. "The barn..."

Cathryn wasn't quite sure what kind of reception she'd expected from the kitchen crew, but it certainly wasn't the warm hug Rita Sims gave her.

"Cathryn O'Malley, you are a most welcome sight," the woman exclaimed.

Suki Edwards passed by, arms loaded with pots and pans. She grinned and winked at Cathryn. "Don't let her sweet-talk you. There's a ton of potatoes needing to be peeled."

"I'll peel potatoes," Cathryn offered, "especially if they're going into my grandmother's potato salad."

"That they are." Rita ushered her to a nearby low stool in the shade of a flowering dogwood. Several sacks of potatoes rested against the tree trunk; several gleaming, water-filled pots awaited the peeled potatoes. "Here you go. Best seat in the house. You can still join in the kitchen chat while you watch the building crew smash their thumbs."

Oh, joy. Cathryn sat on the stool. Just what she needed. An unobstructed view of the building crew with its leader, Jacob Matthews.

"I'll be back to help you once everyone's settled in their tasks," Rita promised as she bustled off in search of new recruits.

Cathryn picked up the paring knife and reached into a sack of potatoes. She was being silly. What kind of an adult was she if she couldn't handle the casual sight of a man who meant no more to her than... than... than whom? For the life of her she could think of no one with whom to compare Jacob.

In irritation, she squinted into the now-bright morning sun. Jacob, as if her thoughts alone had drawn him into her line of vision, strode across the yard, a half dozen two-by-fours balanced on his shoulder. Oh, my. The man had stripped off his work shirt, and now his broad chest was covered with nothing more than a tight, faded navy T-shirt.

Cathryn swallowed hard. Were pastors supposed to look like *that?*

"Well, now, dear," Rita Sims said, reappearing unexpectedly and pulling a stool next to Cathryn, "that took no time at all. Let me help you so we can get these potatoes into salad by the noonday meal."

Resigning herself to the fact that her solitude was over, Cathryn noted that conversation with Rita would at least keep her from staring at the disconcerting pastor. And, if truth were told, she could have a far less pleasant KP partner. Rita Sims had always been a warm and cheerful woman, a farmer's wife who looked the plump and welcoming stereotype. Cathryn had at one time baby-sat for the ever-expanding Sims brood. But Rita and she hadn't spoken since Cathryn had left Jacob Matthews waiting at the altar five years ago.

As if reading her thoughts, Rita pointed a paring knife in Jacob's direction and said, "Quite a man, our Pastor Jacob, yes?"

"Yes," Cathryn agreed softly, wondering whether Rita's remark constituted a sly accusation.

The two women worked in relative silence for over an hour, their conversation confined, after Rita's puzzling opening statement, to the storm, the difficulties of feeding and sheltering several hundred people day after day, the prospects of a quick recovery and, at last, Rita's sentiments that the folk of Grace Everlasting truly appreciated the work of volunteers such as Cathryn.

Cathryn, beginning to scrape the mounds of peels into the now-empty potato sacks, looked up in surprise.

Rita smiled gently. "What? You don't think we appreciate you, Cassie, girl?"

"I'm not certain how people in Sweet Hope feel about me," Cathryn responded, abandoning all pretense. "Especially the members of Grace Everlasting."

"Well, I can tell you one thing...we appreciate anyone who's not afraid to roll up their sleeves and work. Like you. Not like *some people.*" Rita nodded in the direction of the farmhouse steps.

There, all fashionable splendor, in a folding lawn chair, under a beach umbrella, sat Missy Able. Ellie's daughter. Cathryn hadn't seen her since they'd gone to school together years ago.

"Missy Able?" Cathryn asked.

"One and the same. Freshly divorced. On a day trip down from Chattanooga. Come to *help out* for the day." Rita snorted. "A fat lot of helping she's done. She arrived and plopped herself in that queen bee chair of hers and hasn't stirred since." She inclined her head toward a large hamper next to Missy's feet and whispered dramatically, "She's guarding the crown jewels."

Cathryn smiled. Rita never did have any use for Missy Able. Had thought her too pretty and prissy to be of any use in the real world. "What do you suppose is in the hamper?"

Rita quirked an eyebrow. "Why, I do suppose it's a catered lunch...for her and our Jacob. Since her divorce—her most recent divorce—Miss Missy's shown a remarkable devotion to her old parish...and its new pastor."

"Well, what do you know. Things never change." Cathryn didn't expect the little twinge her heart underwent as she contemplated Missy Able's renewed interest in Jacob.

"No," Rita replied pointedly. "Things don't change. That's why I think, Cathryn O'Malley, you need to freshen up and pack your own picnic basket for two."

"Rita!" Cathryn's hand flew to her throat in dismay. "Have you been talking to Alice Rose?"

"I might have been." Rita put plump hands firmly on even plumper hips. "But I might just be smart enough on my own to see the sparks that've been flying between you and Jacob these past few days."

Cathryn stood in what she hoped was a proper display of indignation. "Well, I'm not about to create more *sparks* by getting into a tug-of-war with Missy Able over him." She brushed errant scraps of peel from her jeans and felt unexpectedly plain and workaday in light of her former schoolmate's cool, crisp glamour.

"Suit yourself," Rita replied, rising also, "but Jacob's not going to wait forever."

Cathryn was about to retort that she hadn't asked him to wait *at all,* when Rita reached out to rub her back in a motherly gesture. "I'll clean up here, honey. You go take a stretch and clear your head."

Well. She didn't need to clear her head. It was already clear enough. But she sure could stand a stretch and a breather. Perhaps when she'd composed herself, she'd hunt up Belle and help with the children. With a thank-you to Rita, Cathryn wandered off to the line of parked cars, far enough away from the mess tent so that she needn't engage in conversation, and far enough away from the barn so that she didn't have to monitor her view and her thoughts of Jacob.

Someone slammed a truck door behind her, spoiling the solitude. Rhune Sherman rounded Boone's truck and stopped in his tracks when he spotted Cathryn. He wore a wildly colored tropical shirt, sunglasses and a day's growth of beard. She noticed now that his hair was not so much real auburn as a sun-streaked chestnut. He looked every inch the nomadic surfer rather than a responsible emergency-room doctor. His lazy, seductive smile, however, made him look every inch the ladies' man.

As she turned to retreat, he called to her. "I think we need to talk."

Now, what in the world did she and old bedroom-eyes Sherman have to talk about?

Before she could speculate, he'd stepped to her side and said, quite candidly, "I know you don't like me."

"Why, Mr. Sherman, I barely know you."

He pushed his sunglasses into his hair. "You seem to know me well enough to have decided you want nothing to do with me." He'd dropped the provocative gaze. In its place was candor, pure and simple.

If he'd remained seductive and sure of himself, Cathryn would have turned a rude back on him without a word of explanation, but his forthrightness gave her pause. "It's not that I don't want anything to do with you, specifically. It's just that I'm not in the market for a relationship with any man at the moment."

"Not even the good pastor?" The rascal nodded his head in the direction of the barn.

Well, he had her there. She'd been telling herself for five years that she wasn't ready for a relationship. She'd been insisting just that to her family. And now she'd gone and voiced it to a near stranger. But with Rhune's nod of the head toward Jacob, why did those words seem like such a sham at the moment?

"Look," Rhune continued, "I'm not one to push where I'm not wanted. But, quite frankly, I'm not used to being treated as though I had a rare, communicable disease, either. Is it the shirt?"

Cathryn felt as if she needed sunglasses to look at his shirt. She smiled. "No. The shirt...well, the shirt would do Arnold Schwarzenegger proud."

Rhune laughed aloud. A sexy, infectious laugh. Cathryn could see where other women might find him a charmer.

But she didn't. He was too easy with the charm. Too transient. And now that she stood close to him, she saw in the depths of his sexy eyes a flickering haunted look. The kind of look she'd seen in war veterans. A look that said he'd seen too much. And wanted to party the memories away. Well, she was no party girl.

His own laughter still hanging in the air, he regarded her with a quizzical expression. "So, this is the official brush-off, Cathryn O'Malley?"

Suddenly, released from any sexual expectations, Cathryn felt strangely at ease with this chimerical Mr. Sherman.

"Yes, sir. This is the official brush-off." She grinned to soften her words.

"But we're bound to see each other again. Sometime. Through Belle, I mean."

"Oh, I rarely come back to Sweet Hope."

"But you might." The sexy, come-hither smile had returned, even after Cathryn's brush-off.

She sighed, supposing his Don Juan persona simply surfaced as second nature. "If I did, it would be a slim chance of running into you, now, wouldn't it? You practice in D.C., didn't Belle tell me?"

"If you hadn't given me the *official* brush-off, Miss O'Malley, I'd construe that as interest."

"You can construe that as making a point. The point being we *won't* be seeing each other again."

"Not necessarily true." He sobered. "I'm thinking of moving to the Sweet Hope area."

Cathryn's mouth popped open.

"It's only a thought," he insisted quickly. "But if I do..." He smiled slyly. "I'll need to know what our relationship is to be. That is, short of you finding me wildly attractive."

"You're incorrigible!" She couldn't help but think, however, he'd make a fascinating brother. "If you behaved yourself, I *might* consider you a friend."

Rhune did a mock shiver. "Not friends. The relationship kiss of death. I get offered friendship when someone dumps me. Hard. You only gave me a brush-off."

Cathryn chuckled. "Rhune Sherman, I have work to do. I can't stand here discussing the terms of a relationship that may never have an opportunity to develop." She glanced at his waist and at the lack of a tool belt. "Don't you have work to do, as well? Or are you an escapee from a crew?"

"You wound me." Rhune threw his hand over his heart. "I'll have you know I'm one of Pastor Matthews's best workers. I merely came to retrieve my shades." He patted the top of his head, then lowered the sunglasses to his eyes. "We medical guys must preserve the old eyesight."

Yeah, Cathryn thought, skeptical. For scouting the babes. Despite her cynicism, she felt oddly satisfied with her chat with Rhune. He'd come on to her at first, but she hadn't fled. She'd stood her ground, and they'd hammered out a truce. Of sorts. This was definitely a milestone for her. Of sorts. Having dealt with Rhune Sherman, perhaps she was ready to deal with another, less easily dismissed man....

"Well, well," Rhune mused, peering across the farmyard. "If my twenty-twenty doesn't spot the aforementioned pastor heading this way." He turned to look at Cathryn. "You don't suppose he's watching over you?"

"No, I don't," Cathryn retorted in a denial that didn't ring true. "I'm sure, like you, he has to retrieve some valuable piece of equipment from his truck."

With his gaze fastened intently on her, however, Jacob didn't look as if he had equipment of any kind on his mind.

Jacob strode toward Cathryn and Rhune.

What kind of a man was he that he that he couldn't keep a resolution for a full twenty-four hours? He'd vowed not to involve himself emotionally with Cathryn. Not if she showed a determination to keep him at arm's length. And here he was, without having yet constructed his flimsy excuse, storming across the farmyard, as if pulled by some invisible magnet, to interrupt Cathryn's conversation with Rhune.

And a peculiar conversation it had seemed from his vantage point on the barn-raising crew. He'd seen Rhune come around Boone's truck. Had seen, too, Cathryn's reaction. A definite startled reaction. But something Rhune had said had made her stay. And, in staying, her facial expressions and her body language had changed visibly. From nervous and skittish, to defiant, to pensive, to laughing with the ease of one who'd signed a truce.

Jacob wasn't quite sure which of Cathryn's reactions to Rhune had unsettled him more.

Both Cathryn and Rhune had seen him coming. He was within yards of them and about to utter a greeting when Missy Able intercepted him. Where had she come from? He'd thought her out of reach in Tennessee.

"Why, Jacob," she purred, reaching out and linking her arm with his, "you look positively exhausted. Mama says you've been simply killing yourself with storm cleanup."

Your mama should know, Jacob thought caustically. She's been trying to deal the death blow. But aloud he replied evenly, "Missy, it's good to see you. Have you come down to check on your mother?"

"Why, no. Mama's just fine." Missy smiled sweetly. "She suggested I come on down from Chattanooga to...help out." Her tone of voice grew sweeter than her smile. "And I thought, what better way to help out than to bring a real meal to Grace Everlasting's embattled pastor?"

Out of the corner of his eye Jacob could see Cathryn and Rhune observing this scene in startled fascination. "That's very kind of you," Jacob offered, trying to keep his frustration in check, "but Alice Rose O'Malley in the church kitchen has seen that no one goes hungry. Of course, you're more than welcome to join *your mother and family* for the noon meal." He hoped Missy caught his underscored inflection.

"Oh, pooh." She pouted. "If I'd wanted cafeteria food, I could have eaten at my Genna's elementary school." She squeezed his arm. "I brought you a real meal, Jacob Matthews. Catered by the best little bistro in Chattanooga."

He just bet. Missy Able was never one to do anything others could do for her. So why had she, over the years, determinedly set her cap for him? A pastor of modest means. Why had she, except for the few short times she'd been married, thrown herself at his head? Come to think of it, even when she'd been married, she'd flirted shamelessly.

He was never a man for social games. Especially not now when he wished desperately to talk to Cathryn.

"Missy, I don't mean to be rude...." That wasn't true. At the moment he wished to be especially rude to both Missy Able and Rhune Sherman. He wished to throw the two of them together while he spirited Cathryn away. "But I have a barn to raise."

"But you have to stop *sometime* to refuel that big strong body. And when you do, my lunch and I will help take your mind off your troubles."

Lord, help him. He had no experience extricating himself from these stupid situations. He had two loves in life: his parish and its community...and Cathryn. All else rang hollow. He scowled. How much time had he now wasted on this inane, fruitless conversation?

"Hello." Rhune Sherman stood before Jacob, but looked Missy Able in the eyes.

Despite the fact that Cathryn seemed to have disappeared, a slow grin spread across Jacob's face. He'd just now asked the Lord for help. Who knew the answer would come in Rhune's form? Jacob shook his head as he prepared to make the introductions. The Lord's ironic sense of humor never ceased to amaze him.

"Missy Able, Rhune Sherman," he said, inhaling deeply, unable to contain his visible satisfaction. "Missy has come all the way from Chattanooga to minister to the physically exhausted. She has a picnic hamper with your name on it, Rhune."

Missy unwound her arm from Jacob's and stood back in wounded horror. "Why, Jacob, I'd expected you'd need it most."

Jacob saw the opportunity to press on. He threw his arm around Rhune's shoulder as if they'd always been the best of friends. "Well, if you're looking for the person who needs it most, you've found him." He thumped Rhune on the chest. "I've never seen a man work as hard as Rhune here. I've been trying to get him to take a break, but he won't. Insists he'll work till the job is done, or he collapses."

Both Missy and Rhune shot him disbelieving glances. Okay, maybe he'd laid it on a little too thick. He tried to retrieve his sincerity.

"Look at him, Missy." He lifted Rhune's sunglasses. "If he doesn't look exhausted, you tell me who does."

"He looks as if he could use a shave and a haircut," Missy muttered as if Rhune were not present.

Jacob glanced at Rhune and saw from the roguish, what-next? expression on his face that the man was actually enjoying this farce. "This man," Jacob continued, now feeling only half as guilty, "is an emergency-room doctor. From Washington, D.C. He's using his vacation time to help us—"

"A doctor?" Missy's eyes lit up. "From Washington? My, my. I've never visited Washington."

The up-till-now-silent Rhune came to life. "Well, then, Miss Able, let me tell you about Washington. Over an early lunch. Jacob's right. I have been pushing myself too hard. And now that I've stopped, I find myself suddenly starving."

Missy actually trembled under Rhune's ravenous regard. She cast her gaze to the ground, colored deeply, then turned to Jacob. "This is not what I intended, but I've always wanted to visit Washington, D.C."

"And who better to tell you of it than a doctor?" Jacob couldn't resist this last push.

Missy smiled sweetly at Jacob. "I'll give you a rain check."

"Not necessary." Oh, no. Not necessary at all, Jacob thought as he watched Rhune escort Missy to the picnic hamper.

He cast his gaze heavenward. "If you hadn't wanted me to do it, you shouldn't have dropped him in my lap."

"You all right?" Boone O'Malley stood at his side. "For a minute I thought you were talking to yourself."

Jacob shrugged. "Actually, I wanted to talk to Cathryn."

"She's in the mess tent," Boone said.

"I just wanted to talk to her about...."

"You don't have to make excuses with me, Jacob. I'm on your side."

It was difficult to look Boone in the eye. Ever since Cathryn's return to Sweet Hope, he'd felt emotionally raw, transparent. As if anyone, by just looking at him, could tell his every thought, his every impossible dream.

"Go on. Take care of... whatever... with my daughter." Boone's eyes twinkled. "Get it off your chest. I need you to help me with a clear head."

"You need help?"

"We need to sort through this lumber. Old Jake at the lumberyard must've thought, this being an emergency and all, we wouldn't check the supplies too closely. I've found some seriously defective two-by-fours. If you and I sort through the lot, we can get the good stuff to the crew, and I can take the junk back to Jake and give him a piece of my mind." Boone grinned. "But it can wait a few minutes till you straighten out... whatever."

"Fifteen minutes," Jacob promised, though he had no idea as to the *whatever* it was he had to straighten out. Had no idea, but had a sneaking suspicion the unknown would take more than fifteen minutes. Had more than a sneaking suspicion that despite his resolve he would never remain either detached or neutral where Cathryn was concerned.

Cathryn looked up from the onions she chopped to see Jacob watching her from the far side of the tent. To her surprise, happiness welled within her at the sight of him. Smiling shyly, she looked down at the chopping block and thought, Well, well. Maybe I am conquering this flight reflex, after all.

Hoping she'd correctly read the look on his face that said he'd come to see her, she glanced up only to see him turn as if to leave. She tried to suppress her disappointment.

He stopped, however, in midturn and paused long enough to give the impression of indecision. Then, rather abruptly, he turned again and walked deliberately toward Cathryn.

His eyes had lost their distant, businesslike shield. They were now soft gray and intense and very much a reflection of the warm Jacob Matthews Cathryn had come to expect. Yes, over the years she'd come to expect warmth from Jacob. She hadn't expected the warmth that seemed to seep into her very core each time she now stood before him. *That* had crept up on her. Totally unexpectedly.

"Cassie." Her old nickname rumbled softly in her ears.

She tried to assume a lighthearted attitude. "So, you've come to check on Cinderella in the kitchen?" With the back of her hand she swiped at several tendrils of hair that clouded her line of vision. She only managed to wave the scent of onions too close to her nose. Her eyes watered in reaction.

Jacob reached out to gently brush the wayward locks from her face. "I know it's not your favorite duty."

She tried not to think about his touch. "Trying to teach me humility, Pastor Matthews?" she asked, trying to keep her words light banter, but failing. They came out sounding edgy.

Jacob quirked one dark eyebrow. She could see he wasn't quite sure whether she was playfully teasing or whether she'd issued a challenge of sorts. Too, he wasn't quite certain how to respond. She softened at his discomfort.

She smiled. "I was joking, Jacob."

"Oh. Good." He relaxed only slightly, shoving his hands deep into his pockets. As Aiden did when he felt unsure. "I thought you might like a change of scene after lunch. We had an unexpected opening on the building crew."

"No one's hurt, I hope."

"No." Jacob grinned, and an unmistakably mischievous twinkle appeared in his eyes. "It's Rhune. He . . . I assigned him to another task. That leaves us one person short. How are your hammer skills?"

"About as rusty as my softball skills."

His grin widened. "Then we're in luck."

Cathryn looked down at her hands. She'd actually run out of things to say. How distressing. She and Jacob, as friends those many years ago, could talk for hours. About anything. And during these past few days they hadn't been at a loss for words, even if many of their conversations had been spiced with tension. But now this unaccustomed shyness tied her tongue. What was happening to her?

She glanced up to discover Jacob still in front of her, his grin replaced by a thoughtful expression that unnerved her as much as the silence.

"Where's Aiden?" he asked finally.

Discovering she'd been holding her breath, Cathryn exhaled sharply. "Aiden." She brightened. She could talk to a lamppost about her son. "Aiden's with the other children and Belle. Homer Martin has them building shed doors. Can you imagine?"

"Yes." He filled the single word with an unmistakable pride. "Yes. I *can* imagine."

"You know," Cathryn began tentatively, "I never thanked you for the bedtime story last night. For including Aiden."

He looked at her, puzzled. "Why wouldn't I include him?"

"More than that. For making him a part of the magic." She faltered. "I'm not saying this well. You see, I love Aiden more than I ever believed possible."

"A stranger could see that," Jacob offered gently.

Cathryn felt the heat of emotion tinge her cheeks. "He's loved. And he's loving." She paused. "But he's very sober."

"And sometimes you worry?"

He understood. Cathryn breathed a sigh of relief. "Yes. But last night you brought out a side of my son I seldom see. A mischievous, giggling, four-year-old boy. That's what I want to thank you for."

Jacob reached out a hand to touch her, and then withdrew as if he thought better of it. "Cassie O'Malley," he said, his eyes full of an unmistakable longing, "believe me when I tell you the pleasure was all mine."

He turned to leave, but paused. "When Rita feels she can let you go from kitchen duty, come on over to the barn. Perhaps, before I assign you to a crew, we could sneak a peek at the kids. Together."

Cathryn watched Jacob's retreating back and wondered how a mere word could linger and resonate in the air.

Together.

A word both compelling and frightening.

Chapter Eight

With Boone, Jacob positioned the last piece of roofing plywood onto the barn's now-completed frame. Alone on the roof, dusk enveloped them. It had been a race against Mother Nature to finish up the plywood undercoat before dark, but they'd done it. They'd raised the barn's essentials. Tomorrow a much smaller crew would return to finish.

As he hammered the remaining nails, Jacob could hear the fiddlers tuning up in the yard below. Having snatched food and drink as they could during the day, the volunteers would eat heartily tonight, and dance, and celebrate this successful community effort. No small triumph in the wake of the devastating twister.

Although every muscle in his body ached, satisfaction filled him. Satisfaction and anticipation.

Cathryn had joined the work crew in the afternoon, after she and he had surreptitiously observed Homer and his junior builders. At the sight of Aiden hammering as seriously as any adult, Jacob's heart had swelled with a pride he hadn't known possible. When he'd glanced at Cathryn, she'd seemed to hold back tears. At that moment he'd felt a circle of love inextricably bind the three of them together.

"That's it!" Boone exclaimed. "The last nail. And just in time. I'm parched."

As if on cue, Marshall Sims's oldest boy popped up at the top of the ladder to offer two frosty cans of soda. "From Mama," he explained. "She says to take your time drinking them." He grinned and backed down the ladder.

Both men climbed the roof to the peak, then sat. They opened the cans of soda and laughed simultaneously as spray followed the pop and hiss.

"Lordy," Boone sputtered, "you think that kid could have shaken them up a little more."

"I don't care," Jacob replied with a sigh. "My next stop is the water spigot outside the paddock, anyway." He took a long, satisfying draft of the soda, and relished the cool, fizzy sensation as the liquid slid down his throat. "You show me anyone cleaner than me after today's work, then I'll worry about my appearance."

Boone's disembodied chuckle came to him out of the dusk. "You don't want to drive prospective dance partners away."

Cassie. No, he didn't want to drive her away.

"Boone?"

"Yeah, I think she'll stay for the dance."

Jacob smiled into the gathering night, then sobered. "Since you seem to have the answers before I have the questions . . . tell me what's eating Cassie."

The other man's temporary silence made Jacob think he'd overstepped his bounds. But when Boone spoke, his response was gruff but gentle. "You're going to have to ask Cassie that."

"I have. And I will again. But do you know the answer?"

"No." Boone sounded tired. "I sure as hell wish I did, though."

"Well, that answers one of my questions. I thought maybe I was going crazy. Thought maybe I was reading too much into things. Her leaving me. Her leaving Sweet Hope...her jumpiness with men."

"You noticed that, too," Boone said almost inaudibly.

Jacob's heart sank. He'd wanted to believe he had been reading too much into things. "I can figure out two of the three. I figure she left me waiting at the altar because...well, I know she never loved me."

"She cared for you a heap. We all thought it could be more in time."

"Me, too." Jacob took another deep swallow of the cold soda just to keep his emotions in check. "And leaving Sweet Hope...I suppose she didn't want Aiden to suffer because he didn't have a father. More than that, didn't want him to suffer because of old rumors about his mother."

"Damn. Old gossip dies hard." Boone's voice became steel edged. "Especially when certain folks are bound to keep it alive."

"I'm trying to work on that."

"As a father, I appreciate it. But seems to me you've made some waves where your own position is concerned."

"News travels fast." Jacob snorted. "But I can take care of myself. It's Cassie I'm worried about. The jumpiness thing with men, especially...take Rhune."

Boone laughed out loud. "No! *You* take Rhune!"

Jacob smiled. "Right now, Missy Able's taken Rhune. I figure they're a match for each other." He had to chuckle, but sobered immediately. "But back to Cassie. I couldn't help notice that every time Rhune approached her, she seemed skittish as all get-out."

"Like that time in the gym. When he touched her, she seemed ready to climb the walls."

"Yeah. And when he looks at her, she starts looking for the nearest exit."

"Is she that way with you?"

The abrupt frankness of Boone's question startled Jacob. He took a deep breath. "No. But you have to understand that your daughter sees me as nothing more than a friend. I'm no more sexually threatening—or appealing—to her than a stuffed bear."

There. He'd said it aloud. And instead of exorcising the horrible thought, he'd made it sound too true. And final.

"She respects you," Boone insisted. "Respect is love in plain clothes."

Jacob harrumphed. "You know, when I was five years younger—and a lot hotter under the collar—I accepted that idea more readily than I do now."

"You want more." It wasn't a question.

"I want more," Jacob agreed.

Boone thumped Jacob on the back. "Then let's get off this roof, boy, so you can make a little romance. Those fiddlers aren't playing for their health."

Jacob sure hoped they weren't.

He rose carefully and followed Boone down the steep pitch of the roof, then down the ladder. Compared to the silence of the rooftop, the ground level buzzed with activity and noise. Happy sounds. Sounds of people relaxing and visiting after a hard day's fruitful work.

Optimism filled the air, and Jacob couldn't help getting caught up in it.

Cathryn peered up at the barn rooftop and could barely discern her father and Jacob silhouetted against the evening sky. She watched—and worried—as they rose and slowly made their way off the roof. She discovered when they finally set foot on the ground that she'd been holding her breath. Goodness, where had this incredible, almost possessive concern come from?

She watched, too, as Jacob approached the spigot near the paddock, turned the water on full force, then thrust his entire head under the gushing stream. Trust Jacob not to do things by halves. She chuckled softly, then mentally told herself to look away. It wasn't seemly to be spying on the pastor.

For spying it surely was. Especially when she had no good excuse for it except the warm feeling of pleasure it gave her to watch Jacob.

"Mama?" Aiden appeared at her side. "Will you dance with me after supper?"

Remembering the times as a child she'd stood on Boone's boots to be danced around the room, Cathryn beamed down at her son. "You bet!"

"Will you dance with me, too?" a familiar, deep voice asked.

Cathryn looked up and into Jacob's steadfast eyes as he strode toward them. He'd run his fingers through his wet, dark hair, but a forelock tumbled enticingly over one eyebrow. The neck and shoulders of his T-shirt were damp, and the fabric clung to his muscles. Despite the hard day's work he looked fresh and full of masculine vitality. And very sexy.

Cathryn caught her breath. Now, *where* had that observation come from?

"Will you, Mama?" Aiden piped up.

"Will I what, sweet thing?"

"Dance with Pastor Jacob?"

Jacob cocked an eyebrow, smiled and waited expectantly.

Cathryn ruffled Aiden's hair. "We'll see. First, supper."

"Mind if I join you?" Jacob's words were casual, but there was nothing casual about the feelings that buzzed through Cathryn.

Ever since this morning in the mess tent and her bout of uncharacteristic shyness with Jacob, she'd been puzzling over the fact that her relationship with him had somehow changed over the past few days. When was it, exactly, that she'd begun to lose her detachment?

"We were waiting for you," Aiden insisted, looking up at Jacob.

Cathryn shot him a glance that said, *We were?* But either Aiden didn't catch it or he ignored her. Instead, he reached up first for Cathryn's hand and then for Jacob's.

"I'm hungry," he declared, and pulled them both toward the mess tent now lit by torchlight.

Jacob laughed. "I admire a man who knows what he wants, then goes for the gusto."

Cathryn sensed a double meaning in his words, but when she looked at him, she could see only relaxed pleasure lighting his face. Why shouldn't she, too, relax this evening? Relax with an old friend and savor the fact that today she'd accomplished what she'd set out to do. She'd helped her community begin to rebuild. Nothing more. Nothing less.

It served no purpose to look for hidden agendas at every turn.

She inhaled deeply as she walked across the dusky yard with Aiden and Jacob. "You know, I'm hungry, too," she said. And suddenly she was. Hungry for more than the fried chicken and coleslaw she knew awaited them. She was hungry for a life without second guesses and suspicions. Without the burdensome daily concern for what others might think.

A feeling of liberation washing over her, she looked at Jacob and laughed. "Shall we swing this hungry boy?"

"Yes, do!" Aiden squeaked.

Jacob winked at Cathryn. "I think one good swing would land him right at the end of the food line."

Aiden giggled. "Do it!"

"One," Jacob counted dramatically. "Two."

Cathryn buzzed her lips in her best imitation of a drum roll.

"Three!"

On the count, Jacob and Cathryn swung Aiden between them as they each took a giant step to the back of the food line. When Aiden's feet touched the ground, he'd landed right beside the stack of paper plates and cutlery.

"Again!" he insisted jubilantly.

Homer Martin, last in line, turned around. "Again and you'll be in the jelly mold, young man."

Aiden giggled, and Cathryn started. Three full-fledged giggles in the past twenty-four hours. Life in Sweet Hope had been unexpectedly good for her son.

"Your mama and I will swing you in a dance later," Jacob promised as he passed Cathryn a plate with one hand and lightly brushed her arm with the other. "Won't we?"

She didn't know if Aiden's giggles had worn down her resistance, or if Jacob's strong but gentle touch had made her temporarily throw caution to the wind, but she said, "Yes!" Quickly. Eagerly. Yes. She, too, would like that.

They stood in line, the three of them, and chatted with the other volunteers as they loaded their plates with home cooking. Then Jacob helped Aiden carry his plate to a grassy spot near Rita Sims's herb garden. Cathryn followed as if it were the most natural thing in the world to be part of this threesome.

She lowered herself onto the cool, soft grass and sighed deeply.

"Tired?" Jacob's voice buoyed her.

"A good tired." She watched Aiden dig into his supper. "There's satisfaction in the tired that comes from accomplishment."

"We all accomplished a lot today."

Aiden looked up, his face as intent as Jacob's eyes. "The kids and I 'complished a calf door."

Cathryn smiled. "A calf door?"

"Mr. Martin says it'll go to the shed where the mama cows and their new calves are kept." His little body swelled with pride. "Mr. Sims said our door was a corker, and we could come back when the barn is finished to see the mamas and their calves."

Cathryn almost reminded him that she and he would be long gone before the Sims's cows and calves were established in their new barn, but she didn't have the heart. Instead, she said, the pride showing in her voice, "How wonderful that you built such a fine calf door."

She glanced above Aiden's tousled blond head to where Jacob watched her, a most puzzling, expectant expression on his face. The fiddlers began to play in earnest now, and Cathryn used the opportunity to look away from Jacob's unsettling gaze. To disengage herself mentally from the pull of this easy circle of three.

She ate and watched the couples and the families begin to dance.

My, but she was beautiful tonight.

Jacob deeply inhaled the night air as Cathryn, beside him,

pretended to be engrossed in watching the dancers. It tickled him, this new shyness of hers.

He felt almost as if they were courting.

What a journey they'd traveled to get to this point. Despite her circumstances five years ago, there'd never been a reserved moment between them back then. They'd been friends. Real and true friends. And as such, they could say anything to each other.

But then, for her own reasons, she'd left him waiting at the altar. Left him with a bellyful of hurt. And because of that, they'd gotten off to a rocky start upon her return just a few days ago.

Now things had changed again, although he wasn't at all sure why. Somewhere in the past twenty-four hours Cathryn had softened toward him. Had softened and had caught herself in the act. Her shyness was the result.

A lovely, tentative mood, in which she'd stopped pushing him away. A mood that allowed such a moment as this, wherein Jacob could imagine that Cathryn, Aiden and he were a family.

Aiden, who had jumped up to chase fireflies, came hopping back to where Jacob and Cathryn sat. "Let's dance. Like those people over there."

He pointed, and Jacob could see the Harlen family of four laughing and dancing together in a ring.

Tugging at Cathryn and then at Jacob, Aiden insisted, "Let's dance. Together. Please, please."

Cathryn shook herself out of her reverie and smiled. "But perhaps Pastor Jacob has other things he needs to do."

Rising to his feet, Jacob held out his hand to help Cathryn rise. "No. Nothing more important than dancing. We did promise Aiden."

"Yes, you did, Mama, and now I'm collectin'."

Cathryn laughed gently, and the sound of it was music to Jacob's ears. "Well, then, I guess we'd better dance. Together." She looked up at Jacob before she put her hand in his, and he could see joy in her eyes. He froze with the unexpectedness of it.

When she slipped her hand in his and pulled herself to a standing position, Jacob felt her touch infuse his entire body with warmth. She held his hand and Aiden's as the three of them walked to the clearing used for dancing. He saw heads turn. He looked at Cathryn, who smiled back at him then passed the smile along to Aiden, and felt an overwhelming sense of yearning.

This was right. Cathryn and Aiden and he were meant to be together. As a family. He knew it. He need only find the means to convince Cathryn.

When they'd reached a clear spot among the dancers, Aiden clasped each adult's hand firmly in his own and began to circle to the rhythm of the country waltz. Riveting her gaze on her son, Cathryn, a smile transforming her face, moved gracefully to the music. Jacob hoped the fiddlers would play forever. Would play forever and allow him the luxury of holding this small boy's hand and this lovely woman's hand in his own until he'd memorized the feel of their touch. This memory he wanted to keep forever.

Cathryn began to hum the melody of the familiar waltz. As she hummed, she glanced at Jacob, and her eyes sparkled with the old Cassie magic. Sparkled and included him in the warmth she'd shown her son. Jacob's heart swooped in rhythm to the music.

Suddenly Margaret O'Malley skipped up to Aiden and tapped him on his shoulder. "Aiden."

Aiden shrugged her off. "You can't cut, Margaret."

"I don't want to cut. I want you to come catch fireflies."

Aiden stopped, and Cathryn and Jacob stopped with him. The boy looked truly undecided.

Jacob smiled down at him. "If you want, go with Margaret, son. There'll be other dances."

Very solemnly, Aiden took Cathryn's hand and placed it in Jacob's. "Will you still dance with Mama?"

"If she wants." Jacob's heart squeezed tight. If only she wants...

"Come on," Margaret urged impatiently. "Pastor Jacob will take good care of her."

"I will," Jacob promised. He winked at Aiden, who did a solemn double-eyed wink back before scampering off with Margaret.

Jacob and Cathryn stood in the midst of the dancers, their hands lightly clasped, and looked into one another's eyes. At that moment Jacob forgot everything, except that he held the hands of the most beautiful woman in the world. Not an old friend. Not a young boy's mother. But a woman flushed with the exertion of the dance, the torchlight and life's limitless possibilities. Cathryn O'Malley. Beautiful. Vibrant. And very desirable.

He wanted more than anything to kiss her.

He moved to take her in his arms. To hold her close and waltz as lovers. But when he did so, he felt her stiffen. Saw the light in her eyes change to the shadow of fear.

"I can't," she whispered hoarsely. "I'm sorry, Jacob. I can't."

She jerked her hands from his, then threaded her way around the dancers until the darkness at the edge of the dance space enveloped her.

Standing stunned at first as his parishioners stared, he collected himself to follow her, not because of his bruised ego but because of the worry that gnawed at him. Worry triggered the minute Cathryn's attitude had changed from a lighthearted woman enjoying a dance to that of a startled and frightened creature caught in the headlights of an oncoming car.

Cathryn O'Malley hid a hurt that resurfaced time and time again to haunt her. Having talked to Boone, Jacob was more certain than ever that she'd never shared her dark secret with anyone.

Well, the secrets stopped tonight.

"Cathryn!" he called in the dark to the ghostlike retreating form.

She didn't stop. Instead, she disappeared into the skeleton of the newly raised barn.

He quickened his pace and found her standing near a small detached door, leaning against a pile of two-by-fours. The door to the calf shed. The one that Aiden and the other children had built. She'd reached out her hand to touch the door, and her skin appeared pearly white in the darkness.

"Cassie." Jacob wanted to take her in his arms, to comfort her as he had those years ago. But if it had been his hungry look that had made her flee from the dance space, what would his touch now make her do?

She turned to face him, her hand still resting on the shed door. "Why is it that what is so good for my son so overwhelms me?"

Jacob was unprepared for her frankness. "Tell me what you mean. What exactly is so good for Aiden? What overwhelms you? I want to understand, but you're losing me."

She brushed past him and began to pace. "Everything."

He reached out in the darkness as she moved near him. Reached out and gently but firmly grasped her wrist. She stopped. And stilled. But Jacob could feel her pulse hammering beneath his fingers. "What, Cassie? What?"

She looked up at him, her lovely pale face a mask of uncertainty. The scent of new lumber enveloped them as the fiddlers played on, far away and ghostly. For an instant time froze, and Jacob wondered if Cathryn would ever open up to him. Would ever again let him draw close.

To her secret. To her life. To her heart.

"I came home," she began, "because my family needed me. My real goal while I was here, however, was to protect Aiden from...from my unpleasant memories of Sweet Hope."

"Aiden doesn't seem unduly affected by those memories," Jacob replied softly, moving his hand from Cathryn's wrist to her hand. Instead of drawing away, she slowly twined her fingers in his, where they rested very lightly, feeling right. Very right.

"Aside from his scrape with Howie Mapes, Aiden has blossomed here," she admitted.

"You sound surprised."

"I am. I knew he loved being with the O'Malleys, but he's loved living these past few days in this community. Has loved the freedom, the children, the helping activities... you."

"He's a very loving child." A lump formed in Jacob's throat. "And easy to love."

Cathryn stiffened, but looked Jacob directly in the eye. In the dim light he could still see the wonder that transformed her face.

He took her other hand in his and drew her so that she stood directly in front of him. "All this still doesn't explain why you ran from the dance."

She cast her gaze downward. "It does."

"How?"

She looked up at him again, and he could guess that it took a great deal of will. "Because, as I said, the same things that have been so good for Aiden since we've returned home have overwhelmed me. The sense of community...you."

"Me?" He hadn't meant to overwhelm her. He'd meant to be her friend. No, that wasn't true. He'd wanted more than friendship, but he'd always meant to control his desires. Especially since Cathryn had seemed to want so little from him. But earlier, at the dance...earlier, she'd seemed almost to want what he wanted. And then his powerful longing had become transparent. Had dismayed her. Had forced her to retreat.

"Our relationship has changed, Jacob. Over the years. Over the past few days. Over the hours and minutes, even."

He smiled at her and gently squeezed her hands. "It's a dead relationship that doesn't change."

"That's just what's so overwhelming," she fairly whispered. "Our relationship seems anything but dead."

"And *that's* what made you run from me just now?"

She pulled her fingers from his, then turned her back to him. Crossed her arms over her chest and hugged herself as if she were suddenly cold. "It all happened so fast. One minute we were dancing with Aiden. As friends. The next minute Aiden was gone, and it looked as if...as if..."

He reached out his hand and brushed her hair with his fingers. "As if what, Cassie? Say it."

She whirled around to face him. When she spoke her words were defiant, as if she wanted him to contradict her.

"As if you wished to hold me. Not as a friend... but as a lover."

She'd said it. Finally. He wanted to keep silent so that she wouldn't bolt again. But, now that the opportunity had come, he didn't want to squander it, either. He wanted to lay his feelings honestly before her.

"I did. Want to hold you," he said huskily. "You were so beautiful. Are. Beautiful."

"Jacob..." She turned as if to leave.

"Don't run again."

She stopped. "You use that word a lot in connection with me. *Run.*"

"Does it fit?"

"I never thought of it as running away. In fear. Rather, I thought of it as very practical. Leaving something painful behind. Something impossible. Letting go. Moving on toward a new start."

For Jacob, the old emotional bruises began to ache. "You think of me as painful?"

He heard her sigh. "No, Jacob. I think of you as impossible."

The sigh seemed to come up from the bottom of Cathryn's soul. It made her feel tired and sad and filled with longing all at once.

She was the one who sounded impossible. Prickly. Contrary. Heartless. But she was none of these. Not really. Not since she'd come home to Sweet Hope. Not since Jacob Matthews had reentered her life.

Back at the dance she'd felt happy and free and expectant. To dance with her son and Jacob had been a joy. A celebration of homecoming and friendship. And then, too quickly, Jacob's look had changed. To one of yearning and desire.

And she'd been frightened.

Frightened. But not of Jacob or of his all-too-transparent feelings. She'd been frightened by the feelings he'd sparked in her. Feelings of yearning and desire on her part. For him.

"If that's what you believe," Jacob conceded, his voice flat, "that I'm impossible, then there's nothing more to be said."

Without thinking, she reached out and grasped his arm. "*You're* not impossible. The situation—the situation between you and me—*that's* what's impossible."

"What situation?" His normally mellow baritone was edged with control. "What situation—*exactly*—do you mean?" He was the one to pull away now. His gaze, even in the dim light, was as cool and as clear as ice water, sending an unwanted shiver down her spine.

She answered in a rush of words. "You're the pastor of the largest church in northwest Georgia, and I'm..."

He bent so that his face was inches from her own. Bent and invaded her space. "Yes? Who are you, Cathryn? What kind of monster are you that makes us so unsuitable?"

"I'm no monster, Jacob. But I am the woman who left you waiting at the altar. The woman who humiliated you before your parishioners. That fiasco alone should make us unsuitable."

He stood straight. "Will you for once stop thinking of me as Jacob Matthews, the pastor, and think of me as simply Jacob the man? You never see me as a man."

She inhaled sharply. At the dance she'd seen him as a man. And that's exactly what had frightened her. She'd seen him as a man, an attractive man, and herself as a woman drawn to him.

"I don't always see you as the pastor."

"No. The rest of the time you see me as just a friend."

She responded to the submerged hurt in his voice. "That's not true. Sometimes I see you as more. Much more. And that frightens me...and excites me, if I'm honest." The last few words came out a whisper.

The intensity of his gaze held her immobile in the dusky night air. "*What* frightens and excites you?" He'd heard.

"The impossibilities...actually, the possibilities, even more."

"We're talking in riddles, Cassie." His velvety, coaxing voice and the sound of her nickname on his lips drew her toward him. Just a little closer. "Tell me just one concrete possibility that frightens and excites you at the same time."

The blood pounded in her ears. Her mind tried not to believe what her heart told her. "Earlier. That you might hold me. And kiss me."

She couldn't afford to be distracted by romantic notions.

He grasped her arms, his fingers encircling her flesh with gentle authority. His eyes, shadowed, contained a sensuous flame. "I never want to frighten you, Cassie. Never. Tell me if I frighten you."

His voice, deep and beckoning, sent a ripple of awareness through her. She tried to conquer her involuntary, pleasurable reaction to that gentle, loving look of his. Tried to cling to reality—to the impossibilities—praying that she wouldn't betray her agitation. Her excitement.

She tried to answer, but found herself speechless.

He was going to kiss her.

Unless she told him that he frightened her, he was going to kiss her.

Slowly he reached out, touched her chin with his forefinger, tipped her face just slightly. Just enough so that her lips were vulnerable to his. Slowly, slowly, he lowered his mouth to hover over hers.

"Don't be frightened, Cassie," he murmured, "*This* is Jacob the man."

She wanted this kiss.

As he covered her mouth with his own, he pulled her to him in an embrace that was so warm and strong and loving, Cathryn feared her very bones might melt. In all their friendship, they had never shared a kiss like this. This kiss reached into her sheltered and secluded heart, and sparked a flame. This kiss claimed her. This kiss made her forget the impossibilities. Made her yearn only for the possibilities. This kiss made her feel alive to her very toes.

Without being fully conscious of it, she wrapped her arms around his neck and kissed him back.

She felt his lips curve into the softest of smiles. Felt his lips move away for a moment. Heard him breathe her name. *Cassie.* Felt his arms tighten around her as he pulled her back into an embrace. Into a kiss that drenched her with sensation.

This was not supposed to happen. They were friends. Always before, she'd felt warmth and respect for him. A chaste sort of caring. Not this elemental pull. This desire the intensity of his kiss had ignited.

He deepened the kiss.

He drew her even closer.

She gave herself up to the kiss. To Jacob. To life.

And then the knot in her very soul tightened. The knot around the emotional wound that had pained her for five long years. The wound that would never let her get beyond a kiss. For the scars ran too deep and were too ugly, and would never let her fully be a woman.

She reeled with the knowledge that kissing Jacob might seem like a promise. A promise of more to come. A promise she could never fulfill. With a startled cry she pulled away from him. Pulled away and tried to run.

He halted her escape with a firm hand on her arm. "Cassie, don't run."

"I'm sorry, Jacob. I can't..."

"Can't what?" She heard the pain in his voice. "That's the second time tonight you've said that, and I still don't understand."

She stood and tried to still her beating heart. "We shouldn't have kissed."

"Why not? It felt to me as if we both wanted it."

Cathryn could find no words to answer.

"Deny it." Jacob pulled her toward him. "Deny that the feelings between us are real. Are right. Deny it, and I'll let you walk out of my life."

Again, thought Cathryn dismally. Whatever she owed Jacob Matthews, she at least owed him the truth. "I don't deny it. I felt something, too. But life isn't as easy as a kiss."

"Why not?" He shook her arm. Sounded desperate to know.

"I can never be more to you than a friend," she insisted.

He threw his hands up in obvious exasperation. "Why not? Because you embarrassed me once in front of my parishioners? Because you're a single mother? I'm sorry, Cathryn, but that doesn't make for a compelling argument."

The knot within her tightened, reminded her of her isolation. She'd never shared her pain. Never. Not with Jacob. Not with her family. Had barely brought it to the surface to share with herself. So tightly was it knotted, she doubted she could loose it now if she wanted.

How could she begin to explain to Jacob, for explanation he needed? She owed him an explanation. Not to make up for the way she'd hurt him years ago. But because she cared for him. Cared for him far more deeply than she'd ever before realized.

"Cathryn! Cassie..."

She looked into his face and saw anguish. She moved in an instinctive gesture of comfort, placing her hands lightly on his chest. When she spoke, she abandoned all pretense. "I can never be more to you than a friend," she began, trying to keep her voice from cracking, "not because I'm uncomfortable with you...but because I'm uncomfortable with me. As a woman."

"What are you saying?"

"Your kiss surprised me. It made me feel."

He began to speak, but she laid her fingers on his lips to silence him.

"It made me think what it would be like to be your wife. To be your lover. But I can't be either."

"Why not?" he asked, his words full of despair.

"Because there's a part of me that died five years ago. A part of me that was naturally filled with the ripeness of life, but is now filled with hurt. And loss. And confusion... and shame."

"Shame?" He repeated the word as his expression stilled and his eyes grew very dark.

The knot tightened within her. She had come this far; there was no turning back.

"Aiden is no mere love child, Jacob," she said, her heart pounding in her throat. "I was raped five years ago. Drew Paxton, Aiden's father, raped me."

She watched the horror gather in his eyes, and felt the knot reach out to ensnare her future.

Chapter Nine

Cathryn would never, *ever* forget the look of horror on Jacob's face.

What she'd dreaded for five long years had now come into being: that, knowing of her rape, those closest to her would forevermore look at her differently. See her as different.

See Aiden as different. Perhaps as a child less deserving of love.

Loving her son as fiercely as she did, she'd guarded her secret to protect him. Had rather people thought of her as a fast and loose woman than think of her son as some kind of freak. Society's castoff.

She saw Jacob stiffen. Saw him clench his jaw, his neck muscles, his fists. He would know now why they could never be more than friends. As much as he insisted she see him as a man, he was a pastor. To further a relationship with her and her son would be professional suicide. Like sitting on a powder keg. Someone, at some point in time, was bound to uncover the ugly truth. Was bound, despite Jacob's best intentions, to twist that truth into an explosive weapon.

Hadn't Ellie Able hinted that she had just that weapon? Hadn't she dug up—or thought she'd dug up—something damning enough to stop a wedding five years ago?

"Cassie." Jacob's voice rasped raw. Pained. A disbelieving plea. "Why didn't you tell me?"

The old horror began to wash over her. "I told no one."

"Not even your family?"

Cathryn hugged herself and shivered. Again, as she had that awful night five years ago, she felt unclean. Violated. Alone. "I couldn't tell them . . . especially them."

Jacob reached out to unclench her arms. She recoiled. It was painful to be touched.

He seemed instantly to recognize this now and withdrew. "Cassie, why not?"

The sound of her nickname seared her soul. Locked her in the past, as a frightened eighteen-year-old with one foot still in adolescence and one foot forevermore in a damaged adulthood.

"Why not?" Her eyes filled with hot tears. "Why not? Because all along my father had insisted I was growing up too fast. Insisted I pressed into emotional territory I wasn't mature enough to handle. He was right. And the consequences were disastrous."

Jacob raised his hand as if to touch her, but dropped it helplessly at his side. "Were you afraid of I-told-you-so's? Boone loves you far too much to pull something like that in a situation this grave. His only concern would have been your well-being."

Cathryn hugged herself even tighter. So tightly that her fingers dug painfully into her upper arms. The present pain somehow warded off the ghastly, ghostly pain of the past. "I know Daddy would have been supportive. But I *had been* a fool. A fool and foolhardy. I couldn't face him."

"You sound as if you blame yourself." The rich timbre of his voice cracked with apprehension. "I know enough about rape to know that you were the victim. Not the instigator."

"Perhaps I misled . . ." She choked on a sob and couldn't continue.

"Tell me how you think you misled anyone."

She couldn't look at him. She couldn't speak.

"Cassie, don't shut me out." His words were a tormented appeal. "It's time to bring this into the open. It's time you let someone help shoulder the pain. Let me."

Cathryn began to tremble. Still she could find no words to answer Jacob. Yes, perhaps he could help shoulder the pain. But who would ever—*ever*—help ease the sense of shame?

Damnation! He couldn't lose her now. Silently, frenetically, he prayed to find the right words to draw her out.

Now he knew the answers to all his questions: Why she'd left him waiting at the altar. Why she'd fled Sweet Hope and her family. Why she seemed so ill at ease around the rakish Rhune. But knowing the answers brought him no satisfaction. He—Jacob—and his unanswered questions were not the issue here.

Cathryn was the issue. Cathryn and the trauma she'd tried to deal with all alone.

All alone. He could only imagine her pain. "Cassie..." He tried to draw her out again, but she wouldn't answer. Wouldn't look at him. Wouldn't move.

He hated his helplessness. He wanted to pull her into his arms, to comfort her, to tell her that together they would deal with her past. Together they would forge a future. But he couldn't even touch her. His touch, meant to heal, to show love, would only bring her pain.

All he had were words, and words were proving ineffective.

"Did you at least seek medical help?" he asked, trying to keep her with him in the barn's shell. He feared that at any moment she'd flee. "Counseling?"

She shook her head. He saw teardrops spatter her shirt.

"I've trained in rape counseling," he offered gently. But he'd never been called upon to use his training. Never imagined he would have to use it with someone he loved. He clenched his fists and tried to suppress the ungodly desire to thrash Drew Paxton to a repentant pulp.

She looked up at him, an expression of yearning and indecision washing her tearstained face. "I...need to tell someone. It just won't go away."

Jacob exhaled. Please, God, just keep her talking. We can do this together.

He motioned to a stack of plywood low enough to form a bench for two.

Slowly she unwound her arms from the death grip she'd maintained on herself, then haltingly moved to take a seat. She didn't speak, but looked at Jacob, her eyes brimming with ineffable sadness. And something else. The faint glimmer of an old trust.

Sitting next to her, close enough to impart comfort, distant enough so as not to invade her space, her private pain, Jacob struggled for words. "Let's start at the beginning."

"The beginning's not what you think."

"Don't worry about what I think. Start where you need to start."

She sighed, and Jacob wished again that he could hold her. She swiped at her eyes with the back of her hand. He could see her lower lip tremble.

"One night, at the end of my freshman year of college, I was helping Belle move donated books into her storefront. Daddy was there, doing renovations." She sighed again. "I dropped a pile of books and, with them, my purse. The purse opened, the contents spilled on the floor... including some condoms. I thought Daddy was going to have a heart attack."

Jacob tried to keep his voice even. "So...you were having a sexual relationship when you were eighteen?"

"No!" Her face filled with alarm. "No, not at all! I thought I was being prepared. Thought my preparedness was maturity. But preparedness was a double-edged sword."

"What do you mean?"

"My father, and even some of my classmates, thought I was...advertising. Obviously, Drew Paxton thought so."

"Had you ever expressed a desire to experiment sexually?" Jacob tensed. This was a thornier issue than he'd anticipated.

"Who doesn't talk about sex in college?" Her voice took on a defensive edge.

He hoped his words hadn't sounded judgmental. That wasn't his intention. His intention was to help Cathryn work through her trauma. From the beginning. But he hadn't counted on the details.

"Sure, we talked," she continued, "but my contention was that sex should only be shared by two people committed to each other." She laughed softly. A bitter little laugh. "I wasn't naive, however. I knew about raging hormones."

"And that's where the condoms came in." Lord, he'd witnessed this dilemma time and time again with the teenagers in his congregation. How, as an adult who owed them guidance, could he keep them safe—from unwanted pregnancy, from disease, from the specter of death—without advocating promiscuity?

"That's where the condoms came in. And Drew Paxton."

"Drew Paxton." Jacob repeated the name, unable to keep the loathing out of his voice.

Cathryn reached out and laid her fingers on his arm. Her unexpected touch made him start. "The condoms," she said, "might have been a double-edged sword . . . but Drew Paxton was a mistake from the beginning." She withdrew her hand and hung her head.

"What do you mean?"

"Drew Paxton was a walk on the wild side. Meant to tweak my father." She looked up, and Jacob could see regret in her eyes. "Drew Paxton was much older. Only a part-time student. Dating him was my attempt to prove to my family that I wasn't a child anymore." She began to cry softly. "He certainly dispelled any trace of my childhood."

Jacob thought his heart would break. "He raped you, Cassie. He not only stole your childhood but, by your silence, you've let him steal your adulthood. Your future."

She looked up at him as if he'd somehow betrayed her.

"You are *not* to blame for the rape." Dear Lord, he couldn't let her think he'd turned on her. "Drew Paxton was to blame, and he can still be held accountable. But, you, Cassie . . . *you* must take back your future."

"After all these years, I don't know how to begin."

"Let me help you."

"I need help," she admitted raggedly.

"Let your family help."

"No!" A look of panic contorted her face. "No, my family can't know."

"Why not?" Just when he thought she'd made progress, she threw him a curve.

"Because of Aiden. Dear God, I don't want them to look at Aiden differently."

He felt thunderstruck. Until now he'd only thought of Cathryn. Of her pain. He hadn't thought of the consequences of Aiden's conception on the boy himself. A conception not of love. Not even of passion. Not life affirming. But born of violence. Ugly and life threatening. How would Cathryn ever explain—or would she even try—when Aiden became old enough to ask questions about his father?

"You understand?" Cathryn's voice broke into his frozen state.

"I understand, but that doesn't mean I agree your family should be left in the dark. You underestimate them."

"I've hurt them greatly. I don't want to hurt them further." Her flat tone of voice told Jacob he'd gain no concessions by pushing Cathryn now.

"Then let me help." He couldn't lose the headway they'd made. "I'll check my contacts. See if they know of a rape counseling center in Albany. That's a first step."

"After all these years?" Her voice and eyes expressed extreme doubt. "I think I've gone too far beyond the first step."

"No, Cassie," he replied, trying not to frighten her off with his contradiction, "you've just taken the very first step by confiding in me. The others—all necessary—will get easier the more you take."

He wanted to believe, deep down in his heart, that he didn't lead her on with a lie. He couldn't be certain, but his love for her desperately wanted his words to be the truth.

"I want to believe you."

"Then make the leap of faith." Because he couldn't hold her with his arms, he tried to hold her with his eyes. Tried to comfort her with his gaze. "Together, we'll make a start."

"At what? I'm afraid, in the years of confusion, in the years of thinking only of Aiden, I've lost sight of what *I* might want or need . . . if given the chance."

"You need to feel whole again."

"That seems like an overwhelming task. How do I start?"

"Let go of the sense of shame." Although his words were simple, he knew it would be a complex process for Cathryn to carry them out.

She lowered her eyes. He could almost see a flush on her moon-pale cheeks. He could definitely feel her discomfort. It hung, palpable, in the air.

"How?" she whispered.

"Start with me."

She jerked her head up and stared at him in surprise. "You?"

"Start by remembering how I reacted when I first heard this awful secret."

"You . . . you looked horrified."

"I was horrified. But of you or the act?"

Understanding seemed to dawn on Cathryn. "But you and I are old friends. If I expected anyone to understand, it would be you."

"That's not true." Sadness gripped his heart. "If that were true, you never would have left me five years ago." He needed to pull himself up short. He was wandering into old territory. Territory that had nothing to do with Cathryn's recovery. "The point is that you didn't expect me to understand, but I did. Do. I'm just one person. The first."

"Don't ask me to test others. I can't handle it. Not now."

"I'm not asking you to tell anyone else right now." He made his voice as gentle as he possibly could. "All I'm asking is that you acknowledge the step you've taken and the success of your efforts. You *told me,* Cassie. You told me and I didn't look at you as if you had three heads. I didn't turn tail and run. I didn't lose any of the respect or feeling I hold for you."

If anything, her disclosure had reaffirmed his belief that his future and Cathryn's future were inexorably intertwined. This woman, so strong, so selfless, would one day be his wife.

Was this one of the small miracles of daily life? Jacob's act of reaching out. His act of understanding. Cathryn felt overwhelmed with emotion. For the first time in five years she felt the ugly, painful knot within her loosen. Felt the possibility of wanting something—anything—for herself.

"Jacob..." She choked on his name. "Thank you."

"Don't thank me. You said it yourself, we're old friends."

She looked down at her hands, then stiffened her resolve and looked Jacob in the eye. "I haven't always treated you the way a friend should be treated."

A slow smile creased his strong face. "Cathryn O'Malley, if I teach you nothing before you return to Albany, I'm going to teach you to start each day, each hour, each moment fresh."

The warmth in his voice strengthened her. "You have your work cut out for you."

"I'll have a helper." An unmistakable twinkle shone in his eye.

"Who?"

"Someone right under your very nose. Someone who knows how to adapt. Who knows how to squeeze the most enjoyment out of tadpole eggs, or building a calf door, or dancing, or chasing fireflies." He grinned.

"Aiden." She sighed. Funny how everything in her life had always come back to Aiden.

"Do you think maybe your son is an important enough reason for you to make every effort to heal?"

Cathryn nodded her head and had to smile. "Jacob Matthews, you always did know exactly which buttons to push."

He looked as if he might make a sharp retort, but caught himself. Instead, he said, his gaze intense, "I've only ever wanted the best for you."

They were silent. Finally, comfortably silent. And Cathryn marveled at how Jacob had brought her back from the brink of despair. From the abyss of remembrance. Only a short while earlier she'd felt nothing but pain. And now she was conscious of a smile on her lips. A soft smile that bespoke hope.

He was quite a man.

Over the years she'd wondered at the hole her flight had caused in Jacob's life. Had wondered and had worried about the hurt she'd inflicted. It was only now that she realized the hole she'd created in her own life, the hurt, by not allowing Jacob in.

They'd come quite a distance tonight. She'd thought more about herself than she'd allowed in five years. But now it was time to put on her mother's cap and return to Aiden. He must be exhausted after his full day. She couldn't wait to tuck him in bed. Couldn't wait to feel his arms around her neck in a good-night hug. He was her promise of tomorrow.

Finally she said, "I need to get back to Aiden."

Jacob stood. "I'll walk you back."

"For the time Belle's spent with the children, I owe her big time. Maybe I'll offer to take Margaret for a week in the summer, and Belle and Daddy can go on a cruise. Or something."

Jacob snorted. "The way I see it, Belle and Boone don't need a cruise. Or a week away from Margaret. Or repayment for watching Aiden. They're content, Cassie. With each other. With their family. Right here in Sweet Hope."

"Is this a parable, Pastor Matthews?" she asked, unable to prevent a note of teasing from bubbling through her question.

"If the shoe fits, Ms. O'Malley..."

As they made their way from the barn to the farmyard, their easy banter was interrupted by an overwrought Alice Rose. "Cathryn, dear, thank goodness I found you."

Cold fear rose in Cathryn.

"Aiden's fallen." Dear God, she knew it. "He's all right except for a nasty gash on his forehead."

Cathryn didn't wait to hear the rest. She broke away from Alice Rose and Jacob and raced to a small knot of people in the mess tent. She saw her father in the center of the group, holding Aiden. Holding a cloth to her son's head.

She should have been watching Aiden. Instead, she'd been self-absorbed.

She took a deep breath to steady herself so that her son would not sense her worry, then pushed through the assembled volunteers.

"Mama," Aiden whispered as Cathryn gathered him into her arms. He looked too pale and dazed.

"He was playing tag with the other children," Boone said quickly. "He fell against a plow. We've slowed the bleeding, but he needs stitches."

Stitches. Cathryn mouthed the word.

"I don't want stitches, Mama. I want to sleep."

Boone, who still held the cloth to Aiden's head, shook his own head in an emphatic *no.* "I was just about to take him to the clinic in Sterling."

"I'll take them." Jacob appeared at her side. "Take the cloth, Cathryn, and hold it firmly to his head." He lightly brushed Aiden's cheek. "You're going to be fine, son. Just fine. Your mama and I are going to have to tell you some tall tales, however, to keep you awake on the ride."

Quickly, but calmly so as not to distress Aiden, Cathryn followed Jacob to his Blazer, where he helped them in and gently buckled them both safely.

As Jacob started the vehicle, then slowly made his way out of the Sims's farmyard, terrible regrets assailed Cathryn. She should have been with Aiden. She should not have been wallowing in her past and her pain. Had she been where she was supposed to be—watching Aiden as a responsible mother—this would never have happened.

She cradled Aiden, tucked and buckled between Jacob and her. As she did so, her gaze met Jacob's.

As though he'd read her mind, he said softly, "Cathryn O'Malley, this is *not* your fault."

"But—"

"No buts." He scowled and motioned toward Aiden. When he spoke, however, his voice was calm and reassuring, with even a hint of playfulness. "Right now we need to find out from this wild man how this wreck happened." He reached down and patted Aiden's leg. "It was a wreck you and that plow had, wasn't it?"

"It *was* a wreck," Aiden murmured. "That plow surprised me."

"Well, tonight we're going to the clinic where they'll take care of you. Tomorrow, however, Mr. Sims is going to have to take care of that plow."

Aiden snuffled, but, to Cathryn, it sounded more like a chuckle snuffle than a crying snuffle. She reached over to make sure the cloth she held to his head was still firmly in place.

"Why are we going to the clinic in Sterling?" she asked. "Wouldn't it be faster to go to Dr. Peabody in town?"

"Old Doc Peabody fell and broke his hip this January. He's not mended well, and had to retire. The practice is vacant. No one seems to want to be a country family physician."

Cathryn lifted the edge of the cloth she held to Aiden's head. She inhaled sharply. The gash, on the left top of his forehead along the hairline, had stopped bleeding, but the cloth was soaked with blood. Her son's blood. The sight of it made her queasy. She strove to maintain her fragile control.

"Can't we go any faster?" she asked Jacob, her stomach clenched tight, her mind a crazy mixture of hope and fear.

"Head wounds can be more show than substance," he answered softly. Then to Aiden he said, "Do you have a favorite travel song?"

"'Baby Beluga' makes me sleepy."

"Oh, I don't want you to go to sleep. Do you know 'Noah and the Flood'? I teach it to all my Sunday school classes."

"Sing it."

"You and your mama have to promise to help with the chorus."

Bless Jacob. Not only could he calm a four-year-old, he could calm the mother, as well.

Cathryn only half listened to the song's progress as she struggled with her conscience. Here in Sweet Hope she'd been less vigilant with her son than she was accustomed. Lulled by a sense of extended family, she'd allowed him more freedom than she'd ever before allowed him in his short life. She had let others help raise him temporarily...and just look at the consequences.

Jacob glanced at Cathryn as Aiden and he finished the song. Aiden would come through this minicrisis less scathed than his mother.

He'd seen the gash on Aiden's forehead. It was scary to look at, yes, but he'd seen worse in his experiences on the Grace Everlasting Sunday school playground. Aiden was strong, and would come through even stitches like a trouper. Cathryn and he would see to it. But after all was said and done, it would be Cathryn who needed help. Help in overcoming the obviously terrible guilt she felt for Aiden's accident.

Her face shone pale by the lights on the dashboard. Worry settled in the dark circles under her eyes. Jacob wanted to assure her that these things happened to children as they tested their wings, but he didn't want to dismiss her motherly concern. He wanted to support her at the same time he wanted her to understand that the small amount of time she'd taken for herself back in the barn had in no way contributed to Aiden's present hurt.

"We're here," he said as he pulled into the parking lot of the small Sterling clinic.

Aiden whimpered. "Don't want stitches."

"Do you know what stitches are?" Jacob asked.

"No, but I don't want them. I want to go home."

Cathryn unbuckled her son as soon as Jacob pulled to a stop. "We'll go right home as soon as the doctors check that hard noggin of yours." She kissed the top of his head. "On the way home I'll tell you the story of Mike Mulligan."

"Promise?"

"I promise." Cathryn looked at Jacob as she scooped Aiden into her arms. "Perhaps Pastor Jacob will help with the sound effects."

"Nothing would make me happier," Jacob replied as he ushered Cathryn and Aiden into the clinic's reception area. Nothing except to have this all over with, he thought. To have Aiden patched and to have Cathryn reassured.

The nurse in the outer office recognized Jacob immediately and led the three of them to a small examining room. "We have some paperwork to fill out," she declared briskly, "but we can do it after we look at this young man. Now, if your mama will remove that old cloth, I can see what needs to be done."

Cathryn blanched as she removed the cloth, and Jacob said a silent prayer, asking the Lord to steady the doctor's hand and Cathryn's heart.

He reached out instinctively and clasped both Aiden's hand and Cathryn's in his own. Both squeezed him. Hard.

A young doctor entered. Jacob didn't recognize her. She must have been one of the volunteers from the nearest Atlanta hospital who augmented the one paid doctor on staff. "I'm Dr. Latham. And who might you be?" she asked, smiling directly at Aiden.

"I might be Aiden," he replied soberly from Cathryn's arms.

The doctor leaned close to examine Aiden. "And you're his parents?"

"I'm his mother," Cathryn answered quickly. "Cathryn O'Malley."

And I want to be his father, Jacob said in his heart. Aloud he said, "I'm Jacob Matthews, pastor of Grace Everlasting."

"Well, all I can say," Dr. Latham said as she patted Aiden's shoulder, "is that I feel sorry for the other guy."

"It was a plow," Aiden offered.

"Well, Aiden, we're going to get you fixed up before that plow recovers, that's for sure." She turned to Cathryn. "I'm going to need to speak to you and have you sign some forms." And then to Jacob. "There are some puzzles under the examining table. Do you think you and Aiden could keep busy for a few minutes?" She winked. "Nothing rough. We don't want the bleeding to start again."

Jacob reached for Aiden, and the boy came readily into his arms. "I don't know about you, sport, but I'm a whiz at puzzles."

"Me, too," Aiden answered with a yawn. "Even new ones."

The nurse pulled several from beneath the table and handed them to Jacob. Within minutes Aiden became engrossed in the distraction, allowing Jacob the opportunity to observe this beautiful child. This child whose beginnings were inauspicious. Born of physical pain and mental anguish, this child had brought love and joy and a renewal of wonder with him into the world. Jacob smiled. No small miracle.

Cathryn returned shortly with the doctor and the nurse.

As his puzzles were removed, Aiden protested. As the nurse laid him on the examining table, his eyes filled with fear and tears, and he reached out for his mother.

Her voice even, Dr. Latham said, "Aiden, I need you to hold your mama's and Pastor Matthews's hands so they don't touch anything. Can you do that for me?"

With alacrity, Aiden complied, then strained to see what the doctor and nurse were about to do.

"You need to be very still and look at me, sweet thing," Cathryn said, "so that the doctor can patch you like I patched Boo Bear."

Jacob didn't need to look at Cathryn to tell that she held raw emotions in check. He held Aiden's hand and stroked it with his thumb, then reached across the examining table for Cathryn's free hand. She gave it willingly.

"You and Boo Bear are going to have some tale to tell Margaret," Jacob said. "Perhaps tomorrow we could even find paper and crayons so that you can draw your story."

"I want to use markers."

I'll buy you a paint store, Jacob promised silently, if only that fearful look would leave your eyes. Aloud, he replied gently, "Markers it is."

As the doctor and nurse worked efficiently at Aiden's head, Jacob and Cathryn drew the boy's attention, alternately with gentle banter, reassurances and simple promises. Jacob could tell each time Cathryn's gaze slipped from Aiden's eyes to the doctor stitching, for then her grip on his hand intensified. He had to give her credit, however. Never once did her anxiety slip into her voice. Whatever anguish she felt, whatever terrible regrets assailed her, she hid them under an exterior of loving calm.

His admiration for her quadrupled.

"All done," Dr. Latham said quietly.

Cathryn had never heard two sweeter words.

She smiled at Aiden and then at Jacob and felt her knees wobble. "Aiden O'Malley," she breathed in relief, "you are one super boy."

He scowled. "I have a headache."

"I'm going to give you something for that, Aiden," Dr. Latham said. "And juice boxes and cookies for the three of you." She winked. "You make a fine team."

A fine team.

As Cathryn finished up the necessary paperwork and Jacob distracted Aiden, those three words repeated in her mind. A fine team. Aiden, Cathryn and Jacob. Why did that surprise her?

It hadn't surprised her when Jacob had taken over from Boone in the mess tent. As if it were natural. It hadn't surprised her when Jacob had come into the clinic examining room with them. As if he belonged. And it hadn't surprised her when she'd seen worry edge his eyes at the same time he'd kept his voice strong and reassuring. As if Aiden meant more to him than the son of an old friend.

None of that had surprised her, so why now did the doctor's words startle her? *A fine team.*

This was not the time to begin thoughts in that direction. Four more days of service to Grace Everlasting and she would be on the road again. Back to Albany. Back to her safe and ordered existence. Away from the painful introspection. Away from community scrutiny. Away from the relaxed communal raising of her child—a practice that had courted disaster. She needed to regain her focus: Aiden and his well-being.

She must resist the growing needs that clamored within her. Personal needs. A woman's needs. Needs for which the unsettling Pastor Matthews held out the promise of fulfillment.

Cathryn crossed the final *t* and dotted the final *i* on the insurance form, then put down her pen and looked over at Jacob and Aiden. It would be a lot easier to leave Sweet Hope this time if her son had not grown quite so attached to her *old friend.*

"Ready?" Jacob, Aiden in his arms, rose.

"Let's get this boy home." The word *home* slipped out before she could stop it.

Once in Jacob's truck, Aiden snuggled against Cathryn's side and immediately fell asleep. She stroked his silky hair and sighed.

"You don't have to help me in the office tomorrow morning if you'd rather keep an eye on him," Jacob offered. "Or you could bring him with you. He could play with Molly-the-Snit's kittens."

"Thank you. We'll see how he's feeling tomorrow."

"And how does his mother feel right now?"

Uneasy thoughts fluttered through her mind. Deliberately, she turned her head to look at him. "I'm glad that this is behind us, and very grateful for your help, but..."

"But?" He kept his eyes on the road. The muscle in his jaw twitched.

"But I can't help feel that none of this would have happened if I'd been properly supervising my son."

"Don't do this to yourself, Cassie." His voice was a low, unexpected warning growl. "Don't beat yourself up for something you probably couldn't have prevented."

"If I'd been there—"

"If you'd been there, you would have been watching him play tag. You would have seen him collide with the plow. How does that help?"

"But—"

"Again, no buts." He spoke with cool authority. "No matter how well you supervise them, children get in scrapes." She detected a thaw in his tone. "My father claimed that, while I was growing up, he never once got to watch an entire Super Bowl. Said he spent some part of every one of them in the emergency room with me."

She smiled. "*You* got in scrapes?" Somehow she'd always pictured him, even as a child, as in control.

"Broken bones, sprains, fractures, chipped teeth, you name it. And both my father and I survived to tell the tale."

She wrinkled her nose and shook her head. "Who would have thought it?"

He chuckled. "You know the old saying. What doesn't kill us makes us stronger."

"And that's supposed to comfort me?"

"No." He reached out and stroked Aiden's head. "This child, patched up and sleeping peacefully, should comfort you."

He does, Cathryn thought. And not surprisingly, so do you.

Chapter Ten

Over the top of the filing cabinet, Jacob's warm gray gaze bored into her. Lordy, but the man didn't give a woman a chance to breathe.

"I think we're getting a handle on things," he said simply, handing Cathryn another sheaf of papers.

There was nothing simple in the way her heart responded to his deep, sensuous voice. Nothing simple about the way her thoughts jumbled inside her head. Absolutely nothing about Jacob Matthews seemed simple anymore. Not after last night. Not after that kiss...and her subsequent confession.

She pasted a smile on her lips, took the papers from his outstretched hand and hoped distraction wasn't evident in her every move.

Did he know the reaction he provoked in her? Was that smile truly boyish, or was it disingenuous? Calculated to wear her down.

Well, intending to or not, he'd worn her down for three straight days now. Ever since her return to Sweet Hope.

He'd worn her down with his moonlight softball. He'd worn her down with his unflagging strength and leadership in the face of disaster. He'd worn her down with his good spirits and diplomacy this morning in meetings with countless insurance representatives and government agents. Quite frankly, his energy and his optimism wore her defenses down.

But mostly he wore her down emotionally with those eyes. Those warm, too-intense gray eyes that said he and she had unfinished business.

She breathed a sigh of relief as Jacob turned, then stepped gingerly over Aiden, who, stretched out on the worn office carpet, drew with markers on huge sheets of packing paper. Molly-the-Snit, ensconced in an adjoining storage room, had allowed Aiden only a peek at her kittens. The rest of the morning he'd entertained himself with books—mostly used as building blocks—and makeshift art supplies.

"Mama?" His voice held a hint of restlessness. "Can I go find Margaret? I feel fine. Honest."

The afternoon sun shone through the window on his tousled blond head, highlighting the bandage at his hairline. Cathryn knew she was overprotecting. But he was her only child. She couldn't bear any further harm to come to him.

"As soon as I've filed these papers," she answered, softening, "I'll walk you to the classrooms. I bet we'll find Nonny Belle and Margaret just in time for snacks."

Jacob knelt beside Aiden. "I have just the thing. I should have thought of it sooner." He extended his hand, and Aiden quickly grasped it. "Come 'round my desk."

Once on the other side of his desk, Jacob sat on the floor and pulled Aiden into his lap. Cathryn heard the scrape of a drawer opening.

"This," Jacob said, his tone of voice hushed, "was my treasure drawer when I was a boy. When he was pastor of Grace Everlasting, my daddy kept it especially for me. For the times I'd come play in his office while he worked."

Aiden peered into the drawer. "Wow!" His tone was as hushed and reverent as Jacob's. "Do you still play with this stuff?"

Jacob chuckled. "No. Now that I'm pastor, I don't have time." He picked up a miniature metal race car. "In fact, I'd almost forgotten this drawer. I guess it took a boy like you to remind me." He handed Aiden the car, and lightly kissed the top of his head. "From now on, it's your treasure drawer... when you come to keep me company."

The breath caught in Cathryn's throat. This sounded too close to a generational rite of passage. From grandfather to father to son. Jacob made it sound so natural. So fitting. As if Aiden would be in his life from now on. Permanently.

Jacob didn't sound like a man who expected Cathryn and Aiden to be leaving come Saturday morning.

Her head began to spin with conflicting thoughts. Living in this sardine can of a relief center, she hadn't time alone to sort through the little cherry bombs of revelations and personal epiphanies of the past twenty-four hours. And now Jacob seemed intent on heaping new challenges upon the almost new. Upon the old.

She needed to sort through her own growing attraction for Jacob. She didn't need a new complication staring her in the face: the very obvious bond Jacob and Aiden had for each other. Even as she'd seen friendship between the two of them blossom, she'd worried about the day she'd have to take Aiden back to Albany. Worried about creating yet another separation in her son's short life. But today the stakes had been raised the minute Jacob, working the old Matthews magic, had opened his treasure drawer and passed it on to Aiden.

To Cathryn's eyes this was more than an act of friendship. This was a fatherly gesture, and her son had accepted it willingly.

The papers in Cathryn's hands fluttered and a tiny shiver ran up her spine as someone quickly opened the office door, sending a cross breeze through the room. Cathryn turned to find an obviously irate Ellie Able standing in the doorway.

Without preamble, Ellie launched into her complaint. "I want to know how Marshall Sims can get a whole cow barn raised when people's homes are still in ruins—when I can't get more than a hundred dollars from the church emergency fund. Now you tell me that, Miss Hotshot-From-Albany-Who's-Worked-On-Relief-Efforts-Before."

Jacob rose from behind his desk, and Ellie blanched. Obviously she'd thought she'd found Cathryn alone.

Coming around the desk, he asked, "What seems to be the problem?" in a tone of voice that said with certainty that the buck stopped here. That whatever the problem, it would be settled in this room. He'd see to it.

Ellie's attitude turned from outrage to wheedling. "I can't fix my house on a hundred dollars."

"The hundred dollars is not meant to fix your house," Jacob explained patiently. "It's meant to buy you basic toiletries, medicines, pet food, a change of clothes—small necessary things—to tide you over till you can get back into your house. Your insurance and the federal aid will cover major repairs."

"Then how come Marshall Sims already has a new barn? Did Miss O'Malley here put his applications on the top of the stack as she hid mine at the bottom?"

"That's enough, Ellie." Jacob's gray eyes, normally warm and inviting, were now steely. Full of unmistakable warning. "Cathryn and I only help fill out the insurance and federal forms. For the most part, the wait depends on the individual companies. Marshall Sims happens to have an agent who could assess the damage and write a claims check on the spot."

"So he's lucky once, he gets to be lucky twice and have his barn raised pronto? The cows will be back in their home before legitimate parishioners are back in theirs."

Jacob's voice bordered on lost patience. "We voted on this at Sunday's meeting. The majority felt that since Marshall had the funds and the supplies, it would boost morale for the congregation to participate in the barn raising. A positive, concrete effort that would raise flagging spirits."

"It doesn't raise my spirits to sit in that gymnasium contemplating the mess my home's in."

"We're all in the same boat," Cathryn asserted. "My family hasn't been home since the storm, either."

Ellie Able turned a look of pure contempt on Cathryn. "*Your family.* Your family sticks together like glue. Takes care of its own. Your family, with a member heading up just about every committee of importance, won't have to worry about getting their properties taken care of."

Cathryn's blood began to boil. "If you're hinting at preferential treatment—"

"I could hint at a lot more than preferential treatment," Ellie huffed.

"Enough!" Jacob ordered. "Ellie, I think you owe Cathryn an apology."

The older woman shot Jacob a look that declared, *When hell freezes over.* "You, Pastor Matthews, have been blinded again," she snapped. "I think Grace Everlasting deserves a pastor who gives more thought to his parishioners than to a little out-of-town chit with a sordid past." She whirled around, then flung her parting words over her shoulder. "I'll find someone willing to help me. And I won't forget those who weren't."

Ellie Able left the room far, far colder than she'd found it. Cathryn shivered. The woman still spelled trouble.

"Cassie, I'm sorry." Jacob's words broke the silence just as Cathryn heard Aiden whimper.

She quickly rounded the desk to find her son concentrating on a bag of marbles. His concentration was ineffective, for she saw his lower lip tremble. As part of the O'Malley family, he was used to boisterous voices, voices raised in play or discussion. He was not, however, used to voices raised in accusation and threat. Clearly, the confrontation with Ellie Able had disturbed him.

He looked up at Cathryn. "Why was that lady so mean?"

That was no lady, Cathryn thought bitterly as she scooped her son into her arms. She bit back her angry thoughts as aloud she said, "The people in Sweet Hope have been through a terrible storm, love. The storm hurt them and made them frightened and sometimes angry. It's made them say things they might not usually say."

Although, she thought, Ellie Able, storm or no storm, was just getting warmed up. The very idea made her own blood pressure rise.

"Like the time Gramps hit his thumb with a hammer?" Aiden asked, his eyes wide.

Jacob chuckled and held out his arms. "Come to me and tell me just what Grandpa Boone said. Your mama needs to go kick some stumps."

"Kick some stumps?" Aiden reached out and tweaked Jacob's nose. "That sounds silly. And fun. Can we go, too?"

"No, sir. Your mama needs to let off steam. You and I are going to empty the treasure drawer."

"Okay," Aiden replied with restored good spirits.

Cathryn, her temper still simmering over Ellie Able's gall, eyed Jacob. "And just where am I supposed to find these stumps for kicking?"

"Down the road a piece. In what used to be the old piney grove. The storm leveled it. It's not in anybody's way, however, so no one will think to clear it. It'll be empty." His eyes flashed encouragement. "Just the place to let go of some anger. Aiden and I will give you an hour, then we'll meet you on the church steps for a snack."

The idea appealed to her. She might not do any stump kicking, but she certainly could use the walk to ease the simmering indignation Ellie Able had stirred up. "An hour, then."

She kissed Aiden. Almost kissed Jacob. But, thinking better of it, she raised her hand in a wave before leaving. Coward, she thought. No, not coward. Practical. Before last night's kiss, she and Jacob had been friends who could share a hug or a peck on the cheek. But now...now, just what were they to each other? She wriggled her fingers—in a practical wave—then turned quickly and left Jacob's office.

It wasn't until she was walking along the side of the road away from Grace Everlasting that she realized she'd left Aiden in the care of another. Again. Not twenty-four hours after her vow to keep him by her side. She stopped and waited for the guilt to descend. It didn't. Instead, to her surprise, she felt sure that, rather than leaving Aiden with another, she'd left him with an extension of herself.

Now, *that* little cherry bomb of a thought alone deserved a good stump kicking.

Jacob sat back on his heels and surveyed with supreme satisfaction the town Aiden and he had constructed over the entire office floor. He hoped Cathryn had derived as much satisfaction from her walk alone. He actually did hope she'd taken his advice and had taken out some of her anger on the piney grove stumps.

Unless he'd missed the mark, Cathryn had some long-suppressed anger to deal with. She'd mentioned shame, but she hadn't spoken of anger. To his mind, anger was healthier. He'd bet she'd held hers in because of Aiden. Would bet that she'd suppressed it in order to get on with her life. One could suppress anger. Anger was such a public emotion. Shame was more insidious. Because it was such a private ill, it constantly lurked beneath consciousness. Whispered its bile. Refused to be suppressed.

Jacob had discovered in his career that anger released could drive away shame. But he couldn't do it for Cathryn. She had to do it for herself.

"Pastor Jacob," an unseen Aiden called out, "can you find the bear in his cave?" A muffled giggle followed the challenge.

Jacob smiled. How many times had he called out *Find me* to his own father? How many times had his father put down his work to search for the son? When he'd grown, Jacob had often wondered why his father had put up with the constant interruptions. Today he'd found the answer.

Today he'd discovered the treasure at the end of each search: a boyish grin, a giggle, a warm hug. And a look of trust and affection that could soften the hardest heart.

Not to say that his own heart was hard. No. Jacob suppressed a chuckle as he carefully crawled on hands and knees around his big desk. His heart, if anything, was predisposed to love Cathryn's son, despite the warning he gave himself daily to guard his heart in case Cathryn, true to her word, did indeed leave Sweet Hope again. This time with Aiden.

The first time Cathryn had left she'd been with child. A child not yet born—an amorphous promise. Her leaving then had hurt. This time, with the image of a very real Aiden, a living, breathing little boy with a grand capacity for love, seared upon Jacob's heart...well, he refused to harbor the thought.

Instead, he rounded the desk to discover Aiden crouched in the kneehole, eyes twinkling, hands over his mouth to suppress his laughter. When Jacob spotted Aiden, the boy sprang with a bearlike growl and threw his arms around the man's neck.

Laughing, Jacob tumbled to the floor in a vanquished heap. He remembered his own father, and knew now with certainty that it wasn't so much that his father had interrupted his work to play with his son. He felt certain that his father had thought the process worked the other way around.

Cathryn walked through what used to be a grove of pine trees but was now a tornado wasteland littered with fallen branches and uprooted stumps. She'd found to her surprise that the walk here had not cooled her off. Instead, she felt like shouting her anger to the heavens.

Her anger at the meddling and self-righteous Ellie Able.

Her anger at Drew Paxton.

All the anger she'd kept submerged and out of sight for five years as she'd struggled alone to be a good and loving parent. An upstanding citizen.

She was angry, too, for allowing a sense of shame to creep under her skin.

She had been the victim. She had nothing to be ashamed of. She'd never dressed provocatively. She'd never been one to drink, and so she'd never been out of control. She'd believed in exploring one relationship at a time. Slowly. In order that each person understood the other.

Well, Drew Paxton had surely understood the word *no.* He'd simply chosen to ignore it.

And then he'd bragged of his exploits to his friends.

Anger rose like bile gorge in Cathryn's throat as she remembered how her misdirected sense of shame had driven her out of her hometown. She should have cultivated anger instead. Should have stayed. Should have fought back through all the legal channels.

And then she thought of Aiden. She'd left so that his birth would be untouched by Drew Paxton or his memory.

She kicked a fallen pine. The hateful thing was that Drew Paxton didn't even live in Sweet Hope. But some of his friends did, Ellie Able's son among them. She picked up a fallen branch and hurled it like a javelin into the air, releasing the frustration that she'd let the threat of secondhand knowledge run her out of town. Amazingly, the physical exertion made her feel better.

She kicked a large rock and felt the satisfying *thunk* reverberate through her entire body. "That's for me!" she shouted, giving vent to her anger.

Picking up a clod of earth, she threw it against a stump. "And that's for Aiden!" She grabbed a branch of pine and stripped it of its needles. "And that's for Jacob," she sobbed. A dry, heart-wrenching sob that failed to bring the release of tears. She used the branch as a whip against the ground. "That's for Jacob."

Jacob.

She'd left him five years ago because she'd been afraid Ellie Able could derail his calling...and because she'd been afraid he couldn't love another man's child. She worried still that Ellie could create enough trouble to harm Jacob's position at Grace Everlasting, but in four days she'd seen enough to know that Jacob loved her son.

She'd seen it in his eyes and in his voice and in the tender way he'd helped her care for Aiden when he'd fallen. She'd seen it especially in the way Jacob had brought laughter to her son's lips.

She flung the branch away from her in disgust. For five years of lost opportunity, damn Drew Paxton to hell.

She kicked a stump and, as splinters of wood rained about her, felt her rage energize her. Felt shame retreat before her newfound strength. Her newfound resolve.

She would not let Drew Paxton have another minute of her life.

She would no longer be a victim.

She would hold her head up high and choose her future based upon her own needs as well as the needs of others.

She would not be railroaded by the likes of Ellie Able.

Giving the stump one final kick, she felt tears sting the corners of her eyes and threaten to overflow. Instead of weeping, however, unexpected laughter bubbled up inside her. Laughter and an incredible sense of lightness. As if an enormous weight had been lifted from her heart as she'd given herself these new goals.

She felt release.

"Oh, Jacob," she said aloud, a smile spreading across her entire face, "there's something to this stump kicking."

Suddenly, desperately wanting to see Aiden and Jacob, Cathryn began to run through the tall, still, winter-pale grasses. Startling a covey of mourning doves, she laughed as they took flight sounding as if they needed a good oiling.

It felt so good to have released the anger. The anger she'd forgotten that she harbored. It felt so good to be alive. Alive to explore the possibilities of the future. Had her healing process really begun? Had the first steps really been there all along? Obvious. Simple. Starting with a declaration that she would take back her life. A declaration that it was all right—more than all right—to demand that her own wants and needs be filled.

With an intoxicating sense of buoyancy, she skipped along the roadside until she could see Grace Everlasting.

Until a red convertible barreled past her on the narrow country road, spewing rocks and clouds of dust as it fishtailed on and off the shoulder. My, my. She scowled. Perhaps she wasn't the only one filled with anger today. But at least she'd taken her anger out in an empty piney grove without the chance of harming others. Who was that fool with the Tennessee tags?

The car turned into the church parking lot and squealed to a stop before the administration building steps. She heard a door slam. Heard the engine rev. And before she herself could set foot onto the church grounds, the car flew past her once again, leaving only dust and the smell of exhaust.

And the image of a very irate Missy Able driving hell-bent for leather.

Now, what could that be about? Cathryn turned toward the church complex to see Rhune Sherman slapping the dust from his clothing. He looked up, saw her and gave a rueful, lopsided grin. Cathryn shook her head in return, but couldn't help the smile that crept to her lips. What had this bad boy gotten himself into now?

She strode across the church parking lot. "Mr. Sherman," she called out in greeting.

"Miss O'Malley." He gave his tropical shirt a final swat. "It's been a while since I've been home, but this isn't quite the way I recall Southern hospitality."

Cathryn chuckled. "Let's just say you've sampled the Able brand."

Rhune's eyes crinkled in a wince. "Sounds like you've sampled it yourself."

"Oh, I've had my share of tangles with mama bear Able."

"Then it's not just me? Because I'm an out-of-towner?"

Suddenly Cathryn felt an odd bond with this rascally Rhune. "No. It's the town itself. Small. Sort of like a goldfish bowl. To survive, you have to be true to yourself, develop a thick skin and a sense of humor."

She could barely believe the words she heard her own mouth utter. What release her earlier venting had brought. Bless Jacob for sending her out to kick stumps. She owed him one.

Rhune looked as if he were checking himself for broken bones. "Well, I guess I'll have to weigh all that in the balance if I'm to consider settling down here."

"Rhune Sherman, I can only imagine that a town the size of Sweet Hope would cramp your style."

He looked at her with a mixture of candor and that haunted quality she'd seen only once before. "My style may very well need a change."

Cathryn harrumphed. "Then you've come to the wrong town. In Sweet Hope first impressions linger, making change an uphill battle."

"I take it that's where the thick skin and the sense of humor come in."

"Who needs a thick skin?" Rhune and Cathryn turned to see Jacob approaching, with Aiden riding high on his shoulders.

There was something different in the picture of Cathryn and Rhune before Jacob. He reached up to make certain Aiden was still secure on his perch, and then it hit him: More than the fact that Cathryn seemed totally at ease was the realization that he—Jacob—did not feel jealousy at the sight of her with Rhune. Cathryn seemed much more sure of herself, while he himself had more confidence. Confidence where Cathryn was concerned.

Odd how in the hour they'd been apart they both seemed to have let go of something hard and tight in their lives. Both seemed to have grown. Jacob couldn't be certain what had done it for Cathryn, but for him the calm assurance had come in the form of the small boy riding his shoulders.

Because of Aiden, Jacob felt surer of the path he wanted to take than at any other time in his life. Because of Aiden, he felt certain his dreams were possible.

"Who needs a thick skin?" he asked again as he came to a halt before Cathryn and Rhune.

Cathryn looked up at him, her face aglow with luminescent candor. "We were just talking about how small towns can be tough on the psyche."

Rhune rubbed his neck. "Psyche, hell!" He tossed a sheepish grin in Jacob's direction. "Sorry, Pastor. But I was just thinking small towns can be mighty tough on the body, as well."

Aiden bent and whispered in Jacob's ear. "Pastor Jacob, who is that man?"

Jacob patted Aiden's leg and thought a minute. "Aiden, let me introduce you to Mr. Rhune. I do believe he's your great-uncle on your Nonny Belle's side of the family."

Rhune smiled up at Aiden. "Don't let appearances fool you, Aiden. I do make a great uncle once I get cleaned up."

"That's okay," Aiden offered soberly from his perch. "I like to play in the dirt, too."

Cathryn's laughter rippled on the spring air. "I've just come back from a little playing in the dirt myself. And I'm hungry. Does that offer of snacks still hold, Pastor Jacob?"

"It sure does. Aiden and I were just coming to fetch you."

"Mind if I join you?" Rhune asked.

Jacob looked at Cathryn and saw happiness. A new strength. A return of the old Cassie O'Malley vitality. The sight made him magnanimous. "Not at all," he replied sincerely. "I believe there's room for a great-uncle in the group."

As they turned to enter the building, Jacob, curious, asked, "Cathryn, how was your walk?"

The laughter in her eyes flashed like summer lightning. "Terrific. I owe you one."

Rhune shoved his hand into his back jeans pocket and fished out a twisted pair of sunglasses. He shrugged, rolled his eyes, then leveled a scowl that was more show than substance at Jacob. "If you're interested, *you* owe *me* one."

Jacob examined Rhune's rumpled appearance and thought of Missy Able. It didn't seem as if things had worked out between the two. He felt just a twinge of conscience.

Clapping Rhune on the back, he asked, "How do you feel about cherry suckers?"

After supper Cathryn and Alice Rose joined several dozen parishioners at the far end of the gymnasium as they sorted through piles of donated clothing, tagging them according to size and gender.

"Lordy," Alice Rose murmured to her granddaughter, "I'm dead on my feet. I sure could use a nice hot bath in my own bathroom and a night's sleep in my own bed."

"I'll second that." Cathryn rubbed her sore neck muscles. "Any chance we can get back in your house before Aiden and I leave?"

"Well . . . we could, I suppose. The power's back on for most of the town, and my farm has only minor roofing damage. . . ."

Cathryn brightened at the thought of a little privacy, but then she looked around at the still-full gymnasium. She'd heard the stories of the other parishioners—tales of woe far more serious than anything the O'Malleys had sustained as a result of the storm. She looked at her grandmother, who avoided her gaze. "But there's still so much to be done here, Grammy. How could we leave when we've been relatively fortunate, and others still need our help?"

Alice Rose turned a brilliant smile on Cathryn before she hugged her. "I knew you'd understand. You may live in Albany—*temporarily*—but Sweet Hope is your home."

Cathryn shook the child's pair of jeans she'd picked from the enormous pile. No matter how she tried to avoid it, that undeniable fact kept staring her in her face: Sweet Hope was indeed her home. She folded the jeans, tagged them, then laid them in the children's pile. It was simply tough luck that circumstances prevented her from living at home.

Giggles and whispers from a group of teenage girls nearby jolted Cathryn out of her wandering thoughts. Glancing in their direction, she recognized Brie from the day care and Harriet from the softball game and several of their friends. At first she couldn't determine the object of their blush-filled merriment. Probably one of the high school boys stranded as they all were.

And then she saw Jacob not far from their group.

He was wearing a polo shirt and a casual pair of khakis, and, as the child's mother looked on, he lifted a toddler above his head in fun. Every time Jacob lowered the child, she would clamor for more. It wasn't an unusual scene. For the past four days Cathryn had seen Jacob, when he wasn't working, playing with the children. But tonight the teenage girls next to Cathryn seemed to find the pastor and his activities fascinating.

Cathryn looked more closely. She had to admit that, smiling and tanned and with that midnight lock of hair fallen over one eye, he looked strikingly handsome. The fact that his muscles rippled every time he lifted the child did nothing to detract from the picture. Cathryn blushed, and as she did so, the group of girls looked over at her. Obviously thinking they'd discovered another covert admirer, they burst into giggles.

Cathryn felt mortification intensify her blush.

She turned back to her work only to find Alice Rose staring at her, that infernal Cheshire-cat grin on her face. "Grammy!" she exclaimed.

"There's nothing wrong with looking, child." Her grin widened, if that was possible. "Our pastor sets his share of hearts aflutter."

"You are incorrigible." Cathryn threw her hand over her heart in a mock swoon. "My heart is not aflutter." She scowled at her grandmother. "May I remind you that Jacob and I are *just friends.*"

"Ah, sweet thing." Alice Rose reached out and touched Cathryn's flame-hot cheek. "True love is friendship set on fire."

Cathryn could find no words to answer. How could she when it was becoming more and more evident, hour by hour, that the pastor Jacob Matthews did indeed set her heart aflutter?

All evening Jacob had been mingling with his parishioners, listening to their concerns, offering what comfort and encouragement he could. All evening he'd been torn between the needs of his congregation and his own need to see Cathryn. Now the evening had drawn to a close. It was almost time for lights-out. And Cathryn was within sight.

He said good-night to Sarah Kimball and her two-year-old daughter, Megan, nodded to the group of unusually giggly teenage girls sorting donated clothing, then came to a stop before Cathryn and Alice Rose.

"Hey," he said softly, suddenly feeling tongue-tied.

"Hey, yourself," Alice Rose answered. Cathryn merely smiled before lowering her eyes to a shirt she tagged.

In the silence that followed, he entertained a fleeting thought: What would it feel like after a full day of pastoral duties to be standing here ready to take his wife and son home? At the risk of sounding blasphemous, he thought it would feel heavenly.

Alice Rose made a show of looking at her watch. "My, my, where has the time gone?"

She lifted up some of the clothing that draped over the table edge, and Jacob could see Aiden and Margaret underneath, playing in their makeshift cave. He smiled. That Aiden and his caves.

"Come on, children," Alice Rose clucked. "Time to wash up for bed."

"Aww!" In harmony, the children protested.

"Come on out and give us a hug. Then it's off to the washroom. I'm in charge of your washup tonight, and we might just detour by the kitchen for brownies and milk."

That got a reaction. Aiden and Margaret scrambled out from under the table and threw themselves upon Cathryn and Jacob in hurried hugs. Then Alice Rose hugged first Cathryn, then Jacob. "Good night, you two."

"Good night," Jacob and Cathryn answered in unison.

Before Alice Rose and the children turned to leave, Aiden piped up. "Everyone hugged 'cept you and Pastor Jacob, Mama."

"My, my," Alice Rose agreed, her eyes twinkling. "That's true."

Jacob watched as color crept into Cathryn's cheeks. Before her confession last night he might have taken advantage of Aiden's innocent observation and Alice Rose's matchmaking. But tonight, knowing Cathryn's difficulty with touching, he could only feel her discomfort.

He ruffled Aiden's hair. "It's not time for grown-up hugs. We still have work to do before bedtime. Now, scoot, you two."

Alice Rose cast Cathryn and him a probing glance before she said, "Brownies, young'uns!"

"Brownies!" Aiden and Margaret chorused as they clasped hands and preceded Alice Rose through the crowded gym.

Leaving Jacob standing next to an obviously flustered Cathryn.

He wondered if she was uncomfortable because he now knew her secret...or...after the kiss they'd shared last night, was she uncomfortable because she now saw him as more than Jacob the friend, Jacob the pastor. Was it possible that Cathryn saw him simply as Jacob the man?

If so, did he repulse her, or—Jacob reminded himself that miracles do happen—did he attract her? He needed to find out. Maybe not tonight. But soon. And he needed to gather this information gently, so as not to destroy any progress Cathryn might have made. Gently, too, he needed to show her that friendship could blossom into something deeper. In defiance of the hurt from the past.

"You've worked hard," he said finally. Simply. "I just wanted to stop by and thank you."

She looked up at him, and her clear blue gaze seemed relieved that he hadn't pressed the hugging issue. "I should be thanking you. I really didn't want to come home. But since I've been here, I've learned a lot about myself and my son. Thanks to you."

He smiled. "My pleasure."

"No. *My* pleasure," she contradicted softly, never taking her gaze from his.

His heart did a somersault. Now, this was progress.

Chapter Eleven

Responsibility weighed heavily upon Jacob's shoulders.

He ripped the Tuesday date off his desk calendar and threw it in the wastebasket. Taking a long swig of coffee, he glanced out his window to where the Wednesday sun barely cracked the horizon. The day had just begun, and he'd already made decisions that were sure to rankle some of his congregation.

He held in one hand a list of all the families in Grace Everlasting, ordered from most needful after the storm to the least. As volunteers poured in from all over the south and beyond, he'd organized work crews to help with cleanup. Today two new crews were ready to tackle two more homes.

Ellie Able's home was still far down the list.

After the squabble in his office yesterday, he was tempted to move her up the list. Not to get her off his back, but to get her off Cathryn's.

But fair was fair. The two families scheduled for help today needed aid far more than Ellie. In fact, Ellie, if her grown children Missy and Sonny could see their way to break from their busy lives to help their mother, could be in her home now. Her property had suffered only a few missing roof tiles, a couple of broken windows, some distressed landscaping. But, Jacob guessed, Ellie preferred being at the shelter with her nose in everybody's business, pushing her own agenda, roiling the waters.

By herself, she was merely a thorn in his side. But if she decided to muster support, as she'd implied in her threat yesterday, she could spell real trouble. And Jacob didn't need real trouble at the moment. Not with his congregation's need to get back on its feet as quickly as possible after the storm. Not with his own need to convince Cathryn before Saturday that her place was right here in Sweet Hope. At his side.

No, he definitely didn't need Ellie Able implying that he labored under a conflict of interest. And what would moving Ellie up the list be, if not a conflict of interest? Buying her off, so to speak, to protect Cathryn.

Cathryn had made it clear that she didn't need or want protecting.

He looked down at the list in his hand. The order would stay. In the short term, his decision might cause problems, but in the long term, it was fair. He'd handle any short-term flack Ellie might dish out as it arose. If need be, he'd call Missy and Sonny to get them down here to settle their mother in. Lord, you'd think grown children would have sense enough on their own to see what needed doing.

He heard the door to his office creak. Looking up, he saw Cathryn peeking around the door.

"Good morning," she said sleepily. "What gets you up so early?"

"Good morning." Just looking at her sensuous, sleep-washed face, Jacob felt the day improve dramatically. He shrugged. "There aren't enough hours in the day. I have two new work crews coming in an hour. I just thought I'd make double sure we're ready for them. What are you doing up?"

"Couldn't sleep." She raised a mug of coffee, then stepped around the door and into the room. "I was just coming from the kitchen when I noticed the light under your door. Do you need help?''

''No. You don't need to come in for a few more hours. Go have your coffee with your family. Have breakfast with Aiden and get him settled in the nursery school.''

As much as Jacob wanted Cathryn to stay, maybe even needed her to stay, Aiden needed her more. Living in the shelter, if only temporarily, was a pretty haphazard existence. A four-year-old would need all the stability possible. Like starting the morning with his family.

The beginning of a smile tipped the corners of her pert mouth. Jacob found it difficult not to dwell on the delicious memory of her lips against his in the kiss they'd shared less than forty-eight hours ago.

A quizzical look passed over her face as she gazed steadily into his eyes. ''Do you want to talk about something?'' she asked. ''I can spare a few minutes.''

Do you want to talk about something? Funny how those simple words triggered a host of complicated memories.

How many times during those emotion-packed days five years ago had either he or she asked the other that very same thing? Too many times to count, surely. But every time, the talking had eased the pain or the confusion or the trepidation.

In the past few days, however, Cathryn hadn't often offered to talk. Jacob wasn't about to pass up the chance now.

''Sure,'' he said. ''Pull up a chair.''

He leaned against his desk as Cathryn curled up in an old reading chair under the window, looking for all the world as if she'd just settled down to stay. The sight tugged at his heartstrings. She eyed him expectantly.

He put down his coffee mug and shoved his hands deep into his pockets. ''You wouldn't have a magic wand to clean up this storm mess, untangle bureaucratic red tape, mend old feuds and add a few more sleep hours to the day, now, would you?'' His words came out in a rush.

Her eyes twinkled. ''Jacob Matthews, you're looking to *me* for magic? I'm the practical one, remember? All I have are two capable hands.'' Her expression stilled and grew serious. ''But this week they're at your disposal.''

He was touched by her offer. ''Thank you.'' He smiled. ''You know the Matthews magic is just window dressing. Faith is the real thing. The magic may be temporarily gone, but the faith's still intact. It gets a little jolt of renewal every time someone like you comes along to lend a helping hand.''

Cathryn unwound herself from the chair. ''Well then, today let's use the practical O'Malley approach and take this morning one step at a time. I'll concentrate on the red tape. You concentrate on keeping people's spirits up. We'll share any unexpected task that comes our way. Then, at noon, I suggest we pat ourselves on the back, go meet Aiden and sneak a picnic lunch down by the stream.'' The mischievous sparkle had returned to her eyes. ''Just to check on the tadpoles and the status of small miracles.''

''Cathryn O'Malley, are you asking me on a date?''

She quirked an eyebrow. ''How you do jump to conclusions, suh,'' she answered in a mock drawl. ''I'm merely suggesting we try to grab a few moments of peace and quiet in this goldfish bowl you call a parish. Now, if you'll excuse me to have breakfast with my family, I'll see you at eight sharp for work.''

With a parting smile, she slipped out the door before Jacob could even utter a *See you.*

He felt joy trickle through him and suddenly laughed aloud. Say what she would, a picnic lunch by the stream sure sounded like a date to him.

As the church bell rang twelve, Cathryn rubbed her eyes in relief. What a morning.

It seemed that her ear had been glued to the phone. As the power went on in their little section of northwest Georgia, as crews cleared the roads and as the sheriff's department eased the ban on travel, the parishioners of Grace Everlasting began to trickle back to their homes, either to move in and tough it out, or to assess the damage and return to the church shelter for a few more days. Cathryn had thought that when the period of intense confinement was over, things would become less complicated.

Not so. In fact, it seemed as if the venture back out into the world added a whole new host of worries, a whole new level of challenges. And it appeared that Grace Everlasting was going to be the hub of support for many weeks to come.

Rubbing the back of her neck, she surveyed the office. What a mess. The paperwork generated by the storm had created, if not a tornado, then a veritable landslide.

Jacob entered the room, a man and a woman in business suits and serious expressions in tow. He began an obviously fruitless search under the mound of papers on his desk.

Cathryn stepped to his side. "What are you looking for?" she asked gently.

"Have you seen my laptop?"

Smiling, Cathryn reached into the filing cabinet. "Now, that's a problem I can rectify." She hauled the computer from the *L* file. "A place for everything, and everything in its place," she said briskly, handing him the piece of equipment.

"And that's one place you won't have to look for it," Jacob muttered with a lopsided grin.

"You look as if you could use some lunch," Cathryn whispered.

"Give me fifteen minutes. Tops," he whispered back as if they were coconspirators. "Thanks," he then said in his most businesslike voice. "Now, Mr. Tutwiler, Ms. Aikens, let me show you the figures. I think there's a clear table just outside in the hallway."

Cathryn switched on the phone's answering machine, then stepped into the small lavatory adjoining the office.

At the sink she splashed cold water on her face, then dried it with a paper towel. Glancing in the mirror, she ran damp fingers through her hair. She felt a sudden surge of anticipation mixed with apprehension. What had she gone and done by inviting Jacob to a picnic lunch?

Early this morning her impulsive gesture had seemed merely like one friend encouraging another. But with the butterflies in her stomach and Jacob's teasing question in her ears, it was beginning to seem more like a date.

A date in the middle of disaster. How silly.

It wasn't a date.

Giving her clothing a perfunctory pat, Cathryn returned to the empty office. Jacob, it seemed, was still tied up. She walked to the window and gazed out into the April sunshine. How could it be such a warm spring day while she suffered a case of the goose bumps? She rubbed her arms vigorously to warm them.

"Ready?" From behind, Jacob's deep, rich voice infused with a trace of laughter startled her. "For our date."

Date? With a deliberately casual movement, she turned to face him. If his voice had startled her, his body language unnerved her even more.

His gray gaze riveted upon her, he leaned easily against the doorframe, his dark eyebrows arched mischievously, his infectious grin setting the tone. "Ready?" he asked again.

She managed an offhanded shrug. "I'm ready. But the Lord only knows why you persist in calling this a date."

Grinning, he pushed a lock of hair off his forehead. "Would it bother you if it was?"

"Not at all." She wrinkled her nose and shook her head and tried not to look into his laughing eyes. "I think I've proved to you in the last few days that I can handle far greater challenges than a date...if it was a date...which it's not...." Feeling heat rise to her cheeks, she sputtered and ran out of steam.

He chuckled. The low, throaty, sensuous sound reached Cathryn's ears and made a delicious shiver run down her spine.

"Okay, no date," he agreed. He held out his hand toward the open doorway. "Let's go get Aiden."

She took a deep breath, squared her shoulders and attempted to look all business. But something in Jacob's smile made her soften. Let's face it. She'd never been able to be in the presence of the Matthews smile without feeling...well, *good.*

He wore her down. The man quite simply wore her down.

With a laugh she linked her arm in his. "Come on," she said, smiling up at him. "Let's go get Aiden."

Jacob and Cathryn stood in the noon sun waiting for Belle and the other teachers and volunteers to bring the children out on their way to the dining hall for the midday meal. Cathryn clutched three box lunches that Alice Rose had eagerly provided.

"There he is." Jacob first spotted Aiden and felt the newly familiar joy rise within him at the sight of the boy. Was this in any way what it felt like to be a father?

"Aiden!" Cathryn called to her son, and Belle, with a wink and a wave, dismissed him.

Instead of running to his mother as was usual, Aiden seemed to dawdle, an expression of little-boy dejection written on his features.

Immediately Cathryn laid a hand on his forehead. "Are you feeling all right, pumpkin?"

"I'm fine," he replied, shrugging away from her touch.

"We brought a picnic lunch." She held out the box lunches. "Pimento cheese sandwiches. Your favorite."

Aiden didn't rise to the enticement. Instead, he scuffed the toe of his shoe in the dirt.

"Do you want to talk about this morning in school?" Jacob asked. It pained him to see the boy so unusually diffident.

Aiden looked up into Jacob's eyes. "It wasn't a very good morning."

"Why not?" Jacob held out his hand and Aiden took it.

"At recess some kids wanted to play softball." He shook his head in disgust. "I'm lousy."

Jacob gently squeezed Aiden's hand. "Well, if that's the problem, we have a state championship solution right here."

"You do?" The boy's doubtful expression brightened the tiniest bit.

Jacob glanced at Cathryn, who nodded and grinned.

"We sure do," he replied, beginning to walk toward the softball fields. "Did you know your mama is a softball star?"

"*Was,*" Cathryn interjected.

Jacob winked. "Still is, according to Grace Everlasting scuttlebutt."

"What's *scuttlebutt?*" Aiden squinched up his face.

"Talk." Jacob chuckled. "And the talk is that your mama is still a dazzler at softball."

"Is that true, Mama?"

"I was good," Cathryn answered truthfully. "And I still love the game. But, hey, did you know that Pastor Jacob's not bad either when it comes to softball?"

Aiden began to jump up and down. "Then could you teach me? Could you both teach me?"

"After lunch," Jacob assured him, "we'll begin."

"All right!" Aiden released Jacob's hand, then raced to the nearest softball diamond. "All right!"

Cathryn laughed aloud, and Jacob turned to look at her. "You know," he said, "I may have opened a can of worms."

"How could you have? Look at how happy he is."

"He may grow to love the game."

"And?"

"And I hear tell Grace Everlasting has the most fun softball league for children in the state of Georgia. Bar none." He winked. "If he loves the game, it would be a shame to have him play anywhere else."

Trying to juggle the box lunches, Cathryn reached out and playfully swatted Jacob. "Pastor Matthews, you are incorrigible. Manipulative. Sneaky. And just downright... incorrigible. It's a wonder the Lord lets you retain your position as pastor."

Her laughter was marvelous. Warm, throaty and catching. Clearly, something had changed since Cathryn took her solitary walk yesterday afternoon. The tension around her eyes had disappeared. There seemed to be a new lightness in her step. More laughter in her voice. And, wonder of wonders, she seemed at times to reach out to him. Not so much physically, but emotionally. As with the invitation to picnic in the first place.

Just the three of them.

She glanced at her watch. "Well, if we're going to instill a love of the game in that boy, we're going to have to quit dallying. I figure Grace Everlasting and its demands won't give us much more than forty-five free minutes."

Perhaps not. But Jacob silently vowed to make every second count.

Once seated on the huge equipment box, they wolfed down their food. All three, apparently, were eager to get to the main event—Aiden's softball lesson. Jacob knew, for certain, he was.

Because Aiden insisted he was lousiest at hitting, they began with batting practice. Jacob took the mound. Cathryn squatted behind the plate. Aiden, his batting helmet askew, hunched over the plate and glared at Jacob.

"That's it!" Jacob called out to keep from chuckling at the boy's intensity. "First rule in good batting—put on your most ferocious face."

"Jacob!" Cathryn objected. "What kind of ball are you teaching my son?"

"Aww, Mama." Aiden tapped the bat on home plate. "Let me do it. It's the thing I'm bestest at."

Laughing, Cathryn lowered her catcher's mask. "All right, you two! Play ball!"

Jacob made a great display of winding up, but he finally lobbed a gentle pitch over the plate. Aiden took a gigantic cut at the ball. And missed.

Neither adult said a word as Cathryn threw the ball back to Jacob.

Aiden smacked the bottom of each of his shoes with the bat. "It's okay. You can say it. Strike one."

Jacob grinned. "You know about strikes?"

Aiden nodded his head dejectedly. "I know all 'bout strikes."

Jacob's heart clenched with love for this solemn boy.

Aiden shouldered his bat, his face set in grim determination, as behind the plate Cathryn, her gaze filled with maternal concern, stared at Jacob. As if the two of them, locked eye-to-eye, could will a hit for her son.

Jacob wound up again. "Ready?"

"Ready." Aiden and Cathryn answered at the same time.

As Jacob released the pitch, Aiden swung, turning in a complete circle before the ball even crossed the plate.

The ball dropped into Cathryn's glove. "Strike two," she announced evenly.

With a dignity Jacob didn't know four-year-olds possessed, Aiden stepped to the plate once more.

Jacob caught the ball Cathryn threw him. "Aiden... son... don't look at me. Keep your eye on the ball. Don't swing till I say, *now.*"

Aiden nodded his head in sober agreement.

Jacob wound up and said a quick, silent prayer. Dear Lord, I know this seems inconsequential, but if you love little boys and softball, this child could use a hit.

He released the ball.

Just as it reached the perfect point of descent in its arch, both Jacob and Cathryn called out, *"Now!"*

Aiden swung and connected. A wobbly little hit that stayed airborne only seconds before it hit the dirt in front of the pitcher's mound. But a hit nonetheless.

"Run!" Cathryn shouted with glee. "First base, Aiden! Run! Over there!" She gesticulated wildly toward first.

With a yelp, Aiden began to run.

Jacob made an exaggerated lunge for the ball, deliberately missing it.

Aiden, looking over his shoulder, shrieked triumphantly.

"Run, Aiden!" Cathryn had turned into a one-woman cheering squad.

Jacob picked up the ball and bobbled it as if it were a hot potato.

Aiden jumped with two feet on the first base bag, raising miniclouds of dust.

"Run to second!" Cathryn shouted. "Go! Go! Pastor Jacob can't control the ball."

His arms pumping madly, Aiden raced down the baseline to second.

As if it were a Hacky Sack, Jacob swatted the ball with his heel, with his elbow, with any part of his body that made him look as if he'd truly lost control. In fact, the laughter that bubbled up from deep within him did indeed make control difficult.

At second, Aiden needed no encouragement to try for third, and then home.

On the home stretch, however, Jacob took control of the ball and made as if he would chase the boy down. Aiden yipped delightedly and detoured far outside the baseline, losing his batting helmet in the process.

"Come on, Aiden!" Cathryn shouted, jumping up and down behind home plate.

Jacob lunged with a mock growl. "No one gets a home run off me. I'm Jacob, the world's greatest softball pitcher." He made as if to tag Aiden, but missed by a mile.

Aiden gave out a tremendous belly laugh, then threw himself on home plate. "I did! I did!" he shrieked in exultation. "I went 'round all the bases, I did!"

In mock defeat, Jacob tossed the ball onto the pitcher's mound. "You did. You surely did," he agreed, unable to contain the joy and laughter within him.

He reached home plate just as a beaming Cathryn scooped her son up off the ground and swung him high on her hip. Aiden wrapped his arms around her neck and planted an enormous kiss on her cheek. Cathryn returned the kiss, then reached out her free arm to encircle Jacob's neck. She drew him close and planted a resounding kiss on his cheek.

Jacob put his arms around both Cathryn and Aiden and drew them close. Drew close the two dearest people in his life.

He felt the sunshine on his back, smelled and almost tasted the dust Aiden's "home run" had raised, heard the sound of birds mix with the heavenly sound of laughter. And saw the smiles on Cathryn's and Aiden's faces.

Could life get any sweeter?

His heart told him no... not unless moments such as this could be a daily possibility. Not unless Cathryn chose to stay in Sweet Hope. At his side.

He reached out to brush a wisp of hair from Cathryn's cheek. She neither shrank from his touch nor withdrew her smile. Instead, she looked at him with an open, blue-eyed gaze that showed undeniable ease. And happiness.

And trust.

Aiden wriggled in her arms. "Let's play some more."

Cathryn gave him a peck on the cheek. "Not now, sport. Pastor Jacob and I have to get back to work."

"And *you*..." Jacob chucked him under the chin. "You have to get back to school to show off your game."

"Yeah." Aiden slithered out of his mother's grasp. Almost before he hit the ground he began to run in the direction of the classrooms. "Come on!" he shouted when it looked as if the adults were going to dawdle.

As they began to head back, Jacob shook his head. "I guess you're just going to have to drive all the way up from Albany twice a week this summer."

"Why's that?"

"Softball for Aiden's age group meets Tuesday and Thursday."

"*You*," she said softly, smiling. But she didn't say no.

No siree, she didn't say no.

Jacob gazed heavenward and grinned. Now, who would have guessed softball could work such wonders?

Cathryn began to turn off the office lights. She glanced at the stack of paperwork neither she nor Jacob had touched this afternoon and the answering machine light blinking furiously. She'd come back only to close up the office, but the practical side of her wouldn't let her leave without, at least, transcribing the messages on the machine. She'd leave a copy on the chair to Jacob's desk and carry a copy with her in case she ran into Jacob at lights-out in the gym.

She hadn't seen him all afternoon.

The minute they'd returned from the picnic and Aiden's softball lesson, Jacob had been called to the hospital. Evan Young, a Grace Everlasting parishioner, had suffered a heart attack while clearing his property. His family feared the worst, and had called for Jacob.

Cathryn had intended to spend the afternoon alone in the office, but Suki Edwards had impressed her into service filling fresh water jugs from two tankers sent from Atlanta. Having spent hours at that task under the warm April sun, Cathryn ached in every part of her body. She crinkled her nose and felt the definite sting of sunburn. After supper, about the only thing she'd thought she had energy for was shutting out the lights in Jacob's office.

But now, faced with an answering machine full of messages, she thought of Jacob and how emotionally drained he must feel by now. She thought, too, of the Young family and their ordeal. Her aches and pains seemed to pale by comparison. The least she could do was to transcribe the messages. She glanced at her watch. It was only eight o'clock.

Sitting in the desk chair, Cathryn switched on the recordings. After several messages she was surprised to hear Jacob's deep voice. Even on tape, she could hear a bone-weary thread woven through it.

"Cassie, it looks as if I'll be here at the hospital through supper. Why don't you close up the office and spend some time with your family. I'll see you tomorrow. And thanks for all your help. I couldn't have done it without you."

Oh, sure you could have, Cathryn thought. You, Jacob Matthews, can do *anything* you set your mind to.

Including setting her pulse to skittering every time he used her old nickname. Ever since Saturday she'd asked him to call her Cathryn, but he hadn't. At first her nickname, bringing a simple reminder of the past, had jarred her. But now, somehow, it seemed fitting on Jacob's lips. And, somehow, deliberate.

She smiled and laid her head on her arms folded on the desk. Did Jacob know the reaction he invoked in her? There were times when she actually thought he'd embarked upon a program of sorts to deliberately gentle her. As one would gentle and tame a wild creature.

Five days ago she would have found that thought abhorrent. But tonight? Tonight, well . . . She sighed and let her eyelids flutter closed. If the truth be known, for five years she'd felt like a skittish wild creature. A little gentling in her life couldn't hurt. And it couldn't hurt to let Jacob call her

Cassie. It felt good. It felt good also to sit in his chair and remember the warm rumble of his voice. It felt good to work side by side with him. To be of help. To feel special.

Cherished.

"Cassie."

Cathryn stretched languorously. How sensuous her nickname sounded on his lips.

"Cassie."

She felt someone gently jiggle her shoulder. Opening one eye, she saw Jacob standing beside her. A feeling of total confusion washed over her. Where was she?

"What time is it?" she asked, rubbing her eyes and remembering that she sat at Jacob's office desk.

"Eight-twenty. Have you been here all afternoon?"

She shook her head to dispel the cobwebs. "No. I just came in to close up." Then she saw the lines of fatigue etched on his face. She stood. "How are things with the Young family. How's Evan?"

"It was touch and go for a time." Jacob ran his fingers through his hair. "But it looks as if he's going to make it." He smiled a weary smile. "Never underestimate the power of prayer. With the size of the Young family, I think you could say we stormed heaven with our petitions this afternoon."

"You must be exhausted."

"I am. But a good kind of exhausted."

"Good? With all the tension of this afternoon?"

"Would you believe that, in the midst of all the worry today, the most joyous thing happened? As we prayed for Evan, Ted Hall brought his wife, Courtney, in to deliver their first child. A healthy baby girl."

Cathryn sighed. "A small miracle."

"A small miracle," Jacob repeated softly. "It kept us all going." He paused. "And do you know what else kept me going?"

Looking into his tired eyes, she knew that whatever it was, she was part of it. And, strangely enough, the thought didn't frighten her. "What else?" she asked quietly.

"The thought that, at the end of this long, tiring, emotion-filled day, you'd be here at Grace Everlasting." As he said the words, he reached out and brushed her cheek with his fingertips.

Instead of pulling away, Cathryn closed her eyes and leaned into Jacob's touch. Closed her eyes and let sensations wash over her. Sensations of peace. And of trust. And of belonging.

She opened her eyes and looked deep into his eyes. Realization jolted her: no man had ever made her feel the way Jacob made her feel.

Loved.

He smiled. His gaze was as soft as a caress. "It doesn't frighten you when I say that?"

"No," she whispered. "It doesn't frighten me."

What frightened her was the thought of losing him again.

He removed his fingertips from her cheek. "Do I frighten you, Cassie? I have to ask. Have to know."

Her heart leapt and her pulse skittered, but it wasn't from fear.

"No," she answered, feeling her breath catch in her throat. "You don't frighten me. Up until now, what has frightened me is the possibility that my feelings for you would carry me only so far. And then my past would twist them. Make it impossible for those feelings to take their full and natural course."

Jacob's face registered surprise and then anticipation. "*Up until now?* Has something changed?"

"I've changed." There, she'd admitted it. "You've helped me change. From now on, I'm going to give some thought to me. To my needs and wants. To the future rather than to the past."

The corners of his mouth twitched in the beginning of a smile. His eyes lost their tired cast and sparkled now with definite interest. "And in this new future of yours, tell me some of the things you won't be afraid of. Specifically."

The sound of his voice, deep and coaxing, made her whole body feel warm and heavy. "Specifically." She cleared her throat to buy some time. She'd come this far; she might as well continue. "Specifically, I'm not afraid to tell you how I feel."

His grin widened. "And how do you feel?"

She tried to look away from his now-intent gaze, but found she couldn't. "I like working with you."

He seemed a little disappointed.

"I also like the times Aiden and I spend with you," she continued. "And . . . I like the times we're alone together."

"As friends," he offered.

Her heartbeat skyrocketed. "As more than friends."

Cathryn had never seen Jacob at a loss for words, but he certainly seemed stunned speechless now. For too long she'd pushed him away, and pushed him away. No wonder the poor man froze now at this apparent turnaround.

Without thinking, she stood on tiptoe and touched her lips to his.

Ah, his lips were anything but frozen. His lips were warm and oh, so inviting. His mouth yielded under hers as she felt him enfold her in his embrace.

This time she felt no urge to flee. This time she knew with certainty that this was where she belonged. In Jacob's arms. She wrapped her arms around his neck as he pulled her closer.

He deepened the kiss and she responded eagerly, feeling a shocked tingle of pleasure. The touch of his lips was a delicious sensation, filling her with warmth and desire. This was no kiss of friendship. Oh, no.

This kiss was for keeps.

Sighing, she pulled away and breathed his name.

He moved one hand to cup the back of her head, holding her so that he could shower feather-light kisses on the corners of her mouth, her cheek, her ear. "Cassie." Her name on his lips was full of tenderness and longing.

In his embrace, she knew full well that the ugly grip of her past had been broken. Tears stung the corners of her eyes. Tears of joy. She stepped back so that she could cup Jacob's face in her hands. So that she could drink in the sight of the man who had brought joy and feeling back into her life.

"Jacob," she whispered, smiling through her tears.

"Jacob," a gruff, disapproving voice interrupted.

Cathryn and Jacob turned to see a tight-lipped Deacon Rush standing in the open office doorway.

Chapter Twelve

Jacob barely had time to catch his breath before Deacon Emory Rush said, "I'd like to talk to you, Jacob. Now more than ever." The man cast a hard look at Cathryn. "In private, if I might."

Emory Rush might be a deacon and one of the most influential members of Grace Everlasting, but Jacob was not about to let him intimidate Cathryn. For that matter, Emory Rush had no business treating Cathryn and Jacob like two teenagers caught in a compromising situation.

Calmly Jacob reached for Cathryn's hand. He squeezed it and said, "I'll be by to say good-night. Thanks for holding down the fort today."

Cathryn met his eyes, and her gaze was strong and clear, without a trace of regret. Only the bright spots of pink that glowed on each of her cheeks hinted at the previous moment's passion. Otherwise, she held her head high with grace and dignity.

She squeezed his hand in return before releasing it. "I'll

see you later." Nodding politely to Emory Rush, she said, "Good night, Deacon," before leaving the office.

Deacon Rush merely grunted in reply.

When Cathryn had closed the door behind her, Jacob asked, "Emory, is there a problem?" No use beating around the bush.

The older man tented his fingers before his ample middle. "Yes, Jacob, I believe there is. But we're willing to talk about it."

"We?"

"Yes. Ellie Able. Edwina and Harry Mapes. Diane and Simon Connors. The Smiths. And myself. We're concerned with the direction your leadership...*ahem*...and your personal life have taken in the past few days."

"I'm more than willing to meet with you to discuss the direction of my leadership." He fixed Deacon Rush with a steely gaze. The older man looked away. "But my personal life—if I've broken none of God's laws nor any civil laws—is just that. Personal."

Deacon Rush's shoulders stiffened perceptibly. When he spoke, it was with clenched jaw. "It's the *seemliness* of your personal life that disturbs us."

"I see." Inwardly, Jacob fumed. Before Cathryn and he had a chance at working on a future, he needed to deal with this persistent and fractious matter. "I don't see the point of you and I discussing this when there seem to be seven other people involved." He drilled Emory Rush with a commanding look. "Do you think you could have the others in my office tomorrow at nine sharp?"

"Why, I don't know," Rush sputtered. "Perhaps. Well, I suppose so. But, you see, I was elected a delegate of sorts."

"To my mind," Jacob declared, trying hard not to let his emotion show, "it seems a little foolish for such a small group to send a delegate when we could have a much more open and honest dialogue with everyone present."

"Well, I don't know if the others would agree."

"I'm extending an invitation to the eight of you to talk tomorrow morning at nine. If anyone chooses not to attend, I will take that as a sign that they've rethought their position."

"Oh, I don't think they'd want you to think that," Rush quickly replied.

"Well, then, I suggest you encourage them to be prompt." Jacob turned to the papers on his desk. "If there's nothing more, I have a great deal of work yet this evening."

Deacon Emory Rush's ears turned hot pink. "No. There's nothing more. I'm sure the eight of us will see you at nine sharp. Good night, Pastor Matthews."

"Good night, Deacon Rush."

When the older man had gone, Jacob counted to twenty before he looked for something to throw. Spying a heavy book, he restrained himself. He would not let this... this *delegate* get to him. Several years ago, when he'd transferred the pastorship of Grace Everlasting, Jacob's father had told Jacob that there would be people who attempted to bog him down with petty matters. His father had urged patience.

But Jacob was quickly losing patience with pettiness.

Mercy, couldn't these people tell the difference between what was of major importance and what was small? Tornadoes were something to get upset about. Putting people's lives back together again was important. A man's heart attack needed attention. And so did the birth of a baby. But to get all hot and bothered over the blossoming relationship between a man and a woman, a relationship born of friendship and of mutual respect... well, Jacob had to admit he didn't understand that one.

He rubbed the back of his neck, and suddenly felt every hour of this emotional day press down upon him.

It was important that his congregation respect him as a man and have confidence in him as a leader. They needed to be able to rely on him. But, as Jacob saw it, this was a two-way street. He needed to be able to rely on his congregation. He was about to take one of the biggest steps in his life, and he needed their support.

He planned to ask Cathryn O'Malley to be his wife.

"Some might say a rash act after only five days of reacquaintance, Pastor Matthews," he said aloud with a grin. He flicked off the office lights. Rash? Not at all. He'd been sure of himself five years ago. It was Cathryn who hadn't been sure.

But the look in her eyes the past twenty-four hours said she might be ready now. Despite her insistence that she would be leaving come Saturday.

He needed to see her once more tonight. To reassure himself he'd read that look right. If he had, there was a good chance he could convince her to stay in Sweet Hope.

He closed the door to his office and headed toward the gymnasium, his heart full of love and optimism for the future.

Cathryn sat in the middle of the empty gymnasium bleachers, nursing a cup of decaffeinated coffee. Except for the bank of lights directly over her head, lights-out had been called. Families, her own included, had settled down for the night in the still-crowded shelter. From where she sat she could see Aiden snuggled in a little ball on his cot. She smiled at the surprising ease with which her son had adapted to their stay in a topsy-turvy Sweet Hope.

For the most part, the room was quiet, and she was alone with her thoughts. Her body cried out for sleep. But her mind simply would not rest.

Thoughts of Jacob and Deacon Rush whirled in her head. Yes, she worried about Jacob. Worried that he might be under attack by a small but mean-spirited segment of his congregation. But Jacob was strong. And principled. He could take care of himself.

The more puzzling thoughts, however, were about Jacob's and her own behavior. Not the kiss in his office. That had seemed so right. Not even the embarrassment of being interrupted by Deacon Rush. But after all that. As Deacon Rush had scowled and fumed his obvious disapproval, Jacob and Cathryn had reached out. Had clasped hands in plain view of the judgmental deacon. And had said by a mutual look that they were not going to keep their feelings for each other under wraps anymore.

Cathryn sipped her coffee. She'd always known Jacob's true feelings. He'd never hidden them. But what about her own? The discovery over the past few days that she had deep feelings—much-more-than-friends feelings—for Jacob had shaken her to her very core. But the realization that those feelings actually made her happy and that she was unafraid of showing her happiness to the world was a thought that boggled the mind.

She smiled and finally admitted to herself, Cathryn O'Malley, I do believe you are in love.

"Is there room for me?" asked Jacob.

Cathryn turned to see him not six feet away, watching her, one foot propped up on the lowest row of the bleachers, his arms crossed and resting on the raised knee. The smile in his eyes a dazzler.

Her whole being filling with a joyous expectation, she patted the seat next to her on the empty bleachers. "There's one seat left, and it's yours."

His gaze traveled over her face and searched her eyes. He must have found what he wanted, because the smile that lit up his face was warm and satisfied. A visual sigh. He climbed the bleachers and sat next to her.

"Did you take care of business with Deacon Rush?" she asked.

"Not yet." He took her hand in his. "We have an appointment to wind it up tomorrow."

"Need a secretary?" She couldn't tell from Jacob's expression if Deacon Rush's business had been unpleasant or if the man himself had merely become unpleasant when he'd found Cathryn and Jacob in an embrace.

"No. It's nothing. Just routine. The meeting should be over by nine-thirty. You can come in then."

The almost imperceptible shadow that passed over Jacob's features made Cathryn pursue the matter. "Are you sure you don't need reinforcements?"

He twined his fingers with hers, then caught and held her with his piercing gray gaze. "Positive. Now, if you don't mind, I've closed the office and have declared the business portion of my day over." His expression softened. "Is Aiden asleep?"

She took a moment to savor the feeling of strength his fingers imparted to her own. "He's making a good show of it, although he's pretty excited. Tomorrow they're making pizza in the classroom."

Jacob's answer was simple yet compelling. "He likes it here."

"Yes." There was no denying it. "He likes it here," she answered softly.

"So, what's keeping you from returning to Sweet Hope, Cassie O'Malley? Returning for good."

Oh, my. She'd asked herself that very question.

Before answering, she studied his face vibrant with expectation. With his gaze he stoked a gently growing fire within her. Jacob. How dear he was to her. The invocation of his name alone made her feel clean and new and bright. With his Matthews magic, with his strength and his faith and his loving persistence, he'd unlocked her heart and soul. Had loosened the heavy, bitter knot that had lain for years at her center. An immovable object.

She loved him. There was no denying it.

And she wanted to return to Sweet Hope.

He sat so close that she could feel the heat from his body, a heat that melted the resolve she'd forged: to take the safe road to the future and return to Albany on Saturday.

"Cassie?" The rumble of his voice pulled her out of her musings. "Tell me what's going on in your mind."

"I'm not used to sharing my thoughts. Not for the past five years, anyway." She raised her chin a fraction of an inch and, in doing so, felt braver. "That's why it comes as such a shock to me to find it's still relatively easy with you."

He made a noise in the back of his throat like a contented purr. "We always seemed right together."

Cathryn looked down at their clasped hands and felt the tingle of a blush creep into her cheeks. "As friends, yes... but did you ever wonder about beyond friendship?"

Jacob chuckled sensuously. "Every day."

She dared a glance at him from under lowered lashes. "I'm not trying to be coy. It's just that...that..." She looked him full in the face. "It's just that you've always treated me with the utmost respect. Except for the last two kisses, I think you could describe our relationship as...well..."

"Chaste?" His eyes sparkled. His mouth curved in a smile of beautiful candor. "Does that bother you?"

"No!" Well, not exactly. But it did have her wondering if life with a pastor was always chaste. At least in tone. "I just wondered if you saw me as a woman, and if you did what, exactly, womanliness meant to you."

"Ah, Cassie." He unwound his fingers from hers, then placed her hand in the palm of his and gently stroked the back of her hand with his thumb. "I have always seen you as a woman. Are you asking me now if I ever envision you as a lover?"

His question seared her senses. "Yes," she answered breathlessly.

There was no mistaking the smoldering yearning in his eyes or the huskiness in his words when he spoke. "If you only knew the unpastorly impulses you've made me feel in the past few days."

She smiled. Somehow the thought delighted her. At the very least, she'd not been alone in her temptation.

His expression grew serious. "If you're asking me whether I envision myself acting upon those impulses outside of marriage, the answer is no. I've always pictured us in the future as husband and wife, friends and lovers. Always those concepts intertwined. Never separate."

Cathryn's pulse stilled. The very air around them seemed charged with electricity. She felt the moment filled with portent.

"What are you saying, Jacob?" she asked, her question barely a whisper.

Taking both her hands in his, he looked deep into her eyes. "I'm saying that I love you, Cassie O'Malley. More now than ever before. And I'm asking you to marry me."

Again.

Why, unlike the time five years before, did her blood now sing? Why did her heart ache in her breast? Why did she feel tears of joy spring unbidden to her eyes? And why, unlike the last time, did she feel her mouth unable to form around the word, *yes?*

"Mama?"

Cathryn swung in the direction of Aiden's voice to see her son clambering sleepily up the bleachers. She hastily dabbed at her eyes. "Why aren't you in bed, sweet thing? You need your sleep for pizza day."

Reaching the bleacher where Cathryn and Jacob sat, Aiden squeezed in between the two adults. "I looked up from my cot and there you were. You and Pastor Jacob. And I wanted to be with you." He looked up at Jacob. "Where were you at lights-out?"

Putting an arm around the boy, Jacob smiled down at him. "I was at the hospital with Evan Young."

"Did he run into a plow?"

Jacob chuckled softly. "No. He had a heart attack, but he's going to be fine."

"Will he have to wear a bandage?"

"No." Jacob ruffled Aiden's hair. "You're still King Bandage Wearer."

Cathryn bent and chucked her son under the chin. "No more questions." She knew this bedtime dawdling technique. "Say good-night to Pastor Jacob."

As Cathryn stood, Aiden climbed up in Jacob's lap and wrapped his small, sturdy arms around the big man's neck. "Good night, Pastor Jacob," he whispered. "I love you."

Cathryn heard Jacob's sharp intake of breath. But without skipping a beat, he replied, "I love you, too, Aiden." The sound of his gentle words rang true and heartfelt in the quiet of the gym.

Hot emotion filled Cathryn. Never in her plans to return to help with the tornado cleanup had she imagined this turn of events. Never had she expected such love. She felt the sting of unbidden tears. Holding out her hand to Aiden, she tried to make her voice even. "Let's go, King Bandage Wearer."

Aiden slid to his feet, and Jacob stood.

As Aiden took Cathryn's hand, Jacob reached up and brushed a tear away from the corner of her eye. "You don't have to answer my question right now," he said softly. "Just think about it all the way till Saturday."

Would she be able to think of anything *but?*

Jacob watched the eight dissatisfied parishioners file into the conference room, and thought of Cathryn. Her silence last night after his proposal hadn't discouraged him. He'd seen the look in her eyes. The look of yearning that had matched the feeling beating deep in his own heart. The look that said, this time, she felt for him what he felt for her.

Because of that look, and because of his innate abiding faith, Jacob faced this morning's potentially difficult meeting with great hope.

With his parishioners seated around the conference table, Jacob remained standing at its head. "I understand you're dissatisfied with my leadership at Grace Everlasting." In turn, he looked each person directly in the eyes. "I want to hear why."

Deacon Rush made a move to speak, but Jacob cut him off. "I don't want to hear from a delegate. I want to hear from you as individuals. Edwina, let's begin with you."

Edwina Mapes squirmed in her seat before she began to speak. "I think you were too harsh with our Howie when he had that set-to with Aiden O'Malley."

"Too harsh?"

Edwina set her chin. "Yes. Howie only spoke the truth. It was the O'Malley boy who started the fight."

Jacob tried to control himself. "Edwina, do you think that if you were four and someone called attention to your fatherless state and blamed it on your mother—a *bad person*—that you might not take a swing at your tormentor?"

Edwina looked shocked, but it was Harry Mapes who, obviously angry, spoke up. "My Howie is not a *tormentor.*"

"Perhaps my language was harsh," Jacob agreed evenly. "Howie was only mimicking words he'd heard at home. Cruel words."

"At home we're not afraid to say what's right and what's wrong," Harry retorted. "We want our kids to know the difference."

"Haven't we as a congregation at Grace Everlasting decided that one of the things we all need to work on is the command to judge not? That the human tendency to diminish another individual is wrong. Plain and simple."

Edwina and Harry had the decency to look uncomfortable.

"Harry," Jacob continued, "have you forgotten two years ago when your sister's boy came to you from Detroit? Came to you because your sister couldn't handle him. Came to you with a drug problem that she hadn't told you about. Do you remember?"

"Of course I remember," Harry grumbled.

"And do you remember how, after initial resistance, initial harsh judgment, the congregation pulled together to help the boy? How we got him into a drug rehab program."

Harry merely nodded his head.

Jacob placed his fingertips on the conference table and leaned forward. "I ask you, is Aiden O'Malley any less deserving of our understanding?"

Both Edwina and Harry were silent. It was Simon Connors who spoke up. "At the very least, Jacob, you run the risk of favoritism. You constantly spend extra time and attention on Cathryn O'Malley's child."

"Perhaps I do," Jacob replied quietly. "Perhaps I do for the very reason that Aiden doesn't have a father. And the O'Malleys—Cathryn and I—are old friends."

"Old friends!" Ellie Able hooted. "Old friends don't create a scene at their wedding, embarrassing the groom and his entire congregation."

"That's history," Jacob replied, quelling an urge to throttle the woman. "If I've forgotten and forgiven, surely you can."

Ellie harrumphed and sat back, pursey-lipped, in her chair. She looked for all the world as if she hadn't said everything that was on her mind. Looked as if she might be reserving her most explosive comments for later.

Deacon Rush smacked his hands on the table. "We're talking conflict of interest here. With so many O'Malleys—special friends of yours—heading up so many key committees, it seems they could sway your decisions when it comes to making up the relief schedule."

"Really, Emory. When was the last time you were suspicious of the O'Malleys? Was it the time last year when Boone provided free labor to help repair the town hall after that pipe burst? Or was it the time Belle held a fund-raiser in her storefront to provide picture books for the kindergarten? Maybe it was the time Alice Rose made doughnuts for the fire fighters after they put out a blaze in her shed." He couldn't help the edge that crept into his voice. "Yes, now I see your point. The O'Malleys always have been a manipulative lot."

"Jacob," Maggie Smith said softly, "there may be nothing to the rumors going around...but this is a church. You're the pastor. And because of that, you must be doubly aware of the truth *and* of the appearance of the truth."

"Ah, seemliness," Jacob replied, stroking his chin. Lord, he prayed silently, perhaps I'm not your man. I have no patience for this pettiness. He took a deep breath. "Now, Maggie, aside from the O'Malleys taking an active role in helping me—the community—with the relief efforts, what in particular has struck you as unseemly in my behavior recently?"

The woman flushed under Jacob's gaze. "Poor Ellie, here, just wants to get back into her house. Every time she comes to speak to you, Cathryn O'Malley stands between Ellie and you. As if she's your official secretary or something. Then, instead of taking care of business, you take an outsider's side against one of your long-time parishioners."

Jacob shook his head, quite simply at a loss as to where to begin in this hodgepodge of secondhand accusations. He decided to bypass the messenger and get right to the source. Pulling a small appointment book out of his back pocket, he skewered Ellie Able with what he hoped was his sternest look. "Ellie, once and for all, I haven't forgotten your pleas. If you'll look in my appointment book, you'll see I have written directly under this meeting a reminder to call your children—your grown, able-bodied children—to get them down here to make the few minor repairs on your house so that you can be out of the church shelter and into your own home by midweek. Will that be satisfactory?"

Ellie quietly seethed in her seat, but she said, her words tight, "That's most obliging of you, Pastor Matthews."

"Now," Jacob continued, turning to the other seven, "let's hear the rest of it. If you think I've behaved improperly, I want to know it."

Diane Connors spoke up. "I for one have noticed that you've been spending a great deal of time with Cathryn O'Malley. Time that's not relief oriented. After the softball game. At the barn-raising dance. After lights-out in the gym." She softened her gaze and leaned toward him over the table. "Jacob, we have such lovely eligible girls in our own parish. Is it necessary to keep company with an outsider?"

Even though he'd suspected this might be coming, Jacob felt as if Diane had struck him. "This is the second time y'all have called Cathryn an outsider. Southern hospitality aside, you seem to forget she's a member of Grace Everlasting. Has been, actually, for longer than you, Diane, and Simon." He nodded at the Connors couple, then looked at everyone seated around the table. "Tell me, do you object to me having a personal life, or do you object to Cathryn O'Malley? Or is it perhaps both?"

Gerald Smith had been quiet so far through the entire meeting. In fact, as he'd entered the room he'd seemed uncomfortable, as if he'd been dragged here this morning. When he spoke now, exasperation showed in his voice. "The way I see it, we've had Jacob and his services pretty much 'round the clock for the last two years. Y'all are beginning to sound like a bunch of children jealous of a parent's attention. The man is human, people. Ever since he took over from his daddy, Grace Everlasting has been his life. He's lived it and he's breathed it and he's yet to take a vacation. Quite frankly, I think I'd have needed a break long before now."

Jacob looked on stunned as Gerald continued. "If the man wants to keep company with a nice young woman, I say it's about time."

Someone, Jacob couldn't tell who, muttered, "It's the *nice young woman* that seems to be the bone of contention."

"Excuse me," Jacob said, his voice steely, "but no one has answered my question. What are the objections to my spending time with Cathryn O'Malley?"

Deacon Rush folded his hands tightly in front of him. "Let's just say, Jacob, that it's an ill-advised attachment."

"Ill-advised attachment!" Gerald Smith was on his feet now. "Is the man supposed to choose his friends by committee? This is getting ludicrous. I was told some serious business needed to get settled here today. This is nothing but a cat fight."

Quite frankly, Jacob had had enough, also. "Gerald, please, sit down. I need a couple more minutes of your time." He looked around at the group and wondered if anything at all had been cleared up this morning. One thing was for certain: He wasn't going to let anyone continue to impugn Cathryn's good name.

"I have an announcement to make," he said carefully, "although I hadn't intended to make it in this way. But perhaps it will clear up the *seemliness* of my actions." All eyes were on him. "I've asked Cathryn O'Malley to marry me."

The silence in the room was overpowering.

Finally Deacon Rush sputtered, "Jacob, have you truly given thought to your actions?"

Jacob actually chuckled. "Only for the past five years."

Diane Connors looked shocked. "But that would make her first lady of Grace Everlasting."

"If she accepts, yes," Jacob replied. "Right now, I'm waiting for an answer."

Gerald Smith leaned over the table and extended his hand. "I hope she says yes, Jacob. You deserve a good woman at your side."

Ellie Able stood so abruptly that her chair fell over. "Are you crazy?" she snapped. "Do any of you know the real history of that woman?"

"No," came Cathryn's voice from the door, "and you, Ellie Able, are not going to tell it."

All eyes turned toward the conference room door where Cathryn stood, a tray of coffee and cups in her hands.

Everyone froze.

Jacob inhaled sharply. He had never seen such a hard look in Cathryn's eyes. He could only imagine what was going through her head. This was exactly the thing she'd feared. That her past would dog her. That rumors would persist and eventually become public. Make their way to her son, tainting his existence in Sweet Hope.

With remarkable dignity Cathryn walked to the conference table, then set the tray on it. Glaring at the assembled group, Jacob included, she turned toward the door.

Jacob's heart seemed to collapse on itself. She was leaving. Again. He had lost her. For good.

Cathryn walked toward the doorway. But instead of walking through it, she closed the door, then turned back to face Jacob and the assembled parishioners. She had no intention of leaving this time with only a vague and hastily scribbled note to explain her actions. This time she intended to clear the air. Once and for all. She didn't, however, intend the entire shelter and day care to overhear.

In a clear voice that belied the quaking in the pit of her stomach, she began. "I have no intention of letting Ms. Able, or anyone else for that matter, tell my story. If it needs to be told, *I'll* tell it."

"You don't have to," Jacob insisted softly.

She looked into his gentle gray eyes and saw worry. She knew it wasn't for himself. She'd heard enough of this meeting from the corridor to realize Jacob had stood up to these people—almost alone—in her defense. No, the worry she saw in his eyes would be for her. He would worry that she wasn't strong enough to tell the tale she must tell.

Five years ago she hadn't been. Five years ago she'd run to protect Jacob and her unborn child. This time, however, Jacob had proved over and over again since she'd come back to Sweet Hope that her past would not drive him off. That he would not allow the rumor and innuendo to sully either his feelings for her or his calling. That his feelings for her, his calling, his faith, his strength and his principles were firmer than the name-calling and the smear tactics. No, her past wouldn't hurt Jacob Matthews.

She couldn't say the same for Aiden.

For Aiden, she needed to clear the air, and then she needed to serve out her promised volunteer duty at Grace Everlasting with dignity before she returned with her son to her carefully crafted life in Albany.

She approached the conference table. Ellie Able, still standing, glowered at her but said nothing. Gerald Smith had sunk into his seat. Maggie Smith and Diane Connors refused to look at her. Simon Connors and Deacon Rush eyed her with suspicion. Edwina and Harry Mapes looked on in unreadable, stony silence.

Only Jacob reached out to her. Touched her arm and, with an expression of strength and support, drew her to his side.

"You think of me as an outsider," she began, "not, I suspect, because I live in Albany. But because my life has been beyond the pale. What has happened to me could happen to you, so, to exorcise that possibility, you create a persona for me. One far removed from your good and ordinary lives. Instead of admitting that bad things can and do happen to good people, you make me out to be a pariah. A loose woman. An outsider. Things that have happened to me, therefore, could never happen to you."

The assembled group, excluding Ellie Able, squirmed in their seats.

"Do you know what happened to me five years ago?" Cathryn asked, controlling with great effort the waver in her voice. "I was raped."

She heard a collective gasp.

Continuing quickly, she tried to keep her voice even. "The man who violated me was no stranger, no criminal by the usual standards. I dated him. Trusted him... and he raped me." She took an enormous breath and forced herself to look each person in the eye as she spoke. "Rape victims are sometimes made out to appear, somehow, guilty themselves, especially date-rape victims. The reasoning being that if we were involved in a dating situation, surely we were, in part, seducer. In no way is that true."

Jacob put his arm around her shoulders, and she drew strength from his touch. Those seated around the table stared at her, ashen faced.

"What's past is past," croaked Gerald Smith.

"That might be true," Cathryn replied softly, "if it weren't for Aiden." She squared her shoulders and felt Jacob tighten his fingers in silent protection. "When I discovered I was pregnant, I chose to have the baby." Tears threatened at the corners of her eyes. "From the ugliest part of my life came the most beautiful."

Diane Connors began to cry softly.

At Cathryn's side, Jacob spoke. "Do any of you feel that your lives have been so spotless that you can now sit in judgment?"

"Live and let live, I always say," Ellie Able snapped, "*but* that doesn't mean I don't expect my pastor *and his wife* to be above reproach."

Cathryn's head snapped up. "Rest assured, Ms. Able, your pastor is above reproach. For three years he's counseled your troubled, visited your sick, welcomed the newborn into the fold, inspired your congregation to take the high road, worked long selfless hours and, with boundless joy, forged a sense of community within Grace Everlasting."

"Amen," Gerald Smith interjected.

Cathryn stared at the others. "You have nothing to fear from me. Saturday, my stint as a volunteer is over. My son and I will return to our home in Albany, leaving you with a pastor I hope you have the grace to appreciate."

"Cassie!" The desolation in Jacob's voice was palpable.

She gently removed his hand from her shoulder. "Now, if you'll excuse me, I have work to do." She turned with all the dignity she could muster and left the room before her own sense of desolation—and tears—consumed her.

Outside the conference room she stormed through the corridors of the administration building, telling herself that this time she was not running away. This time she'd stayed long enough to stand up for herself. This time, in the standoff between herself and the eight parishioners in the conference room, Jacob had seen firsthand exactly why their relationship could never progress beyond friendship. Even if he and his calling could handle her past, she was not about to put Aiden in a position in which he might feel anything but wanted and cherished.

As long as there were Ellie Ables in the world, Cathryn's past was alive and potentially harmful. As long as she and her son remained in Sweet Hope.

Stopping in front of Jacob's office, Cathryn thought of the two full days of service left. She'd said she wouldn't leave until her volunteer stint had been fulfilled. As much as she wanted to pack up right now and head for home, her pride wouldn't allow it. She might have made the decision to return to Albany, but she'd give no one the satisfaction that they'd driven her out of town.

She stared at Jacob's door. How, after the joy and the tenderness and the emotion they'd shared these past few days, could she go back to working side by side with him as just another volunteer? How, after hot kisses and his second proposal of marriage, could they go back to being friends?

She couldn't.

At least, she couldn't this morning. She needed space. She needed her son. Moving past the office door without entering, she headed for the classrooms. Last Saturday she'd come with the intention of helping Belle run the day care. Alice Rose's matchmaking had thrust her in another direction. This morning she intended to take matters into her own hands. Intended to surround herself with children and laughter and pizza. Intended to put her past and the ill will of certain people behind her. Intended to brush aside the image of hearts-and-flowers romance that had begun to creep back into her head lately, and instead embrace reality and practicality.

She had her son. She had her family. She had her health and her God-given strength and skills. Surely that was enough.

Surely she could learn to live without Jacob Matthews.

Chapter Thirteen

Jacob pressed into the gymnasium, fully expecting Cathryn, Aiden and their belongings to be gone.

He would have followed her sooner except for the explosion that had erupted in the conference room after her departure. Half of the group, Ellie Able included, had insisted Cathryn's revelation merely underscored their concerns that her relationship with Jacob was an ill-advised attachment. The other half had turned on Ellie, insisting that she'd used the misfortune of another to further her own selfish agenda. This half had felt misinformed and used and had threatened to bring Ellie up on charges before the church council. Jacob had his own agenda: He'd insisted that not one word of Cathryn's story leave the conference room—for Aiden's sake. It was only after a grueling hour of mediation that Jacob had managed to patch together a truce of sorts.

No one, however, left the conference room happy, least of all Jacob. He could only hope the hour delay hadn't lost him Cathryn.

Not until he spotted Aiden's cot with the boy's sweatshirt and Boo Bear still lying on the pillow did he breathe a sigh of relief. They hadn't left. Not yet.

He'd tried to convince himself that he had indeed heard Cathryn say back in the conference room that she would stay until Saturday. Would finish out her volunteer stint. But the haunted look in her eyes, despite her brave stance and the strength of her voice, had made him dread that she would leave immediately. And when he hadn't found her in his office, he'd feared the worst.

Now the sight of Boo Bear gave him hope that she might indeed stay...unless she'd gone to sign Aiden out of the nursery school. At that thought, Jacob all but leapt over the crowded cots in the gym on his way to the classrooms.

He'd let her go once before because she'd insisted that's what she wanted. He wasn't going to let her go this time, especially not after the past few days when her eyes and her laughter and her kisses had told him she would stay if only he could prove to her it was possible.

If she hadn't left Grace Everlasting already, he had two full days to prove just that.

He couldn't lose her now. He just couldn't. She and Aiden had become a part of the very fabric of his everyday existence. Five years ago there had only been hopes and dreams. For five days now he'd lived snatches of those hopes and dreams, and, like a man who's caught a glimpse of the promised land, he wasn't going to be content with anything less.

Jacob found Cathryn finally in Aiden's classroom, elbow-deep in pizza dough, surrounded by children. The sheer beauty of the ordinary scene took his breath away.

Stepping into the room, he decided making pizza was the most important item on his agenda that day.

"Pastor Jacob!" Margaret O'Malley spotted him first. "Come help us! We have room on our team."

Jacob suppressed a grin. How fortunate that Cathryn headed up Margaret's—and Aiden's—team of five children.

Cathryn looked up, a guarded expression in her eyes. Jacob couldn't help but smile to see a smudge of flour on the end of her nose. Lord, but that woman would look beautiful in a mud pack. He rolled up his sleeves and found a spot between Aiden and Margaret at the table. "What do I do first?"

"Wash your hands," Cathryn replied dryly.

As Jacob bent over to wash his hands in the child-sized sink in the corner of the room, he noticed the giggles of several children watching him. Oh, yes, this was his idea of the perfect solution to an awkward situation. Cathryn wouldn't leave the room now. Having started the project, she knew her leaving would be like a broken promise to Aiden. Jacob had her right where he wanted her. And the kids and the giggling and the pizza would serve to defuse any awkwardness there might be between the two adults. He loved this situation.

Not to mention the fact that he really loved making pizza.

He wiped his hands on a paper towel, winked at the child behind him in line for the sink, and chuckled softly to himself. For a pastor, he could be downright scheming when the stakes were high enough.

Belle passed him on his way back to Cathryn's table. "The storm must be losing its grip," she said, smiling, "if you and Cathryn can take time out to help with pizza."

Oh, I don't know, Jacob thought. Take care of one storm; meet one of a different sort head-on.

"Hurry up, Pastor Matthews," Cathryn called tartly, "if you want a turn at kneading."

Jacob quickly dusted his hands with flour, then thrust them into the pizza dough bowl. He began to knead, and as he kneaded, he wove a story for the children looking on. A story of tiny monsters that live in pizza dough. As he told the story, he squeezed the dough so that it bubbled and popped and extruded through his fingers to a chorus of giggles and *eeuwws* from the five kids in the group.

Finally, he even elicited a chuckle from Cathryn, who obviously tried to remain the mature leader of the group. "I think it's properly kneaded,'' she insisted. ''Plop it on the cookie tray so we can all spread it.''

''What?'' Jacob looked at her in mock horror. ''We're not going to spin it over our heads?''

''Ooh,'' came the response of the children.

''We are *not* going to spin it over our heads,'' Cathryn hissed in obvious exasperation as she snatched the bowl away from Jacob and turned it upside down on the greased cookie sheet.

Jacob shrugged at the disappointed kids. ''Maybe next week, when we're experts.''

''Yeah, next week,'' Aiden piped up. ''Next week's going to be busy. We're all going to see Mr. Sims's finished barn and the calves.''

Margaret sidled up to Aiden. ''Next week maybe I'll be back in my house and you can come sleep over.''

''Awright.''

Next week.

Jacob glanced at Cathryn, who maintained a cool, calm exterior but who wouldn't look at him or at Aiden. ''Okay, kids, let's spread this dough to the edges of the cookie sheet,'' she said cheerfully. A bit too cheerfully.

Ten little hands and four big ones patted and poked and prodded until the dough spread evenly over the sheet.

''Now the sauce!'' Laura Sue Martin crowed triumphantly.

''Now the sauce,'' Cathryn agreed. ''Everyone gets a turn with the ladle.''

As the children each took a turn, spattering as much sauce on the table as on the dough, Jacob trailed his finger through a blob of the red stuff, then looked at Cathryn's flour-daubed nose. The devil must have pinched him, because he couldn't resist the thought that the flour could use an accompaniment of sauce.

She never took her eyes off the pizza-making process. ''Don't even think of it,'' she murmured under her breath, her lips twisting to prevent a smile.

Jacob wiped the offending finger on a paper towel. ''You must have eyes in the back of your head.''

"She does," Aiden insisted, looking up at Cathryn, his eyes full of love. "She's a mom."

The sauce spread, Cathryn moved the bowl well out of Jacob's reach. "Before you arrived, we took a vote. The toppings on our pizza will be cheese and pepperoni."

"Now, that's a surprise." Jacob chuckled. "No pineapple? I know someone who loves pineapple pizza."

Cathryn reached for the containers of shredded cheese and thinly sliced pepperoni. She smiled at Jacob. "I deferred to the will of the majority."

"Well, then," he replied, his voice sounding huskier than he'd intended, "some time soon, I'll have to make you your very own pineapple pizza."

Aiden nudged him gently. "Next week, Pastor Jacob. Everything's happenin' next week."

Jacob saw Cathryn blush, but she didn't contradict her son.

Leaning over to sprinkle cheese on the pizza, Jacob took Cathryn's silence as a good sign and smiled. Smiled and silently vowed that he would use everything in his power to convince Cathryn that her place was here in Sweet Hope. With him. Next week. And the week after. And after that...

In a storm-tossed shelter, he didn't have recourse to the usual hearts-and-flowers courtship accoutrements. His courting would have to take a simpler turn. Pizza. Softball. And the unadorned sterling truth of his love for her.

A love that had only grown truer since her return.

A love that wouldn't admit to the possibility of her leaving him again.

He popped a slice of pepperoni into his mouth, and laughed as Cathryn scowled at him. Pizza. He knew from the start this had been a good idea.

"Pizza's ready!" Cathryn carried the hot cookie sheet out the classroom doorway that opened onto a courtyard shaded by an enormous, ancient oak. As children and teachers of other groups munched their already baked pizza, Jacob sat in the shade with the five children under Cathryn's care and led a raucous clapping game.

Pastor. She harrumphed. That man was more Peter Pan than pastor. Peter Pan with a dash of Pied Piper.

When she'd left the awful confrontation in the boardroom this morning, she'd dreaded that Jacob might follow her. Might try to convince her to change her declared intention of returning to Albany come Saturday. But when he'd found her, she'd felt not one iota of dread. Surprisingly, she'd felt elation at the sight of him.

If he'd launched into a conversation designed to sway her resolve, however, if he'd tried to convince her that the morning's ugly meeting shouldn't drive her from town, she could have resisted him. Could have resisted his reasoning. As it was, she found his pizza making and his delight at being with the children and his simple enjoyment of the moment a far more powerful argument for staying in Sweet Hope.

If only she could....

The children danced and yipped about her like hungry pups.

"Come sit on the blanket," Jacob called to the children with a laugh. "That cookie sheet's hot."

Hot. That's exactly how this exasperating pastor made her feel.

Thankful for the distraction of exuberant children and pizza, Cathryn, carefully balancing the team's lunch, sat across from Jacob in the shade of the giant oak. The protective distraction evaporated, however, as the hungry children quickly cleared the cookie sheet of pizza, then danced off to play with friends. Even Aiden felt the pull of his peers and abandoned Cathryn to Jacob's company.

As the last child scampered away, Jacob stretched out on his side in the grass, his head propped up on his hand, his gaze lazily focused upon Cathryn. Despite his relaxed appearance, she just knew he was going to bring up the ugliness of this morning *and* her announcement that she would be leaving Sweet Hope come Saturday. She steeled herself for a stiff debate, and determined that she wouldn't be the one to begin it.

She deliberately watched the children. And waited for Jacob to begin. And waited. And waited. Finally, stealing a glance in his direction, she was surprised to see him smiling at her. Smiling, at ease and obviously in no hurry to begin the fireworks she felt certain he had planned.

"The kids seemed to like the pizza-making project," he said, his voice husky and low, his gray gaze startlingly provocative.

With a shiver of unexpected pleasure, Cathryn tried to concentrate on his words alone instead of on the sensuous delivery. "Except for that one incident with Howie Mapes," she replied, trying her best to sound casual, "Aiden has loved everything about this day-care situation. As well run as it is, it's amazing to think three-quarters of it is temporary."

"You know, I've been meaning to talk to you about that." Jacob reached out and plucked a long blade of grass, then stuck it in the corner of his mouth. He looked disarmingly boyish, with the emphasis, unfortunately, on his all-too-natural ability to disarm. "Parents from other parishes, who didn't realize Grace Everlasting had a preschool program, have seen a sample of it because of the storm. A large number of them have asked me for applications to our regular program. Now, depending on how many of them follow through, we could conceivably double our preschool enrollment next year."

"Can you handle it?"

A sly smile crept across Jacob's face. "We could... if we restructured our administration. Took on new key personnel."

Cathryn cocked an eyebrow, suspicious that she was being set up somehow. "What kind of personnel?"

"Oh..." Jacob made a show of nonchalance. "One exceptional person would do it. Someone with good people skills. Great organizational skills. Someone who's committed to building a sense of community. You see, Grace Everlasting, as big and active as it already was, has recently taken on a host of new programs and activities. The preschool. The softball league. A challenging music calendar.

A meals-on-wheels proposal. I have a great board of directors, but even with their help I still could use more . . . say, a full-time administrative assistant.'' He grinned unabashedly. ''Someone with experience under fire.''

That man.

He sure knew the buttons to push. If he'd come at her with reasons not to leave—emotional reasons—she would have found it easy to resist. Instead, he'd altered his approach subtly; he'd suggested several very pragmatic reasons to stay. Altruistic reasons. Reasons that smacked of community and belonging. Of being needed. Reasons that pulled mightily at Cathryn.

Now, she had to admit, all those reasons didn't add up to the one that pulled on her heartstrings. Jacob. The man himself. And the love she'd come to feel for him. Impossible love. But had he, right out of the gate, tried to use that too-volatile reason to convince her to stay, she would have dug in her heels and resisted with all her might. But, no, the man had to be calm and rational. Had to appeal to her higher self. Had to make it sound as if he were merely making a logical business proposition. Something of benefit to everyone.

The good pastor didn't fight fair.

''It would seem to me,'' Cathryn replied carefully, ''that, in a sensitive position such as you describe, you'd need someone liked and respected by your congregation.''

Jacob's gaze became dark and penetrating. ''I think my congregation, for the most part, is willing to accept others on the merit of their present work. On strength of character.''

Cathryn thought of Ellie Able and sighed. ''Oh, Jacob, it would take powerful proof for me to begin to believe that.'' She shook her head. ''No. It's simply impossible.''

The hint of a smile curved the corners of Jacob's mouth. ''You forget I have a very powerful Friend. With his help, nothing's impossible.''

It looked as if Jacob were going to reach out for her, but he was interrupted by a man calling his name.

Gerald Smith approached. "Jacob, can I borrow the keys to your Blazer?"

Jacob fished in his pocket for the keys. "What's up?"

"This afternoon Homer Martin and I are going to take care of the repairs on Ellie Able's house. We might need your four-wheel drive to do it, but we're going to make sure Ms. Able can move out of the shelter by nightfall." Gerald actually winked at Cathryn. "Homer and I figured it was our good-neighbor duty to help that poor woman back into her home."

Jacob stood and enthusiastically plunked his keys in Gerald's hand. "Don't let me get in the way of *that* project." Sobering, he took Gerald's hand in both his own, in a heartfelt handshake. "Thank you."

"My pleasure." Gerald tipped his cap as he turned to leave. "Just doing my part for true . . . progress," he added over his shoulder.

Cathryn could have sworn he hadn't meant to say *progress*.

Jacob extended his hand to Cathryn to help her rise from her seat on the ground. "You see?"

Cathryn quickly withdrew her hand from Jacob's. "See what?" She wasn't certain she wanted to see.

"That sure looked like the beginning of proof to me. Maybe a little divine intervention." His eyes twinkled. "Didn't you think Gerald just now looked slightly angelic?"

Harrumphing softly, she turned away from him. "Jacob, it amazes me that you always see the silver lining, never the cloud."

He laid his hand gently on her shoulder. "There you're wrong, Cassie. It's the cloud that makes the silver lining so unbelievably beautiful by contrast."

"I want to believe you," she assured him. "If it were only me, I might chance it, but I have Aiden to consider. If I stay in Sweet Hope, I'll always worry that, in a vitriolic snit, Ellie Able or someone else might say something to hurt Aiden."

"Look at me, Cassie." He turned her around to face him. "Aiden will face his share of hurt in his life. His share of bumps and bruises both physical and emotional. You can't prevent them. You can only prepare him for them."

"I've tried to prepare him by removing him from possible hurt. By taking him to Albany. It's worked so far."

Jacob tilted her chin with his forefinger so that she looked deep into his eyes. "But at what cost to you?"

Held in his probing gaze, Cathryn couldn't answer. This week had proved that, in retrospect, the cost to her had been enormous.

"Wouldn't it be better to prepare Aiden by wrapping him in a family's love? Wouldn't he be stronger if, every day, he saw Alice Rose and Boone and Belle and Margaret... and me?"

Cathryn inhaled sharply. "You?"

"Yes, me. Surely you know I want to be a father to Aiden."

Tears stung Cathryn's eyes, and Jacob released her.

"What's holding you back, Cassie?" Apprehension clouded his eyes. "Do you think I'm asking you to marry me this time out of an altruistic sense of friendship? Do you think I'm proposing a cool and businesslike marriage of convenience? Is that what's holding you back? Or is it your own lack of feelings for me? Still."

Staring down at the ground, Cathryn took a step backward. Her words came with difficulty. "I don't know what to think. I don't know what you feel. Or what I feel."

"Let me tell you what I feel." His deep voice rumbled over her senses, compelling her to look at him. "Then you decide, Cassie. Decide how you're going to live the rest of your life."

She hung on his every word. Her parched heart longed for the shower of words she knew he was poised to say. The words he hadn't said five years ago even though his eyes had hinted at them. The words he'd only written in fun in John Deere green on the overpass. She knew then he'd been afraid to press her. Afraid of frightening her off with the intensity of his emotions. But now—now Jacob looked like a man who wasn't going to let her go until she understood every nook and cranny of his heart. Understood the full depth of his feeling.

And now—now—she wanted to hear. For in his words might be her reason to stay.

"I love you, Cassie," he began simply. There was nothing simple, however, in the powerful timbre of his voice or the fervent look in his eyes. "I need to tell you everything I feel this time, not just for you. I need to tell you for me, too. So that things are absolutely clear between us."

"In what way?" Even to her own ears her voice sounded small.

"If you stayed this time, I wouldn't be satisfied with either a marriage of convenience or a marriage of friends. This time I want it all. I want your friendship and your passion. I want your head and your heart...and your body. Willingly. Joyously."

Cathryn felt her eyes widen as she inhaled sharply.

"I want you to think of me as Jacob the man. The man who thought he was fully alive before your return...but who discovered he'd merely been sleepwalking."

Cathryn smiled shyly. "For a sleepwalker, Jacob Matthews, you exert a powerful influence."

He grasped her arms. Held her, too, with his piercing gaze. "Then imagine what I can accomplish fully awake with you by my side. Imagine what *we* can accomplish. For us as well as for others."

Cathryn shook her head ruefully. "I suppose you see us turning Ellie Able into Alice Rose."

Jacob sobered. "I'm afraid Ellie Able and the Mapes family will decide to leave Grace Everlasting."

Reaching out, Cathryn laid a hand lightly on Jacob's chest. "And how does that make you feel, especially since I precipitated it?"

"Their leaving in anger hurts me, I'll admit it. But I don't regret for a minute not giving in to their emotional blackmail." He smiled and stroked the inner skin of her arms with his thumbs. "I've decided to take a cue from an old friend and be realistic about it. In my three years as pastor, this is my first defection."

Cathryn raised an eyebrow. "Not thinking of ditching your idealism, are you?"

"Not on your life."

At the look of sheer certainty on his face, Cathryn lowered her gaze. "How do you do it?" she asked softly. "Day after day."

He shook her arms gently. "Cassie, look at me." His words were more a caress than a command. "That's the beauty of it. We're given a new day every twenty-four hours. Or we can decide on starting a new moment any time we wish. Yes, we make mistakes. Yes, others hurt us. But we've been given this incredible free will wherein we may *choose* to live life to its fullest. To our potential. Joyously. Celebrating every ounce of our humanity."

"You're talking about love."

A smile lighted his face. "I'm talking about love. In all its manifestations. And this time around, Cassie O'Malley, if you decide you love me, I want *love.* All-the-stops-out love. Because that's what I feel for you. I want no less for myself. I want this...."

Right there, in front of a courtyard full of frolicking children and Grace Everlasting day-care workers, right there Jacob took her into his arms. "I want magic," he murmured huskily before he lowered his lips to hers.

His kiss claimed her. Seared her. Filled her with magic and fireworks and impossible dreams. He made her feel hot and cold. Weak and strong. Filled with hope and hopelessly in love. And just as she slid her arms around his neck, he gently pulled away. Pulled away and left her trembling and yearning.

Oh, my, the pastor definitely did *not* play fair.

Alice Rose's words ran through Cathryn's mind. *True love is friendship set on fire.* Well, her senses burned, all right. Burned while the arsonist stood before his work, looking for all the world as if he hadn't even used all the fuel at his disposal to start the conflagration.

She opened her mouth to speak, but Jacob laid a finger on her lips to stop her.

"I'll be in my office. I want you to think about what I've offered you. What I'm asking of you. Think of what your life would be like if you turn me down this time. Imagine what it will be like if you say yes."

She blinked, felt the flames fanning her body and began to comprehend the magnitude of her decision this time.

He took his hand away from her mouth. "I love you with every fiber of my being," he insisted, his words half purr, half growl, their sound filling Cathryn's thoughts with a sensuous preview of the possibilities of loving Jacob the man.

Turning abruptly, he left her under the giant oak in the courtyard. Left her with her thoughts churning. With her body too hot and longing for his presence, his touch. Left her wanting what she'd denied herself for five years, but wondering how in heaven's name she would work up the courage to take that first step.

As if from a great distance, she heard the laughter of children. She focused on an older group jumping rope. Double Dutch. A girl whose turn it was hung back, intimidated by the swinging ropes, but obviously mesmerized. The bright spots on her cheeks told of her excitement and her fear.

"Just do it!" her playmates called in laughing encouragement. "C'mon, Del. Just do it!"

With a squeal, Del closed her eyes and jumped.

Cathryn shivered and hugged herself. Yeah, Cassie. Just do it.

Jacob had worked in his office all afternoon with the hope that Cathryn would come to him. Would tell him, yes, that she loved him—really loved him—and wanted to be his wife.

But she hadn't.

And it didn't look, now, as if she would.

Where had he gone wrong this time? He'd told her that he loved her with every fiber of his being. He groaned aloud.

That was only half the truth. He loved her beyond himself, if that were possible. She consumed him, his waking thoughts, his sleeping dreams. She fit his life and his desires as no one else ever had or ever would. She was his soul mate.

The thought of living without her made the edges of his existence seem black and thoroughly without joy.

Suddenly a sneeze washed over him. And another. And another. If he didn't know better he'd think Mrs. Wegman's cat, Molly, had come out of her seclusion in the storage room. Considering the misanthropic nature of the beast, that wasn't likely.

But yet again he sneezed as his nose itched unmercifully and his eyes began to water.

Meow. The cry was very real. Rusty but real.

Jacob looked down to see Molly-the-Snit peering around the door to the supply room. And miracle of miracles, she looked as if she wanted company. Round-the-clock single parenthood will do it to you every time, Jacob thought wryly as he sneezed again. As much as he also needed company, he couldn't coexist with old Moll and save his health. He bent to pick her up and return her to the supply room.

"Jacob Matthews, don't you touch that cat. Go wash your hands and face. I'll put her back. That's what partners are for."

Cathryn.

He wanted to swing her into his arms, but she brushed by him, airily waving her hands. "Shoo. Do as I say. I have no desire to accept a marriage proposal from a man with red eyes and a dripping nose."

As she scooped up a startled Molly, Jacob, equally startled, charged into the small office bathroom. Turning on the cold water, he wet his face and his neck. Let the delicious shock sink in. Cathryn had come to accept his marriage proposal. Resting his hands on the cold porcelain of the sink and letting his head fall forward, he grinned into the drain in disbelief.

"Not done yet?" Her bright and teasing voice filled the tiny room. She stood in the doorway, hands on her hips. The old saucy Cassie superimposed onto the new strong Cathryn. "You aren't one of those bathroom hogs, hmm? I see trouble if you are."

He grinned and shook his head and spattered water everywhere.

She laughed, and the sound filled his heart with joy. Extending her hand to him, she said, "Would you mind stepping into the office? I'd rather not say yes in the lavatory."

He clasped her hand and followed her into the office. "Wait a minute," he said, unable to tame his grin. "You said just a minute ago, *That's what partners are for.* I recall saying I wanted more than just a partnership."

Her look sizzled. "Oh, that's just the beginning."

He knew he must look dumbfounded. "But what made you decide?"

She slid her arms around his neck. "There was no decision, Jacob. I love you. With all my heart. It wasn't even a matter of realizing it. It was a matter of admitting it. A matter of acting on it. A very scary matter, I might add."

She loved him. She *loved* him. He could see it in the intensity of her smile. In the sparkle of her eyes. He could feel it in the caress of her touch. She loved him.

Loved him.

Standing on tiptoe, she planted a fairy-light kiss on his chin. "I was a fool once. Never again."

"Are you saying you'll marry me?"

She cocked one eyebrow. "Is the offer still good?"

Let's see if she can interpret this answer, Jacob thought as he bent to capture her mouth with his.

Chapter Fourteen

As Jacob maneuvered the houseboat over the moonlit water of Lake Lanier, Cathryn stood at his side. Slipping one arm around his waist, she sighed and leaned against him, reveling in his warmth and strength.

He kissed the top of her head. "Happy?" His deep, rich voice purred in her ear.

"Beyond belief."

"Me, too." He chuckled softly, and she could feel the rumble in his chest.

She glanced at his left hand, firm on the boat's wheel. Caught the glint of gold. His wedding band. Lovingly, with her thumb, she stroked the band on her own left hand. Out here on the water, under the stars, their wedding ceremony seemed light-years away, not mere hours.

Oh, what a wedding! She smiled to think of it. Alice Rose and Boone and Belle had worked to make it a June extravaganza. And, although Aiden and Margaret, as ring bearer and flower girl, had almost stolen the show, Cathryn couldn't have been happier.

As the strains of organ music had wafted through Grace Everlasting Church, Cathryn, on Boone's arm, had walked down the aisle toward Jacob waiting at the altar. Poor Jacob. The moment she'd stepped through the doorway at the back of the church, the first moment he'd spotted her, she'd seen a look of relief wash over his handsome face. But from that point on, she'd seen nothing but pure joy.

Her family may have planned the wedding, but it had been Jacob who took secretive charge of the honeymoon plans. Not even Boone had been able to pry Jacob's intentions from him. He'd winked and had told Cathryn he wanted to give her the works this time—hearts and flowers, moonlight and magic.

After the wedding reception they'd driven to Lake Lanier in northeast Georgia, where Jacob had taken control of a chartered houseboat. Even now, out on the water, Cathryn didn't know where they were headed.

Who cared? she thought as she snuggled closer to Jacob. She'd waited two months—often impatiently—for this moment when Jacob and she would be alone. Finally. As husband and wife. The thrumming she felt from her toes to her head couldn't possibly be from the powerful engine below deck. It had to come from her love for Jacob. It coursed through her with such energy she felt positively electric with life.

Suddenly Jacob cut the engine, enveloping them in silence. Flipping the lever that released the anchor, he turned to her and pulled her into his arms. "We're here," he murmured, a smile dancing at the corners of his eyes.

"Jacob! We're in the middle of the lake."

"Precisely." His grin was at the same time boyish and seductive.

Holding him lightly at the waist, she leaned back and skewered him with her best stare. "Husband, explain yourself." The moonlight reflecting off the water danced on the ceiling of the wheelhouse, making Cathryn feel slightly giddy.

He bent and feathered kisses along her jaw. "For the past two months," he purred between kisses, "we've lived, first, in a sardine can of a storm shelter. Then, after our engagement announcement, we upgraded to life in a goldfish bowl."

"And so you thought," Cathryn replied, laughing softly, "you'd stretch the fish metaphor one last time for our honeymoon?"

Jacob growled and nuzzled her neck. "No, wife! I tried to think of a place where I could have you to myself for an entire week. No interruptions. No well-intentioned well-wishers. No familiar faces. No strangers, for that matter." He nibbled her ear. "No people at all." He trailed kisses across her forehead. "No traffic." He cupped her face and turned it up to his. "No distractions." He lowered his mouth to hers and gently brushed her lips. "Just us."

Oh, my.

Her knees began to wobble as the haunting sound of a loon floated over the water. "Jacob," she whispered, and stood on tiptoe to receive his kiss.

In the past two months they'd shared kisses, but always with the knowledge that, in their goldfish-bowl existence, they might be interrupted. By children. By family. By Grace Everlasting parishioners. This kiss, however, had the luxury of a very private week stretching before them. A week without interruptions. With that exciting knowledge, Cathryn surrendered to this kiss.

Jacob must have sensed the difference, too, because he groaned and pulled her tightly against him, raining kisses on her eyes and cheeks and neck. Leaving a hot trail where his lips had pressed her skin.

It flashed through Cathryn's mind that it had probably been for the best—the two months of gradually intensifying kisses, the safety net that they might have been interrupted at any moment. Because, for a tiny moment, with these kisses of burning intensity, Cathryn felt a flicker of fear at Jacob's and her own passion. With the darkness in her past, she had thought her body would never feel arousal. The surge of it now was both exhilarating and frightening.

And then she ran her hands over the warm and well-muscled shoulders of the man holding her. Jacob. Jacob who not only loved her and wanted her, but who cherished her. Truly cherished her. She nuzzled his neck, kissed his pulse in the hollow, inhaled the manly scent of him. This was Jacob. Her beloved. She need fear nothing from him.

"Are you all right, Cassie?" he whispered.

Oh, Jacob. He could always read her every thought.

"Yes," she whispered back, twining her arms around his neck, smiling into his face. "I want to savor every minute."

He took her hand. "Come," he said softly, beckoning.

She followed him through the luxurious houseboat to the master bedroom. When he opened the door, she saw a room decorated with magnolia blossoms and sprays of fragrant mock orange. A room bathed in moonlight. A room for giving and receiving love.

"Flowers and moonlight and magic," she breathed, feeling tears of joy sting the corners of her eyes.

Jacob took her hand and pressed it to his chest. "And two hearts. Don't forget the hearts."

Suddenly she felt shy. "Oh, Jacob, I do love you."

"And I love you." He pulled her to him and kissed her lips. Gently at first. Then more passionately.

Cathryn responded to the passion. She opened her mouth to him and welcomed his exploration. Tentatively, she ran her fingers over the smooth planes of his face, down his neck, over his chest as he kissed her now with soul-drenching desire.

She felt his hands claim her. First, pulling her against the full hardness of his body. Then caressing her until she felt soft and warm and not quite solid. She gasped as his fingers slid over her hips and her waist and her breasts. She felt light and alive and almost intoxicated. For the life of her, she had never envisioned physical love as intoxicating. And welcome.

Oh, my, but Jacob's attentions were welcome.

Throwing her head back, she laughed softly, the sound of her own laughter sensuous to her ears. "Jacob, will you always make me feel this wonderful?"

"Either that or die trying," he groaned as he kissed the skin at the very bottom of the V-neck opening of her blouse.

She shivered with pleasure at the feel of his lips on her skin. Suddenly feeling bold, she reached up to unbutton the top button of his shirt. She heard his sharp intake of breath.

Her fingers trembling with anticipation, she slowly unbuttoned each shirt button, and, as she did, she pressed a soft kiss to the warm skin of his smooth, hard chest.

He stood absolutely still. Absolutely silent. But when Cathryn brushed the fabric of his shirt aside, she could feel the thumping of his heart beneath the palm of her hand. The steady, rapid feel of it thrilled her.

An unfamiliar sense of freedom washed over her. A tingling sensation of expectation. And joy. She was free to explore Jacob's body, and he hers. Free. They were in love and married at last. Any physical act between them was now a pledge. An outward sign of their inner feelings. A true union. A promise of forever.

She sighed and kissed the warm, hard flesh above his heart. Felt his fingers twine in her hair. Felt him caress her and pull her closer as the houseboat gently rocked them on the surface of the lake. Soothing. Sensuously hypnotizing. An erotic lullaby.

Bolder, she pushed his shirt off his shoulders, down his arms, then off his hands. And as she did so, she reveled in the hardness of his shoulder muscles, the corded sinews of his forearms, the long, strong fingers of his hands. This man was powerful. But his sheer manliness came from the control he exerted over his physical power. Came from his ability to draw energy from that power to fuel his other attributes. Tenderness. A grand capacity for joy. And selfless love.

"Oh, Jacob," she whispered, "you are so beautiful to me."

She looked up into his face and into a smile of such sensuous brilliance she felt the breath catch in her throat.

"Cassie," he murmured huskily as he reached for the top button of her blouse.

She inhaled sharply, and the fragrance of mock orange blossoms washed over her. Feeling the room begin to float around her, she wrapped her arms about his neck, yielded to the sensation of Jacob, her love, gently, slowly undressing her.

She was his. And he was hers. Forever.

With each article of her clothing that he discarded, she felt the night air caress her skin. Felt his fingertips brush her, leaving a trail of stardust sensation. She would have closed her eyes in surrender to the overwhelming physical and emotional feelings, except, then, she wouldn't see the expression of absolute love on his face. The look of desire in his eyes. The look that promised they would be one.

Oh, my.

Her pulse skittered. Her heart thumped wildly under her breast. She felt an unfamiliar burning at her core. She felt alive.

Jacob bent and scooped her easily in his arms, chuckling softly as he must have seen her eyes widen in surprise. Turning, he carried her to the bed and gently laid her on the silk coverlet. His touch, his intense regard, the feel of the sensuous fabric on her skin sent shivers of pleasure over her body.

She smiled up at him, feeling free and new and daring. Lifting her arms, she beckoned to him. "Come."

She heard his answering soft groan, then watched in fascination as he hastily shrugged out of his trousers and his briefs. This then was manly beauty. Her fingers fluttered to her heart. Be still, she warned it silently, or you will never make it through the evening.

With a smile that banished all her earnest warnings, he lowered himself beside her on the bed and pulled her into his strong embrace. "I love you, Cassie Matthews," he whispered, his words throaty and filled with yearning. "I love you now and forever."

Cathryn found his mouth with her own. Sought to show him rather than tell him of her love. In all their years of friendship, words had bound them together. Tonight she wanted to forge their love with actions, not with words.

His firm, warm lips opened under her own, offering himself up for her exploration. When their tongues met, flames of sensation jolted her entire body, making her more daring. More needful. She deepened the kiss and felt him respond with his caresses.

Sliding his hands over her body, he explored her. Possessed her. Claimed her undeniably as his love. His wife. His beloved mate forever. She, in turn, lost in pure feeling, her mind spinning beyond coherent thought, reached out for him and touched him freely. Intimately. As if he had always belonged with her. As if this were a true homecoming.

"Jacob," she moaned softly.

At the sound of her voice, at her touch, his body surged and pressed hard against her. His hand swept over her belly to the tender skin of her inner thigh, raising the tiny hairs along her flesh, sending a hot rippling sensation between her legs. She had given up hope of ever feeling this delicious physical desire for a man. Until Jacob. Jacob and his magic.

Arching her hips, she pressed herself against his stroking hand. Pressed and silently begged release from this spiraling, dizzying desire.

With his tongue he licked a fiery-hot path from her earlobe to her sensitive, swollen nipples. With his breath warm and feathery against her breast, he murmured, "Cassie, oh, Cassie." Slowly, gently, found the nub of her passion and stroked until she cried out with pleasure.

Shimmery starlight began to pool behind her eyelids. Her body, beyond her control, shivered in a shower of moondust. Her blood pounded in her ears. This then was ecstasy. Heightened by Jacob's love for her and hers for him, she lost herself to the sensation of wanting and being wanted. And the sheer physical magic Jacob performed on her body.

She gasped as he lowered himself over her.

"Cassie, look at me." His deep, rich voice came to her through the sea of turbulent sensations that tossed her. "Look at me, love."

Opening her eyes, she gazed into Jacob's face transfigured with love and desire. "Yes," she breathed as she smiled up at him, certain that her smile was filled with all the radiance that transformed her. "Yes, yes, yes..."

He lowered his mouth to hers as he entered her. Caught with his lips the cry of sheer pleasure that escaped her own.

Flesh to flesh, they were as one.

Together they moved. And together they found the tempo that brought them into exquisite harmony. Together they soared on the wings of love and desire. Together they cried out, and Cathryn found herself falling from the dizzying heights of passion into the sweet abyss of total self-abnegation.

Jacob...

Jacob...

Jacob.

Breathing in hot, tiny pants, she lay in his arms and felt the essence of her melt and pool and reform into something new. She was no longer just Cathryn. She was Cathryn who loved and was loved. Forevermore, she now belonged with Jacob.

She smiled dreamily and wrapped her arms around her husband.

"I love you," Jacob crooned as he kissed her eyelids. "I love you," he repeated in a whisper as he kissed her cheeks and her lips and her chin. "I love you," he murmured a third time as he drew her into his loving embrace. "I will never, ever stop loving you."

Reaching up to touch his face, she said nothing. There would come a lifetime of chances to tell him in words that she loved him. She kissed his jaw, his throat, his chest with sated little nibbles. Just now she had shown him.

She nestled against him and felt the urge to purr.

Cassie, oh, Cassie. Sweet Cassie. Her name thrummed in his head as the sight of her, the scent of her, the feel of her ignited his senses. He could even taste his love for her. He knew now why poets described passion in terms of hunger. In this one aspect of his life he had been, truly, a starving man. Famished. He smiled and trailed his fingers along the curve of Cathryn's hip. She sighed and wriggled closer in his embrace.

Ah, but now his hunger had been satisfied. He grinned. For the moment.

Cathryn reached up and outlined his smile with her finger. "What goes on in that head of yours, Jacob Matthews?" she asked, her voice soft and low and love soaked.

He looked deep into the night-darkened blue of her eyes. "I was just thinking how that wise grandmother of yours always insists that true love is friendship set on fire." He chuckled. "I'd say five years' worth of kindling made a heck of a bonfire, my sweet friend. One heck of a bonfire."

Cathryn laughed softly, and her breath tickled his shoulder. She drew back a little and Jacob could see mischief clearly sparkle in her eyes. "Do you think we're burned out?" she asked, cocking one eyebrow. "Do you think that's it? Once for the record, then up in smoke?"

Jacob felt his body rouse. "You wound me," he growled playfully, pulling her close again, nuzzling her neck. "At the very least, you underestimate my private stock of kindling."

Cathryn pressed herself against him. Against his renewed hardness. "Oh, my!" She giggled against his chest. "There is absolutely nothing about you that I underestimate."

He stroked her bare back and whispered in her hair, "What about us, Cassie? Do you underestimate anything about us?" He knew the answer. Deep down. Instinctively. He just wanted to hear her confirm it.

"Nothing. Not now." She rubbed the palm of one hand over his shoulders, over his chest, over his hip. "Absolutely nothing," she purred as she set his skin to tingling.

She slowly drew away from him and lay on her back on the bed, touching only his fingertips with her own. The cool night air that replaced her presence chilled his skin. Made him long for her return. But looking at her, lying next to him, a dreamy smile upon her face, her hair silvery in the moonlight and tousled from their lovemaking—looking at her was fair compensation.

She was so beautiful—an inside-and-out kind of beauty—and so vibrant. Like a moonbeam dancing on the water. Her beauty and her vitality and the happiness it brought him made him want to ask the Lord what he had done in his life that had made him deserving of such reward.

Scarcely believing it was his privilege, he reached out and traced the oval of her face. She fluttered her lashes involuntarily and smiled. Did his touch thrill her the way hers did him? Her heartfelt sigh made him believe it must.

"Jacob," she said softly, gazing up at the reflection-dappled ceiling. "I have to admit I was a little afraid...of this."

"This?"

She turned her gaze shyly to him. "This physical intimacy. I was afraid I might fail you. Fail myself."

He felt as if the tentative quality of her voice and the trusting look in her eyes might dissolve his very heart. He brushed a wisp of hair from her forehead. "How could you—or I, for that matter—fail at lovemaking if our love is true?"

She smiled. A sweet and radiant smile. "That's just it. Quite foolishly, I hadn't counted on the power of love. Amazing, isn't it? That power."

He leaned over to kiss her lips. To capture the confection that was her smile. "Absolutely amazing."

Amazing.

He'd thought he'd loved her five years ago. Had thought he'd known the meaning of love. But the feeling that had washed over him when his father, presiding as pastor today at their wedding, had pronounced them husband and wife...well, quite frankly, the feeling had blown Jacob away. *Then* he'd told himself, Now I know what love is. That was until he and Cathryn had made love. Shared love. Exchanged love in a ceremony of passion that had added yet another meaning to the definition of the word. He smiled down at his new wife. Would their love prove ever changing, filled with surprises and challenges, always sustaining them yet sometimes catching them off guard? He certainly hoped so.

Cathryn turned on her side and nestled her back against him spoon fashion. As if she'd read his thoughts, she said softly, "I knew I loved you, Jacob. Loved you from the depths of my heart. But this feeling that I have now... this feeling is like an unexpected gift."

"I know," he murmured in her ear, wrapping his arms around her, pulling her close. Yes, he had known, but was filled with profound joy and a sense of wonder that she felt it, too.

Sunlight, warm and persistent, woke Jacob. Looking down at Cathryn curled in his arms, he blessed the day and his good fortune.

Slowly she stretched, then opened her eyes and gazed up at him. "A penny for your thoughts."

"You need two pennies." He kissed the tip of her nose. "My first thought was that I was going to love waking up like this for the rest of my life."

She ran her fingers down the side of his face. "And the second thought?"

"I was wondering what Aiden's doing."

Smiling, she replied, "Probably racing Margaret to see who can eat the most of Belle's blueberry pancakes."

Jacob nuzzled Cathryn's neck. "That boy is a creature after my own heart. I *love* blueberry pancakes."

"Then, when we get home, you and Aiden can start a tradition of making blueberry pancakes on Saturday mornings."

He flopped on his back and gazed up at the ceiling. Happy. Thoroughly happy. "I can't wait to explore the traditions we can start as a family."

"Yes, a family... I had wished Aiden's adoption papers had come through by the wedding. That way he and I could have changed our last names together."

Jacob heard the tinge of wistfulness in her voice. Reaching out, he clasped her hand in his. "Oh, I think it's going to work out even better this way. This way, you and I had our day—the wedding. When the papers come through, we'll make a celebration that's Aiden's alone. His name day, so to speak."

"Yes, he'll like that." Cathryn rose on one elbow to look into Jacob's eyes. The wistfulness in her voice had quickly disappeared. "A picnic with the family, maybe."

"With softball."

"Definitely with softball." She laughed and threw her arms around him. Buried her face in his neck. "Oh, Jacob, we love you so much, Aiden and I."

Jacob felt the sting of tears at the corners of his eyes. He swallowed hard. "I love you, too. I was wrong when I thought I realized how much joy loving the two of you would bring me. The reality far exceeds the imagination."

Cathryn snuggled closer. "I don't think you realize how much your everyday life is going to change. Car pools. Sleep-overs. Parent-teacher conferences..."

"Putting toys together Christmas eve. Holiday celebrations. Family vacations... you two will be my reason to finally take a vacation."

"Wouldn't Aiden just love this houseboat?"

Jacob cupped her face and kissed her soundly on the lips. "Then we'll rent it for the family next summer. Can Aiden swim?"

"Yes, but, Jacob, you can't anchor in the middle of the lake with a five-year-old."

"Oh, there are plenty of inlets near the shore. As a family we'll explore each and every one of them. The middle of the lake is strictly a honeymoon location." He chuckled. "Great for skinny-dipping before breakfast."

"Pastor Matthews!"

"Your shock disappoints me." He tried to look chagrined. "Boone told me that in elementary school you were known as the-girl-who-never-refused-a-dare."

She laughed. "I'm afraid I did eat my share of nasty things just to uphold my reputation. Thank goodness Aiden is so reasonable."

"Ah, but what might the next child be? And the next? Little Calvin the Climber. Or Hettie the Hair Cutter. Or maybe Denise the Daredevil. They say genes will out, and I was known to break a bone or two—not on a dare, but out of sheer recklessness."

Cathryn groaned. "You have an *in.* Couldn't you inquire of the Lord as to the temperaments of our unborn children?"

Jacob chuckled. "No can do. Child rearing isn't a used car lot. You can't test drive the little darlings."

Looking up at him from under a golden fringe of lashes, she asked innocently, "Did we decide on a larger family?"

"Yes, we did... *and* I think we decided that we were going to approach this in a very mature and logical way."

Cathryn scrunched her nose and eyebrows in a puzzled expression.

"You know... practice makes perfect...."

"Oh, you mean, we'll practice being parents on Aiden before we decide to have more?" she asked guilelessly.

"Don't play obtuse with me," he answered, laughing and pulling her against his morning hardness. "You know very well the practice I had in mind."

"Mmm." The little purring sound she made in the back of her throat further aroused him. "But what about the skinny-dipping?"

"I don't think it's an either-or situation," he murmured, caressing the softness of her skin. "We have all week."

"Correction." She nibbled his jawline as she trailed her fingers over his chest. "We have the rest of our life together."

The rest of our life together. The full import of her words hit him, as well as the catch in her voice. An emotional catch that bespoke measureless love. Love not of need or of convenience, but love straight from the heart. Who would have thought that, from their inauspicious beginning five years ago, their tentative liaison of friendship and need, would arise this true and mutual love?

A soft breeze blew through the open windows, circulating the fragrance of flowers. The houseboat rocked gently, the sound of water lapping against the hull a mesmerizing music. A dragonfly alighted on the window screen, its wings iridescent and fragile. To Jacob the world seemed to slow down, giving two newlyweds a chance to absorb the beauty of the choice they'd made. Looking into Cathryn's smiling face, he saw openness and expectation.

They would be friends. They would be lovers. They would be parents. They would be partners. They would be sensible at times, and passionate at others. They would squabble and make up. They would rejoice and despair. Plan and change those plans a hundred times. They would learn new things about each other every day.

And always they would love.

"I love you," he said simply. His heart was too full to say anything else.

"I love you, too," she replied as she tipped her face to share a kiss, the token of that love.

Epilogue

"Mama, Daddy, look! Uncle Rhune has a pet rock!"

With a chuckle, Jacob set the baby carrier with Hannah in it on the kitchen counter, then bent to examine Aiden's find.

Those two. Cathryn shook her head, but couldn't suppress a smile. "Aiden Matthews, we're here to help your uncle Rhune move in. Not to rummage through his belongings." She gave Hannah a teething biscuit and wiped a little bead of perspiration from the baby's upper lip. My, but it was warm, even for September.

"Now, Mama Cass, don't fuss at my nephew." Rhune came up beside Cathryn and chucked Hannah under the chin. "I don't think he can do it any harm."

Cathryn blinked and shook her head at the sight of Rhune's wild tropical shirt. "Why, pray tell, does a thirty-two-year-old man—a doctor, no less—have a pet rock?"

Rhune winked. "With my schedule the past ten years I needed a pet that would thrive on neglect."

Carrying a cardboard box filled with cooking utensils, Alice Rose walked through the doorway of the new double-wide trailer. "Well, Rhune Sherman, it looks as if you'll have your pick of pet rocks now. Fifteen acres' worth. Now, why you couldn't wait for Boone to build a house on your property, why you couldn't, at least, live in the apartment above your office in town until the house was finished, why you had to plunk yourself down in a trailer in Tornado Alley—those are questions that need answering."

"Alice Rose," Belle called out as she, Boone and Margaret entered, carrying picnic hampers, "don't try to figure my baby brother out. He is impetuosity itself. He bought this land, now he wants to live on it. He probably figures the fish in that newly purchased pond of his simply will not wait for a house to be built."

Rhune spun his sister around the kitchen in an impromptu waltz. "That's what I love about you, Arabella. Your understanding nature."

"Stop jostling the help, and get over here, young man," Alice Rose ordered good-naturedly. "I'm here to teach you the business end of cooking utensils. Or do you plan to eat all your meals at the Hole-in-the-Wall?"

"I thought I'd experiment with an omelet or two," Rhune answered as he came to attention at Alice Rose's side.

Boone rolled his eyes in an I'll-believe-that-when-I-see-it expression.

Cathryn shook her head and smiled. What a family! Especially the two newest members. Hannah. And Rhune. She ducked as Hannah lobbed the now-gooey teething biscuit across the kitchen.

"Eeuwww!" Aiden exclaimed as he nonetheless dutifully retrieved it, tossed it in the trash, then provided his sister with a fresh one.

Oh, Hannah, Cathryn thought, you already have the boys running.

"Want to wager which one will set Sweet Hope on its ear fastest?" Jacob's voice rumbled playfully in her ear. She shivered with pleasure. Fifteen months of being married to the man, and he still made her pulse race. "Rhune or Hannah?" he continued, mischief charging his words. "Sweet Hope's newest doctor or Sweet Hope's—"

Cathryn turned and cut him off with a mock glare. Hannah the Hellion. That's what Jacob called their daughter when he was out of earshot of his parishioners. She was not about to encourage that nickname. Although... with Hannah's flashing eyes, her refusal to be ignored and her strong right arm, the girl, at five months, was a handful, to be sure.

And then there was Rhune, her stepmother's brother. Cathryn had never quite figured out what that made him in relationship to her on the family tree. Rhune had insisted that in families there was the original recipe, then in-laws... then outlaws. Cathryn chuckled. Rhune most certainly fit the latter category.

"I think," she said, leaning back against the solid strength of Jacob, "that race will be too close to call."

"Daddy, will you take me down to Uncle Rhune's fishing pond?" Aiden tugged at Jacob's hand.

Lifting their son into his arms, Jacob asked, "Do you want to eat some of Grammy's fried chicken first, or see the fishing pond first?"

"That's a tough one," Aiden replied soberly. Cathryn was caught by how little she saw that sober expression anymore. Suddenly Aiden's eyes twinkled with the more familiar Matthews mischief. "Perhaps we could have both. Drumsticks are easy to carry."

"How can I say no to such a plan?" Jacob laughed and kissed Aiden. Then he bent over and kissed Cathryn soundly. "What do you say to the four of us having a picnic by the pond before we unpack Rhune's one crate of belongings?"

"Hey," Rhune objected. "I have more than one crate. My sailboard counts."

"And the pet rock," Aiden added loyally.

Cathryn slipped her arm around her husband and felt immeasurably happy that her own nomadic days were over. After a long and hard journey, she'd come home. With Jacob's help she'd come home and had rediscovered her own grand capacity for love. Everyone should be so lucky.

Even the restless Rhune.

Cathryn's matchmaking genes kicked into gear. She winked at Jacob, then grinned at Rhune. "You know, Dr. Sherman," she offered, "there's someone I'd like you to meet...."

* * * * *

With all the matchmakers in town, there's sure to be another SWEET HOPE WEDDING *soon. One confused—and lucky—bride is about to find out that A GOOD GROOM IS HARD TO FIND next month—only from Silhouette Special Edition!*

COMING NEXT MONTH

#1039 MEGGIE'S BABY—Cheryl Reavis
That Special Woman!
Reuniting with her lost love, Jack Begaye, gave Meg Baron everything she dreamed of—a husband and a father for her unborn baby. But would their newfound happiness last when Meg's past threatened their future?

#1040 NO LESS THAN A LIFETIME—Christine Rimmer
The Jones Gang
Although Faith Jones had loved Price Montgomery from afar for years, she never dared dream that he'd return her feelings. Then a night of passion changed everything—and Faith wouldn't settle for anything less than a lifetime....

#1041 THE BACHELOR AND THE BABY WISH—Kate Freiman
Hope Delacorte had one last chance to have the baby she so wanted, but there seemed to be no prospective fathers in sight...unless she turned to friend Josh Kincaid. He'd offered to father her child—no strings attached—but that was before they started to fall in love.

#1042 FULL-TIME FATHER—Susan Mallery
Erin Ridgeway had just given Parker Hamilton the biggest news of his life—he was the father of the five-year-old niece she had been raising. Suddenly, being a full-time father and husband started to sound very appealing to Parker....

#1043 A GOOD GROOM IS HARD TO FIND—Amy Frazier
Sweet Hope Weddings
Country doctor Rhune Sherman certainly met his match when Tess McQueen arrived in town. But she had a score to settle, and he didn't want to think about the raging attraction between them—until the good folks of Sweet Hope decided to do a little matchmaking!

#1044 THE ROAD BACK HOME—Sierra Rydell
When Billy Muktoyuk left home, he impulsively left behind his high school sweetheart, Siksik Toovak, the only woman he'd ever loved. Now he was back—and there wasn't anything that would stop him from winning back her heart.

"As the father of six adopted children,

I'm not your typical bachelor. But I may not stay one for long, now that I've met the woman of my dreams—Kristen Fielding. I can only hope she'll grow to love my kids as much as I do. Then I'll make her Mrs. Fernando Ibarra—and when she's the mother of my child, she'll say these words to me..."

HAPPY FATHER'S DAY
by
Barbara Faith
(SE #1033)

In June, Silhouette Special Edition brings you

Sometimes bringing up baby can bring surprises... and showers of love.

TMB696